IGNITE YOU

DIANA A. HICKS

COPYRIGHT

Ignite You

Cover art by Heather Roberts

Publishing History

Print ISBN 978-1-949760-22-4

Digital ISBN 978-1-949760-21-7

Dear Readers,

I'm so happy to share Emilia's and Dom's intense love story with you!

Ignite You was previously published as the standalone novel, Love Over Logic. Now that the Cole Brothers series is complete, I thought it would make more sense to have all installments grouped together.

So it all starts here with Dom and Emilia. You'll briefly meet Derek and Valentina (Unravel You) and Tyler and Mia (Escape You). You'll meet the entire Cole family in Unravel You.

If you like fast-paced reads with a heavy dose of suspense and heat, then you came to the right place. Get ready to fall in love with the Cole brothers.

Happy Reading!

Diana

ABOUT THE AUTHOR

Diana A. Hicks is an award-winning author of steamy contemporary romance with a touch of suspense.

When Diana is not writing, she enjoys kickboxing, hot yoga, traveling, and indulging in the simple joys of life like wine and chocolate. She lives in Atlanta, and loves spending time with her two children and husband.

Connect with Diana on social media to stay up to date on her latest releases.

www.DianaHicksBooks.com

PRAISE FOR DIANA A. HICKS

"Hicks' first installment of her Desert Monsoon series is confident and assured with strong storytelling, nuanced characters, and a dynamic blend of romance and suspense."

— **KIRKUS REVIEWS**

What makes any romance a great read isn't the fact that two hot people meet and fall in love. It is the episodes that bring about the falling in love and the unexpected places the experience takes the characters that make it an enjoyable read. Diana A. Hicks knows just how to make this happen.

— **READERS' FAVORITE**

BOOKS BY DIANA A. HICKS

Desert Monsoon Series

Love Over Lattes

Love Over Time

Cole Brothers Series

Ignite You

Unravel You

Provoke You

Escape You

Unleash You

Defy You

Escape My Love

For Hicks.
Because broody heroes are hard to find.

1

FUCK ME TWICE

Emilia

The rustic door of the Roadrunner Bar creaked opened, and a mix of motorcycle fumes and hot Arizona air bustled into the restaurant. From behind the bar, I fisted a dishcloth and wiped the counter with rough strokes while I kept my attention on the dark figure crowding the threshold.

Another step and the halogen lights touched his face. The face of yet another customer, not the guy who'd promised me answers. *Fuck me.* The lowlife had stood me up. And just like that, I was back to square one.

Maybe he got cold feet. Maybe he was smarter than I thought.

"Stop that." Alex, my pretend boss, came around the bar and pressed her palm against my hand. "I think the counter is clean now. Come on, do a shot with me."

Right. One of the perks of bartending? All the shots we could handle. "I've had enough for tonight."

"Oh, come on. It's your last night. We gotta get you properly wasted." She placed a glass in front of me and poured another Silver Cuervo.

She was right. What would it hurt to let my hair down for a night? Okay, maybe not the whole night, but I did need to let go for a bit. Regroup and come up with a new plan because this half-cocked idea of taking a job at the Roadrunner to catch a killer and save my cousin Jess was a total bust.

The idea that she'd sent me on a wild goose chase tugged at the back of my mind, but I pushed it away. Jess was family, and she needed my help. As much as she feared her husband, I truly believed she was ready to do the right thing this time. I took the shot Alex offered and knocked it back.

"Yeah! That's what I'm talking about." She patted me on the back. "While you're at it, go help the hottie that just strolled in. He looks lonely."

I barked out a laugh. "No. Thanks. That's a whole bag of trouble I'm not looking for right now. Or ever."

"I've been doing this a while, girl. I never forget a face, especially not one that looks like that. He was here last week, same smile, same hot blue gaze. Holy shit. If he turned that panty-dropping stare this way, I'd be clawing your eyes out to get you out of the way."

"No clawing necessary. He's all yours." I grabbed a couple of dirty glasses off the counter, rinsed them, and placed them in the dishwasher.

"You know him." Damn, she was good. How did she pick up on that? I was going to miss having someone to talk to without having to actually talk.

I nodded. "Law school. It's been a couple of years. He obviously doesn't remember me."

"Are you sure? The first time he was here, he was all Chatty

Kathy with some of my regulars until you came in for your shift. He couldn't get out of here fast enough. I'd say he recognized you." She poured a couple of beers, stuck a ticket to one of the glasses, and set them on a tray for one of the servers to take. "Why do you think he's back? Every time you look his way, he sits up a little straighter. Gets that cute wrinkle in his eye. Maybe he wants to be your friend." She winked.

"That's my point exactly. He hated me when we were in school. If he knew who I was, he wouldn't even be here. Trust me, he does *not* want to be my friend."

She let out a sigh. "I wouldn't mind being his friend. Come on, it's your last day. Live a little." She gave me a nudge before she grabbed a new ticket and got to work on the next drink order.

Was she serious? Did Dom Moretti, the hotshot from law school, want me? That was impossible. We were in the same classes for three years, and he never once looked my way. Well, except for the one time when he almost kissed me. By accident but still. That one moment was my go-to fantasy most nights. I touched a finger to my lips where his mouth had ghosted mine three years ago. Had it really been that long?

I wiped the counter again, shooting a quick glance his way. I'd been bartending for several months now, so I was an expert at scanning the room for trouble, picking up details in a few blinks. Details that had to do with my cousin Jess and her deadbeat husband, not my nonexistent love life.

He met my gaze. I squeezed my legs together and waited for the spark of adrenaline to dissipate. What would he think if I told him I had a vibrator named after him? No, I couldn't do this. Dom was a complication I didn't need right now.

My cousin's life was on the line. I had to stay focused.

I ambled over to him when he waved a hand to get my attention. The more he stared, the more I was convinced he didn't know who I was. All he saw was a bartender with deep cleavage wearing tight leather pants. Alex dressed like this for the tips. I did it to get customers to talk to me, to get them to give up information I needed badly.

"Hey, hon. What can I get ya?" I leaned on the bar, and he adjusted his weight on the barstool. Yeah, okay, Alex was right about him. He wanted this version of me.

"Silver Cuervo, please." His voice was low and sinful.

Jesus. Was that recognition in his eyes? I swallowed and poured him a shot. I held my breath, but it was too late. I had already inhaled a full dose of Dom's intoxicating smell, a mix of sandalwood and spearmint. The same scent from that day when he almost kissed me.

"Would you have one with me?" He hadn't changed at all. Same soulful, deep-blue eyes, thick eyebrows, and a full mouth that made all kinds of promises every time he smiled.

I needed to get home to *my* Dom. Safe and reliable, battery-operated Dom. I gave him a quick smirk like I could take it or leave it and as if incredibly sexy men offered me drinks all the time.

"Sure." I grabbed another glass and filled it. "I've never seen you in here before. What brings you in? We're not exactly on the beaten path."

"New client wanted me to look into something." His gaze dropped to the notification displaying on his phone screen before he swiped it away. "You celebrating something, doll?" He pointed in Alex's direction, a reference to our shot from before.

"Last day on the job," I said. Alex had been kind enough to

let me bartend, poke around, and ask questions, but she only gave me three months. She didn't want the cartel and Jess's husband to get the wrong idea about her restaurant. My time was up.

"Moving on up, huh?"

"Something like that," I said.

He stood, and I got a good look at him. The man could wear a suit. His biceps stretched the sleeves of his suit coat with every move. And with every move, his body heat lapped at my skin in places that had me blushing. I bet he was all smooth muscle under there. I slanted a glance at the clock. Was it quitting time yet? His gaze followed mine, and his Adam's apple bobbed a little. Did I just give him the impression I wanted to leave here with him?

"Congratulations." He cheered me and took the shot.

"Thanks." I raised my glass and drank.

"What time do you get off?"

The what? I swallowed and coughed at the same time, sending the tequila up into my nasal cavity. Nothing had changed. Dom Moretti was completely and utterly a bad idea. Playing the cool bartender wasn't a game I could keep up with for long. I filled a glass with water and drank to ease the burn in my throat and sinuses. Great. Just fucking great.

"I'm sorry. Didn't mean to throw you off." He rubbed two fingers along his jaw. His beard made a scratchy noise with every pass. "Just thought if you're free later, we could hang out." He lowered his gaze to the lapel of my leather top and furrowed his eyebrows for a second. "What do you say? Anna?" *Anna?* Right. My name tag with my fake name. He definitely didn't remember me. It stung a bit though that gave me a surge of courage.

"I'm closing today. Midnight?" The Cuervo was definitely putting words in my mouth.

He braced his hands on the bar, his gaze intense like he had a million things going through his mind. Something in his slow smile told me one of those things was me naked on this counter. Okay, maybe that was the image going through *my* head. Pushing off, he took a couple of twenties out of his wallet and put them under his glass.

"I'll see you in a couple of hours." He spun and sauntered out the door.

Holy fuck, I have a booty call with Dom Moretti.

"I gotta get out of here." I wiped the counter several times, threw the rag in the sink, and headed toward the back door.

"Oh no you don't." Alex blocked me, arms out, legs hip-width apart. Dammit. What did I do? "You finally did the right thing, *something for you*. You're not backing down."

"I can't have sex with a total stranger."

"Ah, but he's not a stranger. You guys went to school together."

"I've seen him before. In class. We never really talked. I can't." I stepped forward, and she stood taller. This wasn't the time to tell her I'd had a huge crush on Dom when we were in school. Along with half the girls in our class. The bad boy from Jersey.

"Get to work." She nodded toward the door at the new customers streaming in. "You have two hours."

What could it hurt? After tonight, I'd have no reason to come back to this bar and no reason to see Dom ever again. "Ohmigod. I'm doing this."

"Yes, you are." Alex picked up the new drink ticket and

shoved it my way. Maybe Dom would change his mind and stand me up. He wouldn't be the first guy to do that today.

The clock struck midnight, and it was as if the cosmos had given their blessing because the last customer stumbled out of the bar the second Dom's Harley rumbled into my line of sight in the parking lot. Alex held the door open, mostly so she could enjoy the eye candy.

Dom sat back on the seat for a second before he killed the engine and took off his helmet. His thick thighs hugged the bike as he raked a hand through his hair. I'd seen this display before. Dom all hot and delicious in a black leather jacket and tight jeans. He'd changed clothes for me.

A giggle swirled around in my chest. For a change, I played it cool and didn't let it out. Alex, on the other hand, made no effort to hide the fact that she was ogling the guy. She didn't even back down when Dom walked toward the door and met her gaze.

"Hey, hon." She shot a glance in my direction before she leaned toward him. "Lock the door behind me."

"Thanks for the tip." Dom chuckled and stepped inside.

The deep sound of his laughter made my knees turn to warm Jell-O. To crush the last of my nerves, Dom let the door shut and flipped the latch.

What the hell was wrong with me? Why couldn't I stop thinking of all the bad things I wanted to do to this guy? Dom was the exact same guy I'd met back in law school. His connection to the Italian mob back in Jersey made him the exact type of guy Mom warned me to stay away from. Was that the reason for this attraction?

"I was sure you'd chicken out." His voice echoed in the empty bar.

"Not tonight." I prowled around the counter. Desire pooled between my legs when his gaze dropped from my face to my cleavage and all the way down to my feet. Yeah, that was the panty-dropping stare.

Jesus. Do I get undressed or do I let him do it?

He shrugged out of his jacket and laid it on the barstool. One, two, three strides, and he stood inches from me. "*Christ*, Emilia, you're more beautiful than I remember." He gripped my waist.

My feet dangled in the air for a second before he plopped me onto the bar, and his mouth landed on my clavicle. Oh my God, he smelled so good. I kissed the smooth skin on his temple, letting his scent numb my senses. My fingers slipped under the sleeve of his T-shirt and kneaded his shoulder and bulging biceps.

Heat spread fast from his hot lips on my chest to every inch of my body. Something he'd said wasn't right, but what was it? His mouth moved down, soft and demanding, while his hands pushed my legs farther apart so he could position himself where he wanted.

Wait, what?

I pushed at him. "What did you just say?" I asked out of breath.

He looked up at me, lips slightly parted. "You're more beautiful than I remembered."

My eyes went wide. "Before that."

"Emilia?"

Fuck me twice. "You know who I am?"

"We shared classes for three whole years, yeah I know who you are." He chuckled, sliding back into place.

I shoved him away and jumped off the counter. "You need to leave."

"Why? I thought you wanted this."

"That was when I thought you didn't remember me. Oh my God. I'm so embarrassed." I pressed a cold palm to my forehead.

"No need to be embarrassed, doll." The amusement in his tone cured whatever insanity had taken over me. I blinked, and the room came back into focus. This was a huge mistake.

"I have an appointment I forgot about. Sorry to make you come back all the way out here." Words spilled out of my mouth like kittens in a box, fast and all over the place.

Dom raised both eyebrows, arms crossed. His gaze followed me around the room while I collected my things in a hurry. "So, let me get this right. You were ready to jump into bed with me when you thought I didn't recognize you. Why is that?"

"It's not that. I just have somewhere to be. That's all." I couldn't look at him.

"You haven't changed at all, have you? You know, when I saw you here, I thought you'd finally decided to let loose a little. But no, you're the same. Little Miss Proper can't be seen with the likes of me. Is that right?" He blew out air and wrapped his fingers around my wrist. The warmth prickled up my arm and stopped me in my tracks. When he spoke again, his tone was low and tender. "Hey, for the record, I didn't come here for a hookup. I wanted to see you. This other thing came out of nowhere. You never looked at me like that before. I—"

"What?" I turned around and came face to face with him. His smell sent the flutters in my stomach in every direction.

"You hear that?" He scanned the room, placing a finger over his lips.

Before I could process what was going on, he placed a hand over my mouth and slammed me against the wall. His body covered me like a shield. Dom played the bad boy in school. All the girls, me included, loved every bit of his act. Except, I knew his act wasn't an act. Dom was the real deal, running around with the Italian mob in Jersey. He was one of them, though I never pegged him for someone to use force to get what he wanted from a woman.

I shoved and struggled against him but froze when I met his gaze—intense and menacing. Oh shit. Something was wrong. I'd let down my guard, pining over a hot guy, and forgot about why I was here in the first place.

The window shattered and broken glass splattered everywhere as a bullet zoomed by us. The first shot felt like it came in slow motion, but if that had been a warning, the rest of the shots were not. They bombarded us like rain pelting a tin roof.

In a single motion, Dom had me on the floor with my head nestled in the nook of his neck and shoulder. He looked up, taking in the room, calculating an exit. When he glanced down at me, he shook his head.

"I had plans for you tonight." A half-smirk pulled on his lips. "Minus the bullets, of course. Friends of yours?"

He had plans for me? "No. You?"

"Maybe. Fuck my life." He pulled his legs in and sat on his haunches. I stayed flat on the wooden planks, trying to catch my breath, while he peeked over the counter. More shots rang out. "Is there another way out?"

"The stockroom has a door that leads to the back alley."

He nodded. "Okay, go. Now."

"What? No. I'm not leaving you here."

Brows furrowed, he grabbed my elbow and pulled me toward him. "How 'bout that? You care." Tightening his hold on me, he made a break for the door next to the bathrooms in the back. More bullets broke through, shattering what little glass was left in the windows.

I let him drag me with him. One, he seemed to know what he was doing. And two, I had no idea how to get us out of this.

Now I understood why my informant didn't show to our appointment earlier. No doubt he got cold feet and decided to warn his boss instead. Or maybe, he was found out. *Oh my God.* The element of surprise was the only thing we had going for us. Jess's drug lord husband didn't know I was helping her. If the men out there grabbed me tonight, Jess's chance to get her life back would be over. If her husband found her, she'd be done.

And so would I.

If he found out I was still alive, he'd do whatever was necessary to finish the job he started ten years ago when he killed Dad and left Mom and me for dead.

2

TOO MUCH OF THE SAME THING

Dom

Every. Fucking. Time. I start thinking with my cock and it all goes to hell.

Vic had been right. If my new client's soon-to-be-ex-wife was up to something, Vic would've figured it out. I should've let him look in to this lead alone, especially after Emilia had shown up at the bar out of nowhere. Of all the women in the world, why did it have to be her?

After two years of trying to get over her—trying and failing—I couldn't let her mess with my head again. This case was too important, and the key to leaving Jersey and my old life behind for good. A life I had to stay away from because it turned me into the worst version of me. I had to stay focused.

My phone buzzed again with a text notification. That would make five texts from Vic in the last two hours. He was pissed at me. Sometimes the line between right-hand man and babysitter got blurry with him. In this case, he wasn't wrong. I shouldn't've come back. Relationships were a bad idea for me.

Wasn't that why I let Emilia go the first time I realized I had feelings for her?

I didn't want her to get caught up in my world and all the bullshit that came with it. Mickey and his Jersey crew had been out of my life for five years now. I needed to keep it that way and not give him any reason to come after me or think I'd gone soft. I'd seen firsthand what he could do to someone who had too much to lose. Like love, family, and all those things normal people took for granted.

I peeked through the gap between the threshold and the door. Only two guys were out in the parking lot. Either today was our lucky day or this show was merely a warning. Emilia pressed her breasts against my back, craning her neck to get a better view. *Christ.* I squeezed my eyes shut...one, two, three...I had to stop thinking about what almost happened. Emilia wanted me as much as I wanted her.

After she'd spent the entirety of fucking law school looking down her nose at me, I'd been surprised to find her at this bar of all places, pretending to be someone else and looking at me like I was something to eat. Yeah, I'd been surprised and so turned on, but now, it seemed there was more to Emilia than I'd first thought. I didn't buy her bullshit story. The assholes out there were shooting at her. For once, I wasn't the target.

If this was the first time someone pulled a gun on her, she certainly wasn't showing it. I slanted a glance at her. Her cleavage rose and fell in my peripheral vision, those dark eyes wide open and alert. She felt a healthy dose of fear, but she was cool and collected. Who the hell was Emilia Prado?

"This is hardly the time for you be staring down my top. Can you just focus on getting us out of here?"

"It's going to take a minute to recover from what almost

happened, doll. If I hadn't recognized you tonight, I'd have my hand down that top right now."

She swallowed, and a trail of goosebumps sprung across her chest. Good. She was still interested.

"If you hadn't recognized me, we'd be dead right now." She flung the door open and rushed out, blending into the shadows, every step soundless and calculated. I followed close to her. She stopped at the end of the sidewall and peered around for a second. "Looks like they're getting ready to make a move. Got any ideas?"

"Let's split 'em up." I picked up a rock and threw it ahead of us, pressing my body against the stucco. When the first guy came over to investigate, I got him in a lock position and squeezed until he passed out. This wasn't my first rodeo. Was I showing off? Maybe.

"The other guy went in." She sat on her haunches next to the man on the ground and patted him down. "This is our chance." She pulled a blade out of his back pocket and flipped it open before she stood.

Well, fuck.

"Grab his gun," she said out of breath.

"I don't do guns." I didn't trust myself around them anymore.

"Okay." She grabbed the weapon, discharged the magazine, and tossed it in a dried-up bush ahead of us. "Ready?"

I nodded and scurried toward my Harley. Heart pounding, I walked it away from the building while Emilia slashed the fuckers' SUV tires. I straddled my bike and a second later Emilia's body slammed against mine. An electric charge blasted between us. She was pumped just like I was. With a firm kick, the engine came to life, and we careened out of the bar's parking lot. Emilia's arms were wrapped around my waist and her legs squeezed me tight as her ragged breath brushed the nape of my neck.

Holy fuck, she felt good.

Her laugh rumbled, sending flutters to my navel as we got on I-17 South and headed toward Phoenix. Whatever this was needed to stop but taking her home would be a mistake. If whoever was looking for her found her at the bar, no doubt they also had her address. Not to mention that I had a few questions of my own. What the hell was she up to? By anyone's definition, this wasn't my problem, but I couldn't leave her alone after what happened. I sure as hell didn't want her to stop rubbing against me either.

I slid my hand up and down her arm resting on my stomach and she coiled herself tighter around me. No, I wasn't ready for this night to be over. I stayed on the freeway to give the two of us time to get our bearings and come up with a real plan. I had a lot of questions for Emilia. One thing was certain, though—she needed help.

"Take the next exit," she shouted in my ear. Nodding, I put on the signal and hopped onto the ramp. When I stopped at the light, her lips brushed my cheek. "Take a left here."

After the turn, I glanced at her over my shoulder. "Where are we going?"

"Just here. Pull over."

We were in the middle of nowhere, and it was dark as fuck. A cold shiver crawled up my back. This place wasn't my idea of a safe house after a run-in with a couple of hired guns.

"What the hell is this place?"

"I'm hungry. Come on. This guy has the best hot dogs." The bike bounced when she swung her leg out and got off.

"People are shooting at you and you're hungry?" I followed

her through an alley. A single streetlight marked the spot at the end of the road where a hot dog cart was parked.

She stopped in her tracks and spun to face me. "What?"

"Cut the bullshit, doll. You know those assholes were after you. What did you do?"

"Don't call me that. I'm not a doll. God, you haven't changed." She ran a hand through her thick, dark curls. I'd never known what her hair looked like. In school, she always kept it up in some kind of bun like a ballerina.

I chuckled. "Don't change the subject. What the fuck did you do?"

"I needed answers for a case I'm working." She crossed her arms and her tits went up a bit.

I stepped toward her. "When I saw you last month, I thought maybe you had changed careers." She intrigued me. What kind of an attorney goes undercover for a client?

"You wish. You're still number two in our class. I'm number one." She flashed me a row of white teeth.

"I don't know if you've noticed, but school let out a couple of years back. It's anyone's game now."

She shrugged, rubbing it in without words as she strutted toward the hot dog cart. The closer she got to the circle of light cast on the sidewalk, the more I was treated to a perfect view of her ass. The ass that'd tortured me for an entire semester in ethics class when she sat in front of me. Every time she bent over to get something from her messenger bag, my cock would twitch.

"*Buenas noches.*"

The hot dog guy stood at attention when he spotted her. "Ms. Prado, good to see you. The usual?"

"Two, please. I brought a...a guy."

"Dom." I waved at him. He nodded and got to work on our dinner.

Emilia turned to face the deserted street, taking in the scene. She appeared relaxed, but her eyes scanned every inch in front of her. This version of Emilia was certainly not the Emilia I met back in school. Was it possible that her life was as fucked up as mine? Vic had warned me about her. Up until tonight, all his information had sounded so far-fetched. I walked up to her. "So it's true what they say about you?"

"What's that?"

"That you're a cartel princess."

She chuckled, and for a split second, she looked down at her hand as if trying to remember the right answer. "Do I look like a cartel princess to you?"

"Back at Columbia? No. You were the typical rich girl, annoyed that Daddy couldn't get her into Harvard. Walking around like she was better than the rest of us. But tonight. You've shown me a different side. Which version of you is real?"

She straightened her back, rubbing the inside of her wrist. "People change."

"Not this fast." I reached for her hand. "If you're in trouble, I can help you, but you need to trust me. Tell me the truth."

She met my gaze, and her lips parted. "Wait 'til you try these *dogos*. You'll be hooked." She strolled back to the cart and grabbed the two paper plates. "There's guac on here, bacon, jalapeños, salsa, Peruvian beans, sour cream."

"So basically nachos but on a hot dog?"

"Yeah, I guess." She furrowed her brows and took a big bite, mouthing *so good* in between bites.

She made such a big deal out of it, I had no choice but to try it. The blend of flavors was kind of brilliant. "Okay. Yeah. That's pretty good."

"I told you." She wiped her hands and mouth on a paper napkin then froze. Her movements were slow as she stepped toward the trashcan a few feet away. She dumped her dinner in the can and took off running.

Shit.

For reasons I couldn't fathom, I chased after her. When she crossed the street, a shadow moved along the brick building and made a break for it. Was this the reason for the *dogo* expedition? I should go home and call it a night. Emilia could deal with her case on her own. Why was I still here? Curiosity? Or the fact that I didn't want Emilia to die tonight? She needed help, even if she hadn't gotten around to asking for it yet. She brought me in when she agreed to a hookup. Now she was stuck with me until we figured this out.

Emilia trailed her guy down the street. I bolted toward the back alley to corner whomever the hell she was after. I turned when I reached the next street over, and sure enough, Emilia was still in hot pursuit heading my way. I stopped, placed both hands on my hips, and waited. Emilia did the same, all sweaty and sexy as she tried to catch her breath.

The runner took another minute to catch on, keeping his eyes on me. *That's right, asshole. I'm with her.* He rounded on her, paced back and forth a few times, and then threw his arms up in the air. "I don't know anything."

"I haven't asked you anything." She smiled. "Do you know who I am?"

The guy nodded, rubbing his side. "You're the lawyer helping Jess."

"What else?"

"You run so fucking fast." He braced his hands on his knees.

She rolled her eyes, letting out a breath. This look I knew well. She was losing patience with the asshole.

"You're the hotshot lawyer from New York, Emilia Prado. If I were you, I'd split now. Fancy lawyers can't handle the Arizona heat."

Something told me he wasn't talking about the fact that it was a hundred degrees out at two in the morning. Emilia relaxed her shoulders, pursing her lips to hide a smile. How was this good news?

"Tell your employer that if he has something to say to me, he can call my office and schedule an appointment." She raked her fingers through her hair and big curls bounced all over the place. "Go!" she yelled at the guy when he didn't move.

With a quick glance at me, he sprinted down the street and disappeared into the alley.

"As entertaining as all that was, can I please take you somewhere safe for the night?" Why did I get the feeling that keeping Emilia alive would require more than a safe house?

"You're right. I can't risk going home right now. Can I crash at your place?" She looked drained. The kind of tired left behind after an adrenaline rush.

"Of course."

"Thank you. I know you didn't have to stay with me. I appreciate it."

"I couldn't leave you hanging. It's not who I am." I stuffed my hands in the pockets of my jacket. "Come on. We have a long drive. I'm up north."

"Fancy." She grinned, and my chest squeezed tight. This woman was all kinds of trouble I didn't need in my life.

I hopped on the freeway, and we rode in silence the rest of

the way. Emilia wasn't holding onto me as tight as before, but she had her arms around me, our bodies pressed together in a perfect fit. I took my time getting us back to the hotel. The place I'd called home since the beginning of the summer when my friend, Cole, talked me into moving to Arizona to help him out with his divorce. Now there was a guy not afraid to risk it all for the woman he loved. Not all of us were deserving of the family life—a home.

"You're staying at the Tapatio Cliffs?" She stirred behind me when I pulled into the resort. "Um. You're sleeping on the couch, right?"

She was thinking about it too.

"I can sleep anywhere you want."

"I want you on the couch." She jumped off the bike the second I stopped in front of the valet podium.

With Emilia several feet away from me, I could think again. I took my time with the valet, though our exchange didn't last long. The guy was in a hurry to jump on my Harley, but I couldn't worry about him. For fuck's sake, Emilia almost got killed, and to think I'd sworn I'd never go back to that bar. For days, I managed to keep myself in check, keep away from her. Tonight, my need to see her again won over. If I hadn't gone looking for her, Emilia would've had to face the shooters alone. Yeah, she knew how to handle herself, but she didn't know what it was like to deal with assholes without a soul. Or did she?

In the lobby, Emilia waited for me by the elevator bay. When she saw me, she pushed the call button and stuffed her hands in the back pockets of her pants, taking in the room. "I'm guessing you're an attorney these days."

"I am. I recently moved my practice to Phoenix."

"Really? Why Phoenix?" She stepped into the elevator and

relaxed her shoulders when the door slid closed. All the telltale signs of someone on the run.

"I have a friend who talked me into moving here. He needed my help, and Phoenix seemed like a good place to start fresh." And that was the truth. This far away from New York and everything that was Jersey, I felt like I could breathe again— relax. "How 'bout you? How did you end up here?"

"This is home for me. I wanted to come back." A crease appeared across her forehead when she trained her gaze on me. "How did you do it? How did you get out?" She placed a hand over her mouth. "I'm sorry. I didn't mean to pry."

An alarm blared and flashed a warning in my head. After what I saw her do tonight, it was obvious the best thing to do was to stay away from her. Emilia's behavior was too familiar. Been there, done that...never fucking going back.

"Here we are." I stepped out of the elevator and gestured to the grand suite at the end of the hallway.

Her eyebrows shot up for a moment, and suddenly I wanted to be everything she thought was worthy of her praise. "You must be very good."

"I never lose." I tapped my wallet to the door and pushed it open. Her smile and the way she looked at me made me glad I'd gone with a two-bedroom suite. No way I could spend a night in the same room as Emilia and actually sleep. "There's a spare bedroom through there. If you need anything, I'll be in the other room. Goodnight."

"Goodnight." She bit her lip, rubbing the inside of her wrist. Could she possibly be thinking about not sleeping tonight? Not freaking likely...she made it clear before. I wasn't supposed to be more than a one-night stand, and I agreed with her. Emilia and I were a bad mix. Too much of the same thing. "Thank you for saving my life. I promise. I'll be out of your hair first thing tomorrow."

"Right. Of course. Hey, it was good to see you again. I hope you stay out of trouble from now on."

What a lame goodbye, but I was tired, and I needed to sleep. Emilia wasn't my problem. In a few hours, she'd be gone, and it'd be like tonight never happened. I had to let her go.

She waved from the threshold of her bedroom and closed the door.

3

SICARIO

Emilia

I hung up the phone and fell back onto the pillow. My deposition today was scheduled for noon. If I tried really hard, I could still get an hour of sleep. Fat chance. Not with Dom sleeping in the next room. I bet he slept naked.

What was wrong with me? I almost got killed last night and all I'd been able to think of since I went to bed was Dom and *all the plans* he had for me. Too bad he didn't get to do any of it. A light knock on the door made me jerk out of my insanity. Shit. He was up. I threw the covers out of the way and jumped to my feet, my heart pounding. Another knock. Louder this time.

"Emilia? You up?" His voice rumbled while I stood naked in the middle of the room. My gaze darted from the bed to the chair in the corner. What did I do with my clothes? "Emilia? Are you okay? I'm coming in."

"No." I practically squealed. *Jesus.* This guy had a way to make me lose my mind. "One second." I grabbed the sheet off the bed and wrapped it around me, gathering the excess fabric in front of me like my life depended on it. Turning the knob, I peeked through the gap. "What is it?"

My knees buckled when Dom's mouth fell open. He cleared his throat before he swallowed. Good. I wasn't the only one who'd spent the night tossing and turning. Gosh, I wished I'd brought my vibrator with me. Bracing a hand on the threshold, he leaned closer. "You sleep naked?"

"No. I just didn't have anything else to wear. You try sleeping in leather pants."

He chuckled. He looked sexy in the morning. Hair all messy, lips puffy. "You have a delivery."

"That was fast." I glanced at my watch. Huh? Did I spend an hour lying in bed thinking of Dom? How did that happen? "I'm gonna be late."

Letting the door swing open, I tiptoed to the living room where several shopping bags were scattered on the sofa. I grabbed them with my free hand and spun to face Dom, who was still by the door, arms across his chest, a satisfied grin on his face.

"What?"

"Exactly how naked are you under there?"

I squeezed my legs together. His words 'I had plans for you' from last night swirled in my head. The now familiar desire spread from my core down to my feet. I had to get out of here. Two men almost killed me last night because my focus wasn't in the right place. Dom made my head all fuzzy, and Jess needed me focused on her case.

"Oh please, grow up." I sneered at him and scurried back into my room, shutting the door in his face.

Dropping the sheet on the floor, I dumped the contents of the bags on the bed. Not bad. The concierge had managed to find a decent suit for me to wear, complete with bra and panties, and even a pair of Manolo lacy pumps. Anything for the guy staying in the grand suite.

I jumped in the shower. No time to relax under the warm water. Making quick work of the shampoo and body wash, I rinsed and hopped out. In my bag, I found some tinted moisturizer, mascara, and lip gloss. That would have to do. I blow-dried my hair and put it up in a bun. Back in the bedroom, I tore the tags off the gray pencil skirt and the matching belted jacket and got dressed in record time. I took another five minutes to tidy up the room and collect my things before I headed out.

"There's the Little Miss Proper I remember," Dom said from the dining table where a massive breakfast laid in front of him.

"Don't call me that." My pulse quickened as I scanned the room. What the hell? I came in last night and didn't do my usual routine—didn't check for exit routes, locked doors, or furniture placement. I met Dom's gaze. Did I trust him that much?

"Sorry." He put up his hands in mock surrender. "Would you join me for breakfast?"

"Thanks, but I can't. I'm late for a deposition." I stepped toward the door, trying to memorize the place. The plush sofas in cream colors, the fresh flowers on the fireplace mantel, and Dom sitting at the head of the table looking more freaking delicious than he had the right to be. I wanted to stay, but I'd already stayed longer than I needed to. "Thanks again for letting me crash here."

"Anytime. I'm leaving in a few minutes too if you need a ride." His hot blue gaze put all kinds of crazy ideas in my head. The drive downtown was a good thirty minutes, longer if traffic was bad. Plenty of time to...

"No, I'm good. Got a car waiting." I strutted out the door

doing my best Little Miss Proper impression. That act had served me well for years. No reason to give it up now. Though I was glad Dom had had a chance to see a different side of me last night. The real me.

Outside the resort, my cousin Jess waited in the back seat of her black Escalade while my coworker, Jack, fired questions at her. She was already flustered, scared to see her soon-to-be ex-husband, Levi, at the deposition. Last time they saw each other, he left a shiner on her that took weeks to fully disappear. How she'd been able to put up with his temper since high school was beyond me. Ten years of marriage and a baby girl hadn't helped their relationship in the slightest. Some assholes were just that—assholes. A loving woman and a family weren't good enough reasons to change, to be decent, but his time had come. I was done hiding.

I climbed in the car and kissed Jess hello. "Jack, thank you for doing this today."

"Don't mention it. You're right. Levi will be less defensive if a man is asking the questions." He winked at me, making notes on his legal pad.

Yeah. Less defensive. Also, I wasn't ready for him to know who was really helping his wife. As far as he knew, I wasn't alive. I wanted to keep it that way for a bit longer.

"You'll be fine." I squeezed Jess's hand.

She nodded. Jess was two years older than me, but we had been close growing up. We were inseparable in high school until I had to move away to New York. "I know you're risking a lot just by being here, but you're the only one I can trust."

"Don't mention it." I made eye contact with her driver in the rearview mirror. He nodded and put the car in gear. "We're meeting Levi at his attorney's office. Jack will be with you the entire time. I'll be here when you get out."

Jess's case was like hundreds of others that passed through family court each year. On paper, anyway. Levi wasn't the typical husband. He had money, and more importantly, he had several corrupt politicians in his pocket, along with the backing of the Sonoran Corridor Cartel. A world I knew well, the same world I'd been trying to forget since Dad died.

We came to a stop on Seventh Street in front of a tall building in downtown Phoenix. The offices of Levi's attorney were located on the top floor. A lump churned in my stomach. Just like Jess, I hated the idea of being this close to him. Even surrounded by other people, I didn't feel safe.

Jess hugged me. Deep creases appeared on her forehead, eyes watering as if she were on the way to her execution. Dammit, she couldn't go by herself. When she climbed out of the car, I followed.

"Stay here. It's safer that way," she said under her breath.

"I'll stay out of sight. I promise," I whispered, falling a step behind her when we entered the frigid lobby, which was scattered with real ficus trees and leather sofas that gave the place a contemporary upscale feel. Well maintained but not over-the-top fancy.

"All set?" Jack ushered Jess toward the elevator bay on the right side.

My heart pounded when the doors slid open, and I slipped in behind them, standing on the opposite side like I didn't know them. When we reached the top floor, Jess and Jack went right toward the receptionist desk. I trod in the opposite direction to hide in the bathroom. The anvil lodged in my chest coiled itself deeper and blocked the air to my lungs. I washed my hands in cold water and pressed them on my forehead, breathing through my mouth. Was he here yet? I hadn't seen Levi in over ten years. Not in person anyway.

I paced the bathroom. Dammit. I wanted to be there. I wanted to see his face and tell him I was coming for him. I spun on my heel and went out the door. When I reached the receptionist desk, I froze. In the conference room across the way, Levi sat with his back to me, facing Jess while Jack whispered in her ear. She was almost in tears when she met my gaze through the floor-to-ceiling glass panel. Levi leaned his arms on the table, oozing confidence, certain he'd get what he wanted... Jess's daughter. It was a matter of time, of going through the paces, and keeping up the appearances of an upstanding citizen.

Levi's attorney whispered something to him and casually turned in his chair, following Jess's line of sight—straight to me. What was Dom doing here? He was helping that asshole? I turned on my heel and rushed back to the elevators.

Shit. Shit. Shit.

I rubbed a hand over my forehead. Dom's visits to the bar were not a coincidence. He was there for me. Was he there as a favor to the Sonoran cartel? I punched the call button with the side of my fist several times. A hand touched my shoulder, and I slapped it off before I turned.

"Oh. I'm sorry. I didn't mean to startle you," the receptionist said, her cheeks red, eyes wide.

"It's okay. I'm just in a hurry." I pushed the call button again. Where was the freaking elevator?

"Well. Mr. Moretti asked me to escort you to his office."

"I can't. I have to go."

"Actually, his exact words were *don't let her leave.*" She

showed me Dom's text. "Sorry. He says it's important." The woman looked mortified but determined to follow Dom's orders.

"Fine." I had a few questions of my own.

She let out a long breath and escorted me down the hallway on the right, away from the conference room. I swallowed the lump in my throat when my escort opened the door to Dom's massive office. I walked in, sidestepping the boxes scattered all over the place. He had large paintings leaning on the bare walls, piles and piles of manila folders on his desk and on the floor.

The door closed behind me. I didn't bother to check if it was locked. No doubt Dom's receptionist would stand guard until he showed up. I stood in the same spot—waiting. *Dom isn't Levi. Dom isn't Levi.* I repeated the words in my head until Dom sauntered through the threshold. Squeezing my hands into fists, I rounded on him and hit him square on the chest.

"It was you, wasn't it? You went to the Roadrunner to what? Get rid of me? Gain my trust? What?" It felt good to yell.

He slammed the door shut and gripped my waist, walking me backward until we reached the opposite wall. Dropping his gaze from my face to where his hands were, he whispered, "I think we both know why I went back to the bar last night, but this is about you. Why did you string me along? Were you hoping I'd concede to you on this bullshit Levi Smith case?"

Was he still playing the *I want you* card?

"That is *not* how I win cases. That asshole deserves to be in jail for what he's done to his family." I slipped a hand between us and shoved him hard, but he didn't budge.

He slow-blinked and let out a breath before he released me. "I'm not gonna lie. A small part of me wished you were here to see me, but I'm confused. You rushed out of my place this morning to make this deposition, then you don't go in. I saw enough of you last night to know you have a reason for all this sneaking around. Start talking."

"How did Jess do in there?"

"She pretty much recanted her whole story. A family court judge won't have a problem giving Levi full custody of his daughter. Emilia, you don't have a case."

"He hits her."

"Hearsay. You have to do better than that. You know that."

Dom had the right of it. This was a bullshit case. I knew it from the beginning, but it was at least buying us the time we needed to expose Levi for what he was. If I told Dom the truth, would he understand? Or would he save his client instead?

"He's a Sicario."

"*What?*"

"A hired gun for the Mexican cartel."

"I know what a Sicario is. I wanted to make sure you said what I thought you said. *Jesus Christ.*" The furrow on his forehead got deeper. I stepped back. Dom could be intimidating when he wanted to be. "You accuse him of that, I'll have to sue you. You understand that? I just started working here. Losing a cake case isn't exactly the best way to prove myself. Levi will take his business elsewhere if I don't win this for him." He paced the length of his office. What was he thinking? "If I bring in another big account, I could make partner by the end of the year. Phoenix could be home for me." He stopped and met my gaze. "Do you even have proof of any of this?"

"No."

"Is that why you were at the Roadrunner? Trying to find something to pin on him?"

"Yes."

"Fuck, Emilia. I'm going to need full sentences here." He

braced his hands on his hips. "Do you know why I went to the bar last month?" I shook my head and he continued. "Levi knew there was a woman looking into his business. I went to check it out, but no one would talk to me. I guess they didn't trust my looks." He placed his index finger under my chin to make me face him.

Outside the window, puffy white clouds shifted across the sky. Suddenly, the room was bathed in bright light. Dom's features softened, and I relaxed my stance without meaning to.

"I can't think straight when you're near. I was particularly dim at the bar with you looking at me the way you were. I was an idiot for not seeing that you were the one asking questions about Levi. Emilia, if he's what you say he is, you can't fuck with him. Stay out of it."

Shit. Blood rushed through my body, making my legs weak. I needed to tell him the truth. After last night, I knew I could trust Dom, but could I trust him with a case that could ruin his hotshot lawyer career? I opened my mouth to speak, but he put up his hands. "Tell me why you're hiding from Levi."

"Because he thinks I'm dead. Because he knows I know all his dirty little secrets, including the double life he's been living since he married Jess."

"Jess knows?"

I nodded. My cousin wasn't perfect. Of course, she knew. And she liked it. She liked the money, the power. If she put up with Levi's temper all these years, it was because she was afraid to be left with nothing, without a home and her family.

"She came to me when I moved back to Phoenix four months ago. I don't even know how she found me. I hadn't seen her in years. She's afraid for her daughter and her life. I became a lawyer because I wanted to make a difference. It pains me to see I can't do anything for her." Tears stung my eyes. I couldn't let Dom see me like this. Losing my shit. I rubbed my arm and counted to ten, and then another ten until I calmed down. "I'm not asking you to concede. All I need is time."

"Time." He turned away from me, rubbing his thumb on his trimmed beard. "I can give you time, but I want in."

"In? Oh no. I don't need you up in my business." I placed my hands on my hips. Yeah, I needed Dom's help, but I also needed him away from me.

"You want my help? That's my price."

"I don't *want* your help."

A sexy smile spread across his face. "But you need it." He sat at the edge of his desk, crossing his arms. "You don't even have to say please. Just say yes."

"Why do you even want to get involved? This isn't your fight."

"I can't help myself."

He relaxed and braced his hands on the tabletop, biceps straining against his dark suit, long legs in front of him. I swallowed, rubbing the spot on my neck where he'd kissed me last night.

"I'll figure out another way." Turning on my heel, I scurried out of his office before I changed my mind.

4

THE DEEP WEB

Dom

"God, you're as stubborn as ever," I yelled at the closed door.

Fuck, she wasn't wrong. I had no right to insert myself into her life like that. Why would she trust me anyway? I was opposing counsel. However, organized crime was something I knew well. If her cousin's husband was involved with the local cartel, someone needed to make sure Emilia didn't go after him. She could end up in some ditch along the Nogales border.

I hit the intercom button on my phone. "Stop her."

April's response was immediate. "She's gone. Took the stairs this time."

Dammit. Last night, I'd thought I was done with Emilia, but after this mornings shit show of a deposition, there was no way I was letting her go. The shots fired at the Roadrunner were meant for Jess's attorney, and they were meant as a warning only. If Vic was right about Emilia and she was a cartel princess, she could be in real danger. Is this why he warned me to stay away from her back in law school? He knew getting involved with Emilia could become a one-way ticket back to Jersey for me. What was I supposed to do?

I walked around my desk and sat in front of my laptop. From the bottom drawer on the right, I fished out a burner phone and plugged it into my computer to jam any sniffer programs on the deep web. Old habits died hard. Logistics had been my thing on Mickey's crew. I had a knack for sniffing out the bad guys. The assholes coming after us, anyway. We were all bad guys here.

Browsing my go-to sites, I stumbled into the usual chatter. Nothing on me. It'd been so long since I quit Mickey's crew, I doubt anyone remembered my name. I did a quick search on Emilia Prado. Again, nothing. A few more clicks and the throng led me to a fairly active chat room. There was a new hit on Emilia Avellanos. Big money, high stakes. The kind of win that could earn anyone a promotion within the cartel. Could it be that these two Emilias were one and the same?

I entered the Avellanos name in Google and sat back, watching the engine spin its wheels. After several seconds, it came back empty. Too squeaky clean as if someone had wiped out any references to the name. Was Emilia seriously some kind of cartel princess in hiding? She'd denied it when I asked her, but why would she want Levi to continue to think she was dead?

I entered Emilia Prado in the engine next, which produced more normal results. Twitter profile, Instagram pics, the usual.

I should stay away from this one, but my interest was piqued and I'd yet to figure out how to walk away from a good fight. Until I knew for sure Emilia Prado was who she said she was, I had to assume there was a price on her head.

Did Emilia keep tabs on the chat rooms in the deep web like I did? Pulse beating fast, I stuffed the Levi case folder in my briefcase. This couldn't fucking wait. I shut down my laptop and jerked to my feet. With a bit of luck, she went straight to her office.

"Late lunch?" my assistant asked from her desk.

"Yes. If anything comes up call me." I pressed the button for the elevator and hopped on when the doors slid open. As far as plans went, I didn't have any, but Emilia had to know something ugly was coming for her.

Down in the garage level, I climbed into my car, input Emilia's work address in the nav system and drove off. As luck would have it, she was only a few blocks from me. How long had she been working at this firm? It seemed, one way or another, Emilia and I were meant to run into each other again. I shook my head and smiled like an idiot. Cole would be happy to hear his divorce brought me back to Emilia.

I parked outside the building and waited. If I went up, no doubt my presence would raise questions among her coworkers. The best thing to do was to be patient and wait for her to come out.

I messed with the satellite radio while excitement built up in the pit of my stomach. God, Emilia had always had that effect on me. Back in law school, I sensed there was more to her icy persona, that underneath the Little Miss Proper act was someone not too different from me. Could she sense it too? Was that why she avoided me like the plague? I picked up my phone off the center console and dialed her firm's number.

"Gallardo and Associates," a male voice answered on the first ring.

"This is Dom Moretti, I'm handling the Levi Smith case. Could I speak with Ms. Prado?" That was innocent enough.

"She's in a meeting. Could I take a message?"

"No. I'll call back later. Thanks." *Or I'll just wait out here until she goes home.* I hung up and dialed Vic. If anyone could dig up information on Emilia Avellanos, it'd be him.

"Dom. Make it quick." Vic's voice boomed over the speaker. Talking on an open line made him nervous.

"Need help finding someone. Can I shoot you a name?"

"Send it to the usual inbox," he said and dropped the call.

"Good talk." I tapped the end button, emailed him the information I had on both Emilias, and settled in. My eyes glared at the main entrance to the building while I ignored the tiny voice in my head telling me this was the creepiest thing I'd ever done —stalking a woman who up until last night had pretended I didn't exist.

Just fucking awesome.

I put the car into gear. Maybe I could send her a text to warn her about the chatter on the deep web. She'd made it clear she didn't want my help. I wasn't required to do more than tell her about what I saw, right? But then, I wouldn't be able to see her again. And fuck me if I didn't want to see her again. I killed the engine and rested my head on the headrest.

The whispers in my head grew louder as I sat there. Before I had to answer any of them, Emilia strolled out of her building and climbed into the black sedan that met her at the curb. I turned on the engine and followed her. An hour later, the car dropped her off at a house up in North Scottsdale, a swanky part of Phoenix. Judging by the size of her home, Emilia was doing well for herself. I waited at the end of the street. If they had security cameras, I couldn't see them. When she crossed the threshold, I climbed out of the car and walked the rest of the way to her house.

As I took the stone steps up to the massive front door, I rehearsed in my head what I would say. What was the best way to let someone know there was a mark on their back? When I reached the entrance, though, the doors stood wide open. An eerie stillness blanketed the space around me. Out of habit, I reached back for a handgun that wasn't there.

I stepped lightly into the foyer. Large framed mirrors lined the walls, directing me toward the living area, where side tables had been knocked over. My heart twisted, pounding hard in my throat. Holy shit. She'd come in not a minute ago. Thirty seconds was all it took to grab someone. I would know. Was someone already waiting for her? I'd come in too late. I should've stopped her the second she climbed out of her car.

A click and the all too familiar cold metal dug into the nape of my neck. *Shit.* How did they sneak up on me? I hadn't felt or heard anyone in the room.

"Why are you following me?" Emilia's voice was strained like she was trying to catch her breath.

My pulse slowed, and my shoulders relaxed. She was safe.

"We need to talk." I turned to face her. She'd taken off her jacket, and a silky beige top with spaghetti straps hugged her perfectly. The click of her gun stopped my wandering mind in its tracks. I shouldn't be thinking of her like that. She stuffed the weapon in the back of her skirt and stepped back, shooting daggers at me. Holy shit, if that wasn't a turn on.

"Stop looking at me like that and tell me why you're here." She scanned the room, her feet slapping the travertine tiles as she strode toward the front door to close it. "You scared the crap out of me."

"Why so twitchy?"

"Isn't it obvious?" She extended her arms, her gaze darted around the ransacked room. "Someone was here."

"And you don't know if they were here for Jess's lawyer or Emilia Avellanos."

"Right." She picked up a side table and put it back in place. She froze and hung her head. "How do you know that name?"

"That's you, isn't it? I mean, you didn't even bother to change your first name."

"It's my dad's name."

"You can trust me. I'm here to help." She opened her mouth, but I pressed on. "This morning, I was ready to let you walk out of my life again, but after everything that's happened here, I can't just leave you. I can help you."

"No. I can do this on my own." She met my gaze, brows furrowed, lips pressed together—certainly not the look of someone who wanted to be left alone, except I was out of things to say or do to show her I was a friend.

The faint beeping of numbers being pressed on a keypad came from behind us. Emilia's eyes went wide but showed no fear. A few seconds later, the bookcase lining the wall split open.

An older version of Emilia stepped out and offered me her hand as if she just hadn't come out of a secret room. "You must be Dom. I'm Sofia, Emilia's mom."

"I am. It's a pleasure to meet you." I smiled, squeezing her fingers gently.

"Did you mean what you said?"

So, she heard the entire conversation. Had she already figured out I had the hots for her daughter? The look in her eyes told me she was on my side. Honesty was the only way to get her to help me talk sense into Emilia. "I was scanning the online chat rooms..."

"You do this often?" Emilia asked, her eyebrows raised as she met her mom's gaze. As if this particular habit proved I wasn't to be trusted. Sofia wasn't buying it.

"It's always good to keep your finger on the pulse. Today's pulse is telling me there's a hit on you."

"Emilia?" Sofia treated Emilia to an 'I'm disappointed' stare. "You said everything was fine. That we had nothing to worry about."

"And we don't. Levi is pissed at Emilia Prado, his wife's attorney." Her light tone was meant to put her mom at ease, but her mom was smarter than that.

"The ad wasn't for Emilia Prado and you know that."

Sofia dropped her head in her hands. "I knew taking Jess's case was too risky for you. Why didn't you listen?"

I'd been wondering myself the same thing. "You both need to leave Phoenix. Tonight."

Sofia wiped her face, eyes stern and determined. "Yes, we do. Emilia. Go pack. Now."

"We can't let Levi run us off again. I'm done hiding, Mom."

"No. I won't lose you too." Sofia gripped Emilia's hand and walked her past the living area, down the wide hallway to the right. I followed them. If I helped them pack, we could get out of here in less than an hour. Sofia stopped at the first door. "Just a few changes of clothes. We can buy more once we're settled." She pushed Emilia's bedroom door opened and rushed down the hall.

"She's right."

I went in first. Emilia's signature vanilla scent hit me square in the face. Maybe this wasn't such a good idea. Emilia and I in the same room, alone, wasn't a good idea. I shook my head to clear it and headed for the walk-in closet. The faster we got out of here, the better. I slid all the hangers together, picked them off the rod, and dumped them on the bed—her bed. Desire pulsed fast and hard through me. Shit.

"Where do you keep your suitcase?"

I turned to face her. She stood in the threshold as if there were some invisible force keeping her pinned there.

"Under the bed." Her voice was hoarse and sexy. Did she feel it too? I braced my hand on the mattress and reached under it, taking in the faint smell coming from her pillows. "I got it." She rushed to my side when I dropped the suitcase on the down comforter and started throwing shit in.

"Fine." I stepped back, giving her—*and me*—space.

Lips pursed, she folded her clothes, dropping each item in a stabbing motion. Her mom had bullied her into this, but it was for the best. Going against the cartel was a horrible idea. What was she thinking?

"How did you know the ad was about me?" she asked after what felt like hours of silence. "A first name isn't enough."

"Wild guess." I shrugged and sat on the edge of the bed, my fingers toying with the silvery knickknacks on her nightstand. "Not so wild, really. You keep poking a sleeping bear, you're bound to wake him up."

"Levi deserves everything coming his way. The man kills for a living for Christ's sake." She slung a dress across the room, balling her hands into fists. "He can't win. I can't let him win again."

"You've been on the run for a while."

"How do you know that?"

"Well, for starters, you have a panic room and you can handle a gun better than any other lawyer I know." I stood and stepped closer, her scent filling me. "Why risk everything to help your cousin. Why now?"

"Jess is family. And I'm tired of running."

"If Levi is who you say he is, you can't go against him. It's too dangerous. This is the cartel you're talking about. Your life means little to them." *The cartel.* Why didn't I think of it before? I shook my head.

"What is it?"

"Why is the cartel going to the deep web to put a hit on you? Why not keep the job in-house? Don't you think that's peculiar?"

I'd been on the other side of the law when I ran around with Mickey's crew back in Jersey. No way Mickey would have ever trusted an outsider, a random bounty hunter, to do his dirty work. And he had a reason for it...he liked things done right. Based on the two attempts on Emilia, we weren't dealing with professionals here. Why risk it? What was Levi Smith trying to hide? Not that it mattered anymore. Emilia and her mom would be out of his reach before nightfall.

"Earlier today you offered to help me. Any chance that deal's still on the table? I don't want to leave."

I didn't want her to leave, but her mom was right. This was too dangerous. She couldn't stay. Although, if she kept looking at me like that, with those eyes full of longing and asking for help, I'd be done. No way I could say no to her. She rubbed the inside of her wrist, looking so lonely and exposed. I wanted to wrap my arms around her and tell her everything was going to be fine. I reached for her hand, and she squeezed my fingers.

"Dom, please. I need you."

Well, fuck.

5

KILL LEVI

Emilia

"Dammit, Emilia. Of course, my offer still stands."

I closed my eyes for a moment, a smile pulling at my lips before I let go of his hand. "First things first. How are we going to get past the Dragon Lady?"

He chuckled. A sexy sound that reminded me Dom Moretti was in my room—and we were alone. "Your mom? She seems like a sweet woman."

"Yeah, until you say no to her." When it came to the cartel, Mom didn't fool around. She'd seen firsthand what they could do and how fast. No way in hell she was letting me stay in Phoenix another night, but I had to. After all this time, I finally had a chance to go after the asshole who killed my dad.

"Why are we saying no to your mom?" He sat on the bed, toying with the small flower vase on my nightstand. Nervous energy.

"Because I'm not going with her."

"Yes, you are. What part of *there's a hit on you* do I need to explain again? You're leaving with your mom. Tonight."

"You said you were going to help me."

"And that's exactly what I'm doing. I'll allow you a continuance. Thirty days should be plenty of time for me to find out who Levi is. If he is what you say, I'll nail his ass to the wall. I promise you that."

He sounded so convincing. If he hadn't used his lawyer voice, I would've believed him. Dom didn't understand who my cousin's husband was. He wasn't just another crook. I kneaded the numb spot below my hip bone where his bullet went through me the day he killed Dad. The scar he'd left behind was an IOU. And it was time he paid.

"You know that's not what I need from you." I threw a pair of jeans in the suitcase, which took up half the bed.

"You're wasting time." He adjusted his weight on the mattress, moved a few decorative pillows out of the way, and then froze. *Oh, shit.* "What is this?" The infuriating smirk on his face said he knew exactly what was in the small lingerie bag he pulled out from under my pillow. Why didn't I hide it better? Oh, yeah, because never in a million years did I think Dom would end up in my room. "Wait. Don't answer that. What I really want to know is why is my name on it?"

"It was a joke."

"How long have you had this joke?" He pressed his lips together, his chest bouncing a little. It was all he could do not to burst out laughing.

"Your inflated ego must be loving this, but trust me, it's not what you think." I resumed the task of folding my clothes and arranging them in my luggage. Maybe if I pretended having a dildo with his name on it wasn't a big deal, he'd let it go.

"There's a vibrator under your pillow with my name on it. You betcha my ego is loving this." He bit the inside of his lip, gripping the contents of the bag. Why was this turning me on? He planted his feet on the carpet and stood, taking his time. His prowl was a promise that the *real* Dom would be a thousand times better than the chargeable device in his hand. "You want me. Why do you push me away?"

He pressed his chest against the side of my arm. I couldn't turn to face him. If I did, we'd end up doing what we had started last night at the bar.

"I've spent the last ten years in hiding because of what my dad did for a living. You saw today what Jess is going through with her husband. I don't want that for myself."

"I am not like them." His tone was terse and cold. "But you're right. You have your hands full as it is. I have no right to spring my bullshit on you. So here's what we're gonna—"

Shouts came from the other side of the house. They were faint, but they unmistakably belonged to Jess. "My cousin is here."

"Time's up." He moved so fast around the room, I felt like I was going in slow motion. I dropped the bathroom essentials into a toiletry bag while Dom stuffed the rest of my clothes in the suitcase and squeezed it shut.

He was right. If Jess recanted her story this morning, it could only mean her husband had gotten to her somehow. Had Levi convinced her to give me up? Selling out family was definitely Levi's MO.

Dammit, Jess. Please don't back out on me now. You owe me.

I threw my toiletry bag in my messenger bag along with my laptop and headed out of the room with Dom behind me, carrying my oversized luggage as if it weighed nothing.

Through the kitchen, in the main living room, Jess fell back onto a sofa chair. The one where Mom sat every night since Dad had died to knit him scarves he'd never get to wear.

"He made me, Tia Sofia. Levi—"

Mom struck her across the face again. "I raised you like my own daughter. And this is how you repay me? By selling out the only family I have left."

"The Dragon Lady," Dom said under his breath, setting the suitcase down.

I rushed toward Jess, standing between her and Mom. *Jesus*. I'd been here before, defending Jess for something she did to me. "Mom. Enough. What's going on?"

"Ask her." Mom pointed at Jess, her eyes red, hand fisted at her side. "No. You know what? Don't. She'll just lie again. Like always."

Mom let out a cry, a desolate sound that cut me deep. When I turned to face Jess, tears streamed down her face, but her eyes didn't show the same pain as Mom. Mom squeezed my hand.

"We have to leave now. Levi knows you're alive. Yeah. She told him."

"Jess. Why?" I kneeled in front of her. "We've gone through this already, and it ended with you spending the better part of your life in a hell your own husband created for you. I'm the only person that can help you. Why would you do this to me? To you?"

Dom stepped into the living room, wrapping his fingers around my forearm. "Emilia, we don't have time for this. Now you know for sure. That ad on the deep web is for you."

I freed my arm. Yeah, we had to leave. Whoever broke in earlier today would no doubt be back tonight. The mess they left behind was more than a warning, it was meant to instill fear in me, to make me lose my shit. I needed Jess to come with us. Even if she'd switched sides yet again. She was the only witness to Levi's crimes. "Jess...I still have the scars from the last time you betrayed your family. I stood by you and Dad ended up dead. You fucking owe me this."

"I'm pregnant."

"*Joder.*" *Fuck.* Mom plopped herself in the chair next to Jess and dropped her head in her hands.

The room turned a couple of times. I squeezed my eyes shut for a moment and reached for Jess's hand. "And it's Levi's?"

She nodded, meeting my gaze for the first time. "I have to think about my kids."

"Levi isn't the answer. Don't back out on me now."

"He's a good dad. Just like Uncle Emiliano was for us."

"Don't you dare speak his name." Mom jerked to her feet, startling Jess. For a woman in her fifties with all the horrible things she'd seen in her life, Mom was still the Dragon Lady. We'd made it this far because of her. Jess stepped back, and Mom continued. "No matter how hard he tries, Levi isn't half the man my husband was. Levi is nothing more than a traitor, driven by greed and petty illusions of grandeur. Emiliano loved him like a son, and he repaid us in the worst way." She let out a breath. "Enough, Emilia. Stop asking her for permission. She's coming with us."

"I can't. Levi's expecting me."

I stood. "You had your chance, Jess. Make no mistake. You're not coming with us as our guest. If Levi wants his family back, he'll have to go through us."

"Holy fuck, Emilia." Dom's gaze darted between Mom and me. "You're kidnapping a Sicario's family? This is a game you can't win. And you know that."

"That's what you don't get. This isn't a game for us." We couldn't spend the rest of our lives in hiding, fearful that one day Levi would come for us and finish what he started ten years ago when he shot Dad and left Mom and me bleeding out. All so he could take Dad's place within the Mexican cartel. The status quo had changed in our favor, and I was more than ready to do some hunting of my own. I faced Mom, and she nodded in approval. "You understand, don't you? I have to stay."

"We'll be safe. I can handle Jess." Mom hugged me and pressed her wet cheek against mine. "Come find us when it's done."

I nodded. "Go."

"And double time it." Dom peeked through the wooden shutters in the home office facing the street. "A caravan of Escalades just came in."

My hands went cold, and I fisted them. Not this again. It was like déjà vu, Levi showing up at my childhood home like this. Chest tight, the floor gave out from under me, and I fell to my knees. Mom's voice sounded distant, muffled by the loud beating of my heart.

The summer after high school graduation, Levi had been sent to make an example of Dad. No one ever left the cartel. Eager to replace Dad within the organization, Levi did as he was told. Without giving a shit we were like family. He would've killed Jess that day too if I hadn't thrown myself in front of her to protect her from his belt. He hit me several times before my words sunk in. Jess was pregnant with his first baby. We'd come full circle, but this time, he wasn't leaving here with my family. This time we were ready.

I took a gulp of air. When my eyes focused, Dom was on his knees in front of me, cradling my face.

"Emilia. We have to go, sweetheart." He rubbed his thumb along my jaw.

"The panic room has access to the outside."

He blinked slowly and scooped me up. "Use it. Now."

"No." I pulled the handgun stuffed in my waistband. Levi wasn't leaving this house. Not if I had a say in it. "Mom. Take Jess."

"Of course. I'll call Carlos on our way there. He'll pick up Izzy and then come find us."

"I'm not letting your driver get my daughter." Jess stood, facing Mom.

"He's the only one that can bring her to us safely. Now shut up and move." Mom gripped Jess's arm and headed for the panic room, the exit route we'd rehearsed every day since we returned to Phoenix.

As if Jess's infuriated look had the ability to shatter glass around her, a buzz whizzed by us just as Mom's bookshelves exploded behind her. Mom didn't flinch but kept going toward the safety of the hidden walls in the house.

I pressed my body against the wall near the window, Dom next to me and his arm across my body. Was he trying to protect me or stop me from going out and start shooting?

"If I have to drag you out of here, I will." He turned and pinned me with his body. His heat should've made feel safer, but it didn't. I needed to end this thing with Levi. "I see it in your eyes, but trust me, this isn't how you get Levi. Look around you. This isn't the mayhem of the shooting from the bar."

"I know that. Levi is a professional. He's got a silencer and bigger guns, but I don't give a shit. This ends now."

"How? He's pissed. You pitted him against his wife. If you thought he was dangerous before, this is ten times worse. You don't want him angry. You want him desperate. That's how you come out on top. Please, listen to me."

His forehead touched mine, and his heartbeat thrummed against my chest. I slammed my head against the wall and let out a breath.

"He deserves to die."

"Maybe. But not tonight." He slid his fingers down my arm and pried the gun out of my hand. "Come with me. If they haven't shot at us again it's because they found a way in."

I'd waited this long, I could wait a little longer for the right opportunity. One that wouldn't get Dom killed because of me. I nodded and made a run toward the panic room as more bullets destroyed what little was left of Mom's knickknacks across from the window. Dom stepped in behind me and shut the door. I entered the security code and stumbled back, holding my breath.

The soundproof room didn't allow the men's voices to carry, and I couldn't make myself turn on the sound, too afraid they'd hear us through the walls. On the security screens, a man stood in the middle of the room, his face distorted in anger, barking orders to his men—no doubt telling them to search every nook and cranny of the house. Jess didn't know about the panic room or our escape route. What exactly were they looking for?

I forced out a breath and turned to face Dom, who stood by the small door that led to the tunnels on the opposite end of the wall.

"You thought of everything." I cocked an eyebrow at the suitcase by his shoe.

"You'd already gone through the trouble of packing. I figured you might need it." He flashed me a bright smile and offered me his hand.

I took it and followed him into the dimly lit passageway that led to a street three houses down. Mom and Dad had built a place similar to this one when I was a kid. Together, they had devised a plan to make sure Mom and I would be taken care of if anything happened to him. We had an exit route, money stashed away in ten different countries, and contacts we could trust. None of which had helped Dad. Ten years ago, when Levi came for us, we hadn't had time to make it out because he took us by surprise. Dad loved Levi. He trusted him, and Levi used that against him.

One thing was for sure, Levi had a lot of connections, a way to get people to do what he wanted. I'd been going about this all wrong and Mom knew it.

'Come find us when it's done,' Mom had said that to me in her goodbye.

When I finished law school, I knew Levi's time would come soon. I knew the law would find him guilty and put him away for life, except Mom knew different. All this time, she understood something I didn't. The system had failed us before. Money and power always won. After years of wishing for justice, I'd finally caught on. I had to take care of him myself...I had to kill Levi.

Dom squeezed my hand. "It's not as easy as you think. Killing a man." He pointed behind him toward the house we'd left behind. "You're angry and hurt, but tomorrow you'll thank me for talking you out of this fucked-up suicide mission. I can't let you do that to yourself. Not ever."

6
I DECIDE

Dom

This day kept getting better and better—and not in a sarcastic way. Emilia turned out to be a different person than I first thought when we met in law school. She wasn't the spoiled rich girl she appeared to be. She was determined, with an uncanny ability to attract trouble. When I woke up this morning, I never would've guessed I'd end my day in a hot as hell tunnel running away from the Mexican cartel. Was I sorry I went looking for Emilia after she left my office? Not one fucking bit.

"What are you doing?" she asked, using her phone to light the path in front of us.

"We need a ride."

"Uber is our getaway car?"

"I parked a block away from your house." An old habit that paid off today. "To get to it, we'd have to go through Levi's guys. I can't risk him seeing me with you."

She sighed. "I should do the same. There's no reason for me to drag you into this. You know, any more than I already have."

"Stop." I took her hand to get her to quit tapping on her screen. Man, she was fast. "I volunteered. And after everything I saw and heard back at your house, I'm glad I did."

"Yeah. Why's that?"

"It made me realize something...made me realize I've been lying to myself for the last five years." My spidey senses were fucking tingling, and I didn't like it. Why did I let my guard down? When I left Mickey's crew back in Jersey and moved to the city, I'd thought it was over and done with, but I should've known better.

No one ever leaves.

Not two weeks after I moved to Phoenix, a Sicario from the local cartel called one of the owners at my new firm and asked for me specifically. A coincidence? Doubt it. At first, I figured my reputation had followed me and Levi knew I was the guy for him if he wanted shit done right.

"About what?" Emilia placed her hand on the door in front of us and pushed on it gently. We were in another home, a pool house in a ranch-style home that looked like it was built in the seventies and hadn't seen a tenant in years.

"Let's focus on getting out of here alive first. We can talk later."

She cocked an eyebrow at me. When I didn't give her any more details, she gestured for me to follow. "Come on. There's a gate at the other end of the yard."

I glanced on my phone. Vic had found us. "Our car is waiting."

As if I had planned the whole thing days in advance, our black car showed up as soon as we arrived at the curb on a quiet street outside the old house. I opened the door for Emilia and climbed in before she had a chance to scoot all the way across. The side of her body brushed mine as I shut the door, and I had to fight the urge to ask her to stay put, but she was quick. Before the car rolled away, she was flushed against the opposite window, too far away from me.

"Where are we going?" She turned to face me.

"My hotel." I flashed her a smile and she swallowed. Shit, I had to stop doing that. She'd made it clear she didn't want anything to do with me in that sense. "It's the safest place for us to go. Only a couple of friends know where I'm staying, and Levi won't think to look for you there."

"Fine. But I'm getting my own suite."

Not fucking likely. "If you're on your own, I can't protect you."

"I don't need your protection, and you know that. What I need is my gun back."

I rolled my eyes at her, reaching for the back of my pants to pull out her fully automatic 9mm. When she took it, she quickly checked the safety button on the side and the cartridge.

"The minute your credit card shows up on the grid, Levi will find you."

"I have cash."

I pinched my nose. "Why waste your money and put yourself at risk when the answer is right in front of you? What is it? Are you afraid you won't be able to resist me if I'm sleeping next door?"

"You wish." A little wrinkle appeared at the corner of her eye. Maybe she wasn't opposed to the idea.

"Does that mean you're staying with me?"

"Yes." She looked away at the oncoming traffic.

I sat back in my seat grinning and met Vic's gaze in the rearview mirror. He shook his head once in disapproval, his hands firmly on the steering wheel. Of course, he was right. As my right-hand man, Vic knew exactly what was at stake here. Getting involved with Emilia, romantically or otherwise, was a bad idea, but I couldn't let her go until my suspicions were proven wrong.

Vic pulled into the resort, past the main lobby, and continued toward the back access. He wasn't taking any chances. To my right, Emilia's gaze darted from Vic to me, and then back to him. I needed to come clean with her. Tonight, before this rabbit hole with Levi got any deeper.

In an uncharacteristic manner, Emilia followed me through the hotel's industrial-sized laundry room and storage warehouse until we reached the service elevator that put us on the top floor on the opposite end of where my corner suite was located. Calm and collected as if she hadn't been shot at two hours ago, she waited for me to open the door to *our* suite.

"Home sweet home." I ushered her inside and flipped the deadbolt. "Can I get you a drink? Whiskey?"

She faced me in that regal way that was all Emilia. "Red wine, if you have it."

"As luck would have it, I do. The hotel concierge leaves me a bottle every night, but I prefer whiskey." I shrugged out of my suit jacket and laid it on the back of the sofa in front of the fireplace. Folding my sleeves up, I made my way to the wet bar near the door. I grabbed two wine glasses and one of the bottles from the small fridge.

When I returned to the living area, Emilia sat on the sofa, typing something on her phone. No doubt telling her mom she was safe.

"It's probably not a good idea for you to be communicating with your mom." I took a seat on the chair adjacent to the sofa and showed her the bottle. "It's a Valpolicella."

She smiled at me. "I wasn't texting Mom. I was disabling my phone."

"Good thinking." I offered her a glass.

She put her nose in it, and then took a long sip. "I love it. Thanks."

I drank too. "How are you doing?"

"I almost got you killed. I'm sorry."

I shook my head. "Don't worry about me. You have your gun back. Now what?"

She trained those big brown eyes on me, pressing her lips together. What wasn't she saying? After all we'd gone through since our night at the bar, she still hadn't figured out she could trust me.

My heartbeat picked up its pace. Only Vic knew why I left Mickey's crew. Why I dropped everything and went to law school instead of accepting Mickey's offer to be his right hand and business partner. I rose to my feet, taking even breaths as I pulled on the rolled sleeves and unbuttoned my shirt.

"Are you serious with this?" She uncrossed her legs, her back erect.

"Relax. I want to show you something." I laid the shirt on the back of my chair and reached behind me to pull off my undershirt. I pinched my lips together when Emilia's eyebrows shot up in surprise. She reached for her glass, and took two big gulps, her greedy eyes trained on my abs.

My ego was enjoying the display, but this wasn't about sex. I glanced down at my hands and pointed at the three scars on my chest and shoulder.

"You recognize these?"

A deep furrow shot across her forehead as her eyes showed recognition. She set her glass down and stood.

"Bullet wounds." If she'd been turned on before, it was all gone. She stepped toward me, mouth slightly parted as she took in the details of my scars. "More specifically, exit wounds."

I nodded. "He shot me in the back."

Her eyes watered. Finally, she understood. "What did you do?" Her voice was barely above a whisper, hoarse and full of pity while her fingers traced the marks. Not what I wanted her to see in me.

I closed my eyes for a moment, letting it all sink in. Saying it aloud made that night all the more real. "I shot him dead."

"Dom." She wrapped her arms around me, her cool lips brushing the skin on my shoulder.

"Not the response I had expected." I cocked my head to meet her gaze.

"I'm the last person to judge. Trust me." She stepped back.

"Why's that?" I'd bared my deepest secret. It was her turn. "What did your dad do to anger the cartel?"

She shook her head once. Strands of hair fanned the side of her flushed cheek. This vulnerable version of Emilia was as beautiful as the kick-ass version of her I saw earlier at her house.

"He quit his post with the organization."

Just as I had suspected when she and her mom got into it with her cousin Jess.

"Levi replaced your dad with the cartel, didn't he? That's why they sent him. It was a test."

She nodded. "Dad was a lieutenant, feared and respected by all. Until he met Mom, and his life went off in a different direction. Or at least he tried to turn things around. It didn't last long though. The minute they found a replacement for him, my dad was dead."

"Why didn't your mom call the police? She didn't have to let Levi get away with it."

She bit her lip and untucked her silky top. My breath hitched when she pulled it over her head. Those breasts trapped inside her bra pressed together as she let the blouse fall on the coffee table and pulled her hair up in a loose ponytail with her hands. She was showing me something, but for the life of me, I couldn't tear my eyes away from the see-through bra, the curve of her tits, and the goosebumps trailing up her arm and neck. *Christ*, she was sexy.

I stepped toward her, my gaze roaming her skin until I found it, a blotchy spidery scar right over her clavicle. She hooked her fingers on the seam of her skirt and pulled down, showing me her second scar on the inside of her hip bone, an inch from her stomach.

"He left us for dead. Calling the police for an investigation would've told him we were still alive."

She exhaled and turned to show me her back. I wanted to punch a wall. No, I wanted to kill Levi. That greedy asshole.

"I'm so sorry, Emilia," I whispered, tracing my fingers up her back where three whitish lines went from the dip of her waist and up into the lace of her bra. She hung her head and let her hair fall on her shoulders. I thumbed the rough edges of each scar, wishing I could erase the memories they'd left behind—the heartache of being betrayed by a friend, the pain of losing her dad, and even Jess.

Her arms went slack at her sides. She relaxed her shoulders and turned to rest her cheek against my bare shoulder, sending my pulse into overdrive. Was she beginning to trust me? Her body nestled against mine felt like home.

I wrapped my arms around her and she jerked as if I had broken the spell. Not the reaction I was going for. She lifted her head, looking around the room, and stepped back. On instinct, I reached out to her, but she shifted out of my grasp fast. The stern scowl that showed every time she spoke of Levi was back on. Okay. So maybe she wasn't ready to trust me, but she'd finally told me the truth about why she wanted to nail her cousin's husband's ass to the wall. For the time being, that was good enough for me.

"We've waited long enough. Levi has to answer for everything he did to my family."

"So instead of calling the cops, your mom bided her time. And now she's decided it's time for Levi to die and for you to kill him and avenge your dad?" I reached behind me and grabbed my shirt off the chair. My cock couldn't handle any more of this show and tell.

"It's up to me." She donned her blouse, covering the red blotches that appeared on her chest and neck. "I decide."

"And you've decided? Is that what you're telling me? Emilia, killing a person will, in time, kill you."

Her eyes welled with tears. She blinked, and a few drops streamed down her cheeks. "I was eighteen. I looked up to Jess like an older sister and even Levi. We were close. Overnight, he chose power over family. He showed up to our house to execute us."

I'd seen scars like hers before, where the exit point wasn't leveled with the entry point. Fighting the picture forming in my mind, bile rose up to the back of my throat. I took my glass and downed the rest of the wine. The alcohol wasn't enough to drown the clear image in my mind.

The night Emilia's dad died, Levi had known Emilia had to go too. That fucking asshole. She was on her knees when he shot her. During my time with Mickey, I saw all kinds of murder scenes. Emilia's scar told a vivid story. Levi struck her with a heavy and thick belt, brought her to her knees, and shot her in what he no doubt thought was her stomach. When she fell to the floor, he put another bullet in her back for good measure, letting her die a slow death. I bit the inside of my lip, swallowing the lump in my throat, replacing the horrific scene in my head with a more pleasant one—Levi's neck between my fingers. He deserved every bit Emilia and her mom had planned for him.

"I can't even get him for domestic violence. What am I supposed to do?"

"Emilia." I wanted to wrap my arms around her, hold her tight against my chest. Instead, I thumbed her jawline.

"No." She slapped my hand away. "The law can't help us. Mom knew that back then. She waited patiently for me to do things my way. Like a stupid good girl, I went to law school to be the better person, to do things right. Get justice without getting my hands dirty. It took me almost ten years, but I've finally caught on. There's only one way to give Levi what he deserves."

I placed my hands on my hips. *What the fuck do I say to that? How do I stop her from making the biggest mistake of her life? How do I help without putting my own freedom at risk?*

"Don't go against me, Dom. Please."

7

IT'S NOT A JOB

Emilia

I met Dom's gaze. His hot blue eyes had a ferocity I'd never seen in them before. Other than my gut and rumors, I never had any evidence to tell me who or what Dom was until now. Why did he show me his scars? Why tell me point blank that he was involved with the mob? It was a risky move on his part. If he'd wanted to gain my trust, he could've offered me the continuance I asked for. Why put himself out there? Because he thought he was out?

The details of what the mob put him through didn't take me by surprise. If anything, it all played out the way it always did. Except Dom had won, and still, he chose to walk away. What made him quit his crew?

For Dad, it was Mom and me. Probably the worst reason to quit the mob or the cartel. If there was anything I'd learned from my family's experience it was exactly that. For Mom and Dad, and even Jess, love had put a target on their backs. It made them vulnerable. It made them weak.

What happened to Dom? Was he shot at before or after he decided to leave? He sat on his side of the sofa, not bothering to button his dress shirt. His muscled chest strained as he found his composure. I turned my back to him, feeling naked.

Oddly enough, it wasn't the way he stared at my chest that had me feeling that way, but the way he'd compelled me to tell him my most intimate secret. A few guys at work had tried. Mostly because guys tended to get annoyed when women didn't act as expected. At twenty-eight, I was supposed to be looking to settle down. Not one of them would've been able to stomach or even begin to understand what I just showed Dom. Outside of Mom and Jess, no one knew that a price was put on my head once and that I'd survived. I donned my blouse and tucked it into my skirt.

"Why?" I spun to face him.

"Well, one, it's illegal."

"No." I pointed at his scar. "Why did they...? Did you try to leave too?"

He rubbed the stubble on his cheek. A smirk tugged the corner of his lips. "No."

"You don't want to tell me. It's fine."

I had no right to ask, but for the first time in the last ten years, I had someone I could talk to about what happened to me. Someone besides Mom, who'd refused to touch the subject since that night.

Soon after the shootout where Dad died, Jess disappeared. Or rather, Levi took her with him and started a family. Mom, on the other hand, turned to stone. Somehow, she managed to put all of it behind and start new. She followed Dad's plan to the letter and moved us to New York, where I finished my under-grad and then went on to law school at Columbia. From the minute Mom's bodyguard snuck us out of our house with our clothes soaked in blood, halfway dead, she asked me to never speak of it again.

I don't remember every detail. Thank God for small favors. Although I remembered Mom holding my hand lying on the bed next to me in the ambulance and telling me over and over that we would survive this. From that moment on, there were only two rules in our household—never mention that night again, and no matter what, survive.

Except now Dom was here. The least likely person for me to trust. And yet, the only one I could trust at this moment, the only one who wanted to talk, who wasn't afraid of the demons hunting me.

"Let's just say they made me an offer, and I refused."

"A test?" I knew the drill. Loyalty was the highest commodity within the cartel. To prove one's worth, one had to prove true loyalty.

"I imagine you know the details of it. Two friends walk in, only one walks out."

I glanced down at my hands and swallowed my tears. After ten years of it, I had become a pro at it. By the way Dom's Adam's apple bobbed with every breath, I'd say he was pretty good at it too.

"Yeah. So what? You didn't want the job. You had someone?" Was that why Dom had never taken anyone serious in law school? Why all women were disposable to him then? He'd lost the love of his life?

"No."

I nodded. This was a secret he wanted to keep, and I had no right to pry. "I'm sorry."

He reached for my hand. "I know you are. Maybe now that

you know I know what I'm talking about, you'll desist. Once you go down that road, Emilia, there's no coming back."

"No coming back?" I squeezed his hand before I released it. "You think I don't know that? When it comes to...them...there's never a coming back. I'm done hiding. I'm done swallowing this anger I've had in the pit of my stomach since that night. Do you understand?" My breath hitched. Shit. Of course, he understood. He'd shown me that. "You know what I mean."

"It isn't your job to avenge your dad's death."

"It's not a job. It's what I want. I've waited long enough."

He jerked to his feet, running a hand through his hair in frustration. "I might've gotten a few details about you wrong, but this..." he pointed at me, "I was right about this. Your way is the only way. God, you're stubborn as all hell."

"What's it to you anyway? You're not my keeper." I rose to my feet and faced him.

"I'm not." He placed both hands on his hips and flashed me a good bit of his abs again. *Jesus.* "However, I am opposing counsel."

"You can't be serious. Why do you even care if Levi lives or dies?"

"I don't. I care about you. So here's the deal." He sat on the couch and gestured for me to do the same.

I plopped myself next to him. "Let me guess, you'll give me a continuance in exchange for his life."

"The continuance is yours. Don't be the one to pull the trigger, and in return, I will help you nail his balls to the wall."

Was he really this naïve? "If by balls to the wall you mean dead, you've got yourself a deal because that's the only deal I'll take. You know how this works. He has to finish the job. That's me and Mom."

"If he goes to jail, he'll be cut off. His boss will be forced to find a new right hand."

Maybe. But that would leave Mom and me as loose ends, and the cartel hated loose ends. As long as Levi was alive fighting to keep his current position and his family, we would never be safe. It was him or us. Levi showed me that today when he sent his men after me. Even if I had no way to prove he was the one who came after us, I knew it had to be him.

He'd only sent a couple of his men to the bar to deal with his wife's lawyer. They were there to scare me into backing down, to stop asking questions, but the crew that showed up at Mom's house had specific orders to get rid of us one way or another.

"What do you have in mind?" I asked.

"I'll look into his financials. That's where most people make mistakes. For now, I'll make sure that all legal communications are either via email or conference call. I have no intention of serving you on a silver platter."

"You called for a face-to-face to intimidate my cousin, didn't you?"

"Up until now, I thought this case wasn't the right case to win a partnership at a new firm. I wanted it over quickly. I'm sorry."

"Yeah, your plan worked brilliantly. Jess recanted and not only that, she outed me."

I leaned my cheek against the back of the sofa. I couldn't be mad at Dom. As a lawyer, I'd employed the same tactic many times. Easiest way to close a case was to get rid of a witness. All cases came down to that, but now I'd lost the only advantage I had—the element of surprise.

"You have no idea how sorry I am." He cradled my neck. His

hand was warm and soothing. "Domestic disputes are not my thing. I just don't have a frame of reference for it."

"This is more than a domestic dispute."

"I know that." He thumbed my jaw as he pulled me toward him. It was a small invitation to lean on him. I closed my eyes and pressed my cheek against his long fingers. He drew me closer, reclining back until his head rested on the decorative pillows, and he held most of my weight.

The pressure on my chest lifted, and air rushed to my lungs. While I was at Columbia, the only thing that kept me going was the hope that one day I'd get a chance to settle the score with Levi. When Jess showed up at our door with a nasty bruise on the side of her face and her daughter fast asleep in her arms asking for our help, I knew my time had come—I had more than hope. I had a plan. However, bit by bit, Levi had stomped out all my moves. He was too powerful.

When Dom showed up at the bar last night, I'd convinced myself the universe had sent me a kindness, a respite, but now, he was more than that. I was running out of choices. Was Dom my only way out?

"I would never do anything to hurt you. You have to believe that," he whispered against my temple as he massaged the nape of my neck.

I met his gaze. "I believe you."

He smiled, and I got lost in the depths of his intense gaze. His free hand wrapped around my waist. He held me as if it were normal to lay with him this way. Was it fear that had me running toward this fantasy that was Dom—the bad boy from law school, the one who never once looked my way? I shifted my body, wedging my arms between us. Dom was a bad idea then. That much hadn't changed.

He took my hand and pressed it against his chest. The warmth from his skin scurried up my arm and down to my core. "I still remember my first day at Columbia. I couldn't believe my eyes when you strolled through the door and sat in front of me. I thought I was losing my mind."

"I remember that day. You had this deep scowl across your face. Do you have a problem with female lawyers?"

"*What?* Not at all. Even now, I can't explain what I felt that morning. In a flash, I could see us having something. And for a moment, I wanted to be normal. I wanted a family. It was a dumb idea, and you let me know it the first time I asked you out."

"You never asked me out."

"Are you kidding me? I sat across from you at the library and asked if you wanted to get coffee. You were so quick to put me in my place. It took me days to recover from the whiplash."

Did I do that? I scoured my memory for the details of that day. He hadn't asked me out. "You didn't ask me out. You asked me to get you a coffee."

"Why would I do that? That doesn't even make sense."

"It kind of did. You walked around campus like you were God's gift to women."

"Believe me when I tell you I'm no gift from God. Quite the opposite. You were right to turn me away. That day had been especially bad for me. I'd asked you out in a moment of weakness. I wanted to get close to you so badly." He gripped my waist tighter, his lips ghosting mine. The same way he'd done after I told him he could get his own coffee. When in my haste to get away from him, I'd tripped over my computer bag and he caught me. I hadn't imagined it. He'd meant to kiss me, or at least thought about it. His ragged breath brushed against my cheek. "I still do. You have no idea how much."

I tugged my hand from under his and kneaded the hard ridges on his stomach. He wanted me to make the choice for us. After the last two nights, I didn't think I had the willpower to push him away anymore.

"Things are different now. There are no more secrets between us. We decide what we do with our lives. So I'm asking again. You and me...why the hell not?"

"We decide." I echoed his words.

"I want to kiss you."

I nodded because I'd been dying to kiss him too. He shoved his hand into my hair and crushed his lips against mine. His tongue, laced with wine, urged me to let him in. When I did, he let out a groan that sent a desire-induced surge through my body. I melted into him, letting his hand guide me into his kiss. He switched between treating my mouth to his soft lips, and the expert thrusts of his tongue. My pulse quickened, pumping hot blood through every fiber of me.

"God, Emilia, you taste so fucking good." He released the grip he had on my waist and skimmed his fingers up my back. Their warmth rushed down my spine and settled at my core. How was it possible to want someone this much? With a snap, he unhooked my bra, while his other hand made quick work of my buttons. Something like a moan escaped my lips. If I hadn't been so subdued by his heated touch, I would've been embarrassed.

"Maybe your battery-operated Dom can make you come, but I can do so much more for you. You and I, we fit so well. I felt it the first time I saw you." His hand settled on my scars, and

I rocked my hips against him, running my fingernails across his chest and *his* scar.

Yeah, I'd felt it too. The electric charge in the air every time he was near. It was why I'd kept my distance all this time. Dom was so much more than I imagined. The intensity of his words, the hardness of his body, and that sinful mouth of his surpassed any fantasy I'd ever had of him.

Jesus. This guy was so out of my league.

"Wait," I whispered.

He groaned into the soft spot between my neck and shoulder and sat up, holding me tight. "Are you sure?"

No, I wasn't sure. I could feel myself drifting. Dom was not part of the plan. If I gave in now, it'd be so easy to get lost in him. Letting my guard down now could cost me not only my life but the lives of the only family I had left.

Not enough had changed between us. Maybe he knew everything about me this time around, but he was wrong in thinking that we had the ability to choose our own paths. Did he really not see that? I buried my hands in his hair and pulled to make him look at me.

8

NO ONE EVER LEAVES

Dom

Kissing Emilia hadn't been my plan when I brought her back to my hotel room. At all. What was I thinking? I nuzzled her neck, drunk off the scent of her skin and the taste of her kiss. She tunneled her fingers through my hair, her chest rising and falling in tandem with mine. Her hard nipples pushed through the silky fabric of her blouse and brushed against me. I ached to squeeze those proud globes, make her moan against my lips again.

"Whatever testosterone cocktail you're serving, my body is definitely drinking." She breathed against my lips, and her eyes fluttered closed.

I kissed her before she got to the "but" part of her sentence. Her lips were made for kissing, for kissing me, and that was exactly what she did. She cupped my face and ran the tip of her tongue along my lower lip before she pressed her mouth to mine. A sigh escaped her as she slid her hands down to my abs. I gripped her hips in a silent plea not to give up on this just yet, but she'd made up her mind. And this was Emilia Prado—the most stubborn woman I'd ever met. If my life didn't totter on the edge of chaos on a daily basis, this goodbye would've hurt a lot more.

"But..." she whispered.

I fell back on the pillows, running both hands over the stubble on my face. "Just give me a minute."

"I'm sorry." She braced her hands on my chest and pushed off me. I enjoyed every bit of her legs rubbing against my crotch.

"Please don't say you're sorry. I shouldn't have done that." I sat up again, putting as much space as I could between us. Though I couldn't come up with a good reason to sit somewhere else. She didn't move either. Maybe she wasn't appalled by my kiss or whatever the hell that was. She finished buttoning her top in silence. Her long, curly hair covered the side of her face and effectively shut me out. After a while, I let out a breath, feeling more like myself again.

"I swear I had a goddamn point before. What are you thinking?"

She tucked her legs under her and turned to face me. Heat still covered her cheeks, and her breath sounded uneven. "Bad things happen when we kiss."

I chuckled. "That was just the one time, and I'm pretty sure those guys would've shot at us regardless. This is the second time you pushed me away..." My phone rang and I grabbed it. Thankful for the distraction. Though Emilia and I were overdue for *the talk*.

I smiled when I saw Nikki's name on the screen. Here was another soul as lost as me. "How you doin', doll? How's Paris?"

"Not there yet. Took a little detour. I need a favor, darling."

Across from me, Emilia threw her long legs off the sofa and

strutted to the door. My heart did a quick somersault. I jerked to my feet but stayed put when she grabbed her big-ass suitcase and rolled it to her bedroom. I sighed at her retreating form. "For you, anything. What is it?"

"My sister's in jail."

I tore my gaze away from Emilia's door. Nikki needed me. Though I'd met her just a few months ago, she'd proven to be a true friend when she helped Cole get his company back. Even if her methods were outside of conventional standards, if not downright illegal. "Holy shit. What happened?"

"She killed a man." Static filled the air. "Or rather, she's serving time for a crime she didn't commit. I promise you, she didn't do it."

Back when I first decided to go to law school, my life had been a collection of bad choices and bad choices with benefits. My decision had surprised my best friend, Cole. He supported me, even if he couldn't find the connection between the Dom that couldn't give a fuck and the Dom who wanted to be a lawyer. The answer was simple. As I got older, the playground got bigger, and the bullies got meaner. It was as Pops had always said, 'Life isn't fair. So it's up to people like us to even it out a little. Do what we can, huh?'

"What do you need, babe?"

"I need to see my sister. Could you help with that? For some reason, her visitation privileges were revoked or something."

"You got it, doll. Give me an hour. Just text me the details."

"Thank you, darling. You're the best. Ciao." She hung up.

I stared at my phone until her message popped up. I forwarded the information to my assistant and hit the call button. She answered on the first ring. "How can I help you, Mr. Moretti?"

The girl was afraid of me. I'd meant to deal with that before, but with all this Emilia business, I'd had my hands full. "How are you doing?"

"Oh. Um. I'm good. Thank you and you?"

I chuckled. "I'm doing great. I need a favor."

"Of course, anything." Her voice still had a shaky quality to it, but it was better.

"I just texted you a case number. Could you print the file and bring it to my hotel?"

"Absolutely. I have it here. As soon as it's done printing, I'll bring it over."

"Thanks." I ended the call and sat in front of my laptop at the head of the table to get started on Nikki's visitation request.

A few seconds later, Emilia came out of her room barefoot, wearing short shorts and a sweatshirt with a Harvard emblem. Just below it and written in smaller letters was *Just kidding*.

I wasn't ready to let her go.

"Are you finished with your call?" she asked. If I didn't know any better, I'd say that was her jealous tone. How about that? She cared. "I mean, I only ask because we have dinner on the way."

"Thank you. I'm hungry."

She grabbed her computer bag and padded her way to the other end of the table. Her long, toned legs were a big distraction. I glanced down at my crotch. Huge distraction.

Now that she was here safe and sound, the implication of what I'd offered her became painfully clear to me. Until the case with Levi was settled, Emilia would live here with me. Sleeping next to my room, possibly in the nude. At least in my head anyway. How the hell was I supposed to stay away from her?

She fired up her laptop and immediately started clicking

away on her keyboard. Jeez, she typed fast. I did the same, doing my best to stay focused on the court order in front of me. I filled in the usual information and the same legalese I knew would get my request fast-tracked. I hit the keys hard and in rapid succession. If she could sit across from me and pretend we didn't just have the hottest kiss in the fucking history of kissing, I could too. I slanted her a glance. The faster she typed, the harder I hit the keys. I saved the document and created a new email to my assistant, asking her to get my request filed before she came over.

Emilia moved on to scribbling notes in a file she'd laid out on the table. She bit her lip and squinted a little, the way she used to do in school when she'd spend all her free time studying in the library. After last night and everything that happened since we met up again, I understood where all her drive and motivation came from.

She wasn't at Columbia to please Daddy or to have a title to add to her name. Her reasons were the same as mine. She needed to be a lawyer. In her mind, she had no other choice. She wanted justice, and law school was her means to the end she had envisioned for Levi.

I fisted my hand, catching myself before I hit send. Instead, I scrolled to the bottom of the email to add a "please" and a "thank you" for my assistant. After my application beeped to confirm the email had gone through, I snapped my laptop closed.

"So, why are you so afraid of kissing?" I asked.

I wasn't about to let her off the hook that easy. Also, if we were going to be sharing a hotel suite, we needed ground rules. Well, I needed ground rules.

"I'm definitely not opposed to kissing." The apples of her

cheeks turned a pretty pink. "I'm just afraid of what comes next."

I joined her on her side of the table, crossing both arms over my chest to keep myself in check. "Sex, you mean?"

She slapped my shoulder, and I caught her hand. With a smile, she laced her fingers through mine. Emilia needed me. More than the hot sex we could be having right now, she needed my friendship. And I needed hers.

"I mean love." She met my gaze.

Love? My mind was still reeling from the *kiss.* Love was something I couldn't deal with right now. I brushed her soft cheek with the back of my fingers, following the path down to her neck to pull on the curl resting on her shoulder. She was so beautiful. Yeah, Emilia deserved a life full of love. A life full of all those things women want.

I'd had this conversation with many women before. The ones who thought they had feelings for me and wanted to move the relationship to the next step. In other words, do the whole boyfriend and girlfriend thing where we held hands and went to picnics with other couples and such. How could they possibly have any real feelings for me if they didn't know the real me? How could they possibly love the real me?

"I think your heart is safe with me." I brought her hand up to my lips.

She smiled, letting me pull her into my embrace. As if I'd held her a million times, she rested her head on my shoulder, and I'd be damned if this small act didn't feel like home.

"It's not my heart that'd be in danger. You know that. It would be your life, and now that I've met the real you, I'd hate to see you get hurt because of me. You asked why the hell not? That's why." She wrapped her arms around my waist.

I held her tighter, wishing I could tell her she was wrong, but that would be a lie. Even if our circumstances weren't exactly the same, our curse was. To love someone was to hurt them. It was the reason why my relationships were short and sweet.

"You knew that about me in law school?"

She glanced up at me. "I recognized the look in your eyes."

"What would that be?"

"I don't know. There's an intensity in your eyes that warns people to stay away. You can be so intimidating and brutally honest. There was also the way you approached the law. Always from a practical sense. Always looking for a loophole. I realized it was because you already knew how criminals were trying to beat it."

"You never considered that maybe I didn't just have the brawn and good looks but also the brains?"

She barked out a laugh. "Oh, wow. I see your ego hasn't changed." She slipped her hand up to the nape of my neck, and a knot unfurled inside my chest. Emilia had always known who and what I was, and she didn't hate me. She avoided me like the plague, but at least she didn't fear me. "I didn't care about any of that. Even after that one girl started a rumor about you running around with a crew from Jersey."

That'd been a particularly tough day. I went home with a girl that rocked my world. During the post-coital high, I felt like we had connected and decided to come clean. In my defense, I was wasted when it happened. Needless to say, she didn't handle the news well.

At first, she thought I was kidding, and even got turned on by it. When she realized I was serious, she couldn't get out fast enough. Fear was the last thing I saw in her eyes before she shut the door in my face. We hadn't connected like I'd thought. If I had to be honest, I just needed a bigger dose of brutal honesty. I hated secrets. The next day, I made an ass of myself and asked Emilia out, hoping for the real thing.

"I knew they weren't rumors," she said.

"That scared you? Tell me the truth." I wanted to hear her say it. Hell only knew why.

"No." She ran her thumb over my lips, her gaze roaming my face as if she was trying to memorize it. Was she fighting the urge to kiss me again? "I didn't want to make you choose."

"Make me choose?"

She nodded. "The way Mom had done with Dad."

"No one can make a man do something he doesn't want. Your dad chose to do right by you."

"His love for us made him weak. It's what got him killed."

"Love didn't get your dad killed. Bad people did. I hope you understand that." I cradled her neck.

She shook her head. "Not that I thought you'd fall for me back then, but why risk it? I didn't want for you to have to choose because it really isn't a choice. No one ever leaves. Not even the great Dom Moretti."

"My case was different. I had a choice." I worked hard to ensure that choice was never taken away from me. Vic did too.

"I have a choice too. And we both know the solution is the same." She shuffled away from me to make her point.

"Killing is never a solution."

I was an idiot for thinking I could change her mind. I told her about Mickey's fucked-up test to show her I knew what the hell I was talking about. I knew what it was like to kill someone. To see the years go by and never be able to make amends with yourself. I didn't want that for her. It could be different for her if she wanted. She deserved better.

"Whether you like it or not, Levi has to pay for what he did. I don't want to spend the rest of my life looking over my shoulder. It's time I live my life the way I want with whomever I want."

"And I agree with you. The asshole has to go. I just don't want you to be the one to do it. At least let me try."

"Fine." She walked to the living room and casually poured herself more of the wine.

"I need your word."

"You have my word. I won't kill Levi unless I have to, or if he's not in jail by the time Jess's case is closed."

"That's the most non-committal promise I've ever heard, but I'll take it."

9

GOOD OL' B.O.D.

Emilia

A knock on the door made me jump like I'd been caught doing something wrong. Was it wrong that I wanted to keep kissing Dom? Kissing Dom the first time was a bad idea. The second? Well, the second kiss felt like it should never stop. I sipped my wine, hoping to find the answers at the bottom of the glass. I had to suppress whatever feelings started brewing when I let Dom get close because if I didn't, Dom and my family would get hurt.

"Why so jumpy?" Dom swung the door open.

I recognized the woman from his office, the one who stopped me from leaving earlier today. Her eyes went big when she spotted me across the room. Why did I feel naked? Why did I feel the urge to explain to her that I was here on a temporary basis? That I had to be here or that Dom made me stay.

"Is this all of it?"

"Yes, Mr. Moretti." She jerked to a halt and faced him.

"It's just Dom. If we're going to be working together, there's no need for reverent bullshit."

"Oh." She stepped back and removed the lid from one of the boxes. "Okay."

"Thank you. You can leave everything there. I got it."

She dropped the files back in the box as if they'd suddenly caught fire and stepped away. Without another glance in my direction, the girl scurried out of the room and closed the door behind her. Dom got to work on unloading the rest of the manila folders, throwing them on the table in different piles. I picked up a box and set it on a chair.

"Whatever did you do to her? Isn't she your assistant?"

"Yes." He shook his head. "She's scared shitless, and I don't know why."

I laughed. He actually cared. "Maybe cut back on the 'shits' and 'fucks'? Just a thought."

"I'll try to remember that." His gaze lingered on my face before he returned to the papers he held in his hand.

"Cold case?" I asked.

"A friend of mine needs help with it."

"Is that the doll who called earlier?"

Okay, that came out a little too catty. I grabbed one of the files to distract myself. I couldn't care less if Dom had girlfriends who called out of nowhere to ask for help. If our living arrangements had any shot at working out, I had to assume Dom would need his freedom to do whatever it was he did when he got bored or...dammit.

I hated the thought of Dom with another woman, but I'd made my bed, literally, and now I had to lie in it. I had no right to show up out of the blue at his place asking for help, tell him we couldn't be involved romantically, and then turn around and also ask him not to see anyone else. Right. We needed ground rules—a protocol book.

"Yes. This is her sister's case," he answered in his lawyer voice. To my disappointment, he buttoned his shirt. Yeah, he meant business now.

I put aside my pettiness and grabbed a folder. "Maybe I can help?"

"You've done criminal?" He pinched his nose. "Sorry. Of course, you have."

"Don't be. What do you know so far? Did she do it?"

"No."

"You believe her?"

"I believe her sister." He lowered himself on his chair. "Problem is, it's been fifteen years since it happened."

I took the seat next to him. "Oh my God. Poor woman."

"And she was practically a child when she was sent to jail. This is the kind of bullshit I can't stand."

His phone rang again. I sat back and braced for his "Hey, doll," instead he only placed the speaker to his ear. After a few seconds, he glanced at me. "Yeah. I'll let her know."

"What is it?" I asked when he threw the phone on the table. "You ordered pizza?"

"I was hungry. I ordered an extra-large in case you wanted some. Oh..." Shit. I hadn't thought when I ordered.

When Mom and I had to leave Phoenix many years ago to hide from the cartel, she was meticulous and never lost sight of her goal—to keep me safe. She did her job so well. Back in New York, I never would've made such a stupid mistake.

"I'm sorry."

"Don't worry. Your call was intercepted by a friend."

A single knock on the door broke the silence. Dom pushed

himself off the chair and strode to the door. He slanted a glance
in the peephole before he swung the door open. A stocky guy
with dark hair and a darker stare shoved my pizza into Dom's
hands.

"I'll have a talk with her," he called after the man, who'd
already disappeared from the threshold. "Good talk." Dom
slammed the door and set the box on the coffee table.

"I'll do better. You don't need to school me." I jerked to my
feet and flipped the box open. The pizza looked like it'd been
shaken and then thrown across the room. "Maybe your Uber
guy shouldn't quit his day job." I picked some melted cheese and
pepperoni off the paper, rolled it onto a slice of bread, and bit
into it like a burrito.

"He's not my Uber guy. That was Vic. The reason I'm still
alive."

"Oh." I chewed on my pizza, feeling like a six-year-old. I'd
messed up bad. In my defense, though, I'd never let my guard
down before. Not at home in New York, at school, or at work but
between being back in Phoenix and Dom, I felt like I was home.

"You're not to leave this room or order any more clothes or
food. You understand?"

I tossed my pizza back in the box and wiped my hands on a
paper napkin. "I agreed to let you help me with Levi, but let's be
clear, I'm not your prisoner. I survived the last ten years just fine
without you. I can take care of myself."

"That was when Levi thought you were dead. Now he
knows the truth, and the only reason you're still here and not in
some ditch in Nogales is because he doesn't know where you
are. How 'bout we keep it that way?"

"I have cases to work on."

"You can work from here."

"What if I have court?"

"I'm sure any one of your coworkers would be more than happy to do you the favor."

"What if I get hungry again?"

"You can place your order with me."

"What if—"

He gripped my shoulders and cocked his head so we were at eye level. "No matter who Levi is, he's still my client. I'm risking a lot by helping you. I could be disbarred. Don't throw that away by getting killed, okay? Whatever you need, you talk to me, and we'll figure it out."

"Okay." My insides twisted. I was asking him for too much.

"Good talk." He looked at the pepperoni scramble Vic delivered and shook his head. "I'm ordering room service."

"Oh, so you can order room service?"

"Yes." He shot me a dark stare. "Is there anything you would like from the menu?

"I'll have the pasta."

"I see we're in the mood for Italian tonight." He smirked and picked up the room phone.

"In your dreams." I plopped myself on the dining chair and shuffled some folders around while I grinned like a schoolgirl.

"Always in my dreams, Emilia. Always." He glared at the phone handset, and his smile faded. "No. That was not meant for you. Could you let the chef know we'll need a service for two tonight? Anything Italian. Yeah, sounds good. Surprise me." He hung up.

"Thank you," I said.

"Wasn't that easy?" He poured himself a whiskey and refilled my wine glass before he took his place at the head of the table again. "Now, how are we going to help Ms. Morrow?"

"With cold cases like this, the best thing to do is to go through every bit of evidence and see what your gut tells you. Unless you have a reason for re-opening it?"

"Nikki is the only reason, really." He scratched the stubble on his cheek. "But that's a good question. What made her want to unearth all this after fifteen years? What changed?" He scribbled notes on his legal pad.

Who was this Nikki? What was she to him? Was she the reason he moved to Arizona? No, Dom wasn't the type to proposition a girl in his hotel room while he had a girlfriend somewhere nearby, but I couldn't care about that. I'd already made the decision, and it was a good one. Dom and I were a bad idea. Me and anyone, for that matter, were a bad idea. I had to stop thinking of Dom in that way. I darted my gaze away from him and forced myself to focus on the files in front of us.

The pictures in one of the folders caught my attention. Image after image of a man lying in a large pool of blood. It was a gruesome scene. A murder committed by someone without a soul. Only a monster without a shred of compassion could do this to another human being. The usual burn furled in my stomach. No one deserved to die like that. I let my gaze roam the picture, taking in every detail. Unfortunately, the only way to do the man justice was to look at him logically. The way I would look at a jigsaw puzzle. I started at his head and worked my way down.

"Do you have a magnifying glass?"

Dom's head snapped up at me. He'd also gotten lost in his own puzzle. "Yeah. Hang on." He retrieved a magnifying glass from the front pocket of his briefcase.

"Thanks."

I scanned the first picture then moved on to the next. On the third image, I found our needle in the haystack.

"You found something?"

I glanced up and met Dom's blue stare. *Jesus, the man was gorgeous.* "I don't know. Maybe. Look at this." I pushed the picture toward him.

He swallowed before he leaned in. "What am I looking at?"

"Right here." I pointed at the man's arm. "Look at the edges of the bruise."

"It's a bruise." The area between his brows furrowed as he looked through the magnifying glass.

"It's makeup. Poorly applied makeup. You don't see it? It's right there." I pointed with my little finger.

He shoved my hand away. "Just give me a minute." After a few seconds, recognition finally registered on his face. "It's a cut."

I nodded. "Right through the middle the skin split open in a ragged pattern. Do you think?"

"Hang on, I have the autopsy report here." His eyes darted across the document while he speed-read it. "They cataloged it as a bruise on the arm, but this isn't just a bruise. I mean I couldn't see it before, but now it's all I see. Like one of those optical illusion images designed to cover stuff up until someone tells you where to look."

"Right?" I smiled at him. "That's it. That's all you need to re-open the investigation. I mean it should be if the family doesn't block you."

"I have a friend who can get us what we need. Thank you." He squeezed my hand and thumbed the inside of my wrist.

"Your girlfriend will be happy. You'll be like her hero." No doubt she'd be full of gratitude for him, and...I couldn't think about that.

"She's not my girlfriend. She's just a friend."

"I don't care." I slipped my hand from the grip of his fingers.

He threw the manila folder on the table and stood, gripping his hips. "Okay, good. You're ready to have the talk."

His hot gaze sent a warm rush down to my core. One look and he had me wishing I'd remembered to pack my battery-operated Dom. Though I didn't think it would do me any good now that I'd gotten a taste of the real Dom.

How did he put it? *I could do so much more for you.*

"What talk?"

"The sex talk."

Could he just stop saying *sex*? Every time he said the word images of him all sweaty and naked flickered in my mind.

"I don't care what you do with your personal life. What we do need are ground rules. If we're going to live under the same roof, I need to know what to expect. We both do."

"That's what I meant." He grinned, crossed his arms over his chest, and leaned against the edge of the table. "Your room is your room. I promise I won't go in, unless of course, you ask."

"I won't ask."

"Fair enough, but if I'm not allowed in there, neither is anyone else."

"I'm sorry?" I shouldn't care if he cared. Or rather, I should be annoyed he was telling me I couldn't have male company. Did he mean it? Or was he baiting me to see how fast I'd jump at the opportunity to tell him he couldn't have girls over either, and effectively show him I was jealous? Why was I jealous?

"Fine."

"Just fine?"

"I wasn't planning on bringing anyone here. My life and Mom's life are at stake. You think I'd waste my time with some guy? It's not worth the effort."

"Right. Why bother with a real person when you have good ol' B.O.D.?"

"What?" Oh...battery-operated Dom. Heat rose to my cheeks. Why did he have to see that? He opened his mouth to speak, but I raised my hand to stop him. "Never mind. I got it." That infuriating smile of his made me want to smack him. It also made me want to lock myself in my room and spend a few hours with the other Dom.

"One of these days, you'll have to tell me how the whole good ol' B.O.D. situation got started." He cocked an eyebrow, his chest bouncing a little with suppressed laughter.

I chuckled at that. "Oh my God, you and your ego." Before I could stop myself, I blurted out the truth. "It was after the almost kiss. I couldn't stop thinking about it." At some point, I had to stop divulging all my secrets to him. Why couldn't I stop?

"It wrecked me too." He reached for my face, and I shuffled back.

"Okay." He put up his hands in surrender. "Just so you don't accuse me of being unfair, I'll do the same. I won't bring dates back to the room."

My heart squeezed tight. Me. Bed. Made. I had to let him go and get used to the idea that Dom wasn't mine. He had every right to go look for company if that's what he wanted. The sooner the better. I swallowed and forced a smile.

"Good. I'm glad we got our sex talk out of the way."

"My door's always open for you. Anytime." He turned his attention to the files in front of him.

The pressure in my chest unraveled. The big bad wolf, Dom

Moretti, needed a friend. I wanted to put my arms around him, but instead, I patted his arm. I didn't trust myself to do more than that.

"Same here. If you want to talk. I'm here."

"Just talk, huh?" He flashed me one of his panty-melting smiles like he knew something I didn't. "Thanks. I'll remember that."

TO FAMILY

Dom

The grin was something I couldn't help. I ignored the idiot staring back at me in the mirror and rubbed the spot just below the base of my neck. I wore my scars and ink as a reminder of what life could turn into when I lost focus, but Emilia's mark on my chest was something else. It was hope that an empty hotel suite wasn't the rest of my life.

I put on my suit jacket and headed out, leaving the bedroom door open so I wouldn't wake Emilia sleeping next door. I smiled to myself. I liked that she was here, that I knew exactly where I'd find her at the end of the day.

"You look like the cat that drank the milk." Emilia sat at the table, fully dressed in her fancy lawyer suit. A breakfast for two in front of her.

I jerked to a halt. "Fuck. You scared me. I thought you were sleeping."

"It's seven in the morning. You have a half day or something?" She sipped her coffee.

"I would've never pegged you for a morning person." I plopped myself on my chair.

Yeah, we now had his and her chairs.

"The secret is in the coffee." She pushed a mug toward me and poured. "Sugar? Cream?"

"Just cream. Thanks." I gripped her wrist as she tipped the creamer. "What are you up to?"

"What do you mean?"

"This agreeable Emilia scares me."

She laughed. "I'm trying to be nice. I've taken over your life. The least I can do is pour you a coffee."

I released her hand. Maybe this was wishful thinking. "I'm sorry. For a moment it felt like you were using your female wiles on me."

"My what?" She coughed into her cup.

"Okay. What do you want?"

"I need to go into the office."

"No."

She cleared her throat and set her coffee down. "I need to go. Jess called the firm and asked to cancel all proceedings on her divorce."

"What?" I raised a hand. "You're still not going. Jess is with your mom. Do you really think the Dragon Lady let Jess use the phone to put a stop to her divorce?"

I'd hoped Levi would take a few days to regroup and strategize, but it seemed he was ready for his next move. Admittedly, this felt too fast, too risky. What was he up to?

Emilia bit her lower lip and lowered her gaze. *Female wiles.*

"I thought maybe Vic could come with me and hang out in the break room?"

"Are you not listening to me? It's a trap." I sat back in my chair. "Not to mention, Vic has things to do today. And so do I. Can I trust that you'll be here when I get back?"

"Fine."

"There's that word again. What are you planning?"

"Fine just means fine. I'll have Jack bring over the files I need."

I threw my napkin on the table. "Not fucking likely. He's not coming here. Write down what you need, and I'll get it for you."

"Why can't he come here? Your admin came over last night."

"Because the cartel is not looking for me. They're looking for you."

Of that I had no doubt. Levi wouldn't have *summoned* me if he wasn't in the mood to do something illegal, something that could potentially damage his chances of getting custody of his kid...or kids. Last week, I would've told him I only took meetings in my office, but now Emilia was involved. I had to find out what he had planned for her, and the best way to do that was to meet with him at a place where his guard would be down...like his office.

I rose to my feet and grabbed a legal pad off the coffee table. "Write down what you need."

She strutted over to the living area. The faint scent of her flowery perfume wrapped itself around my chest. When she handed me the piece of paper, I gripped her elbow and pulled her toward me.

"Please don't go anywhere today. I'll be back in a few hours."

"I'll stay put like a good girl." She pressed her hand on my chest, right over the long scratch she'd left on me last night. Her eyes lingered on my mouth before she glanced upward.

"If I kiss you now, I won't leave," I whispered. She nodded and pushed me away. I had to get out of here fast before I changed my mind.

Vic stood by the valet podium waiting for me. When he spotted me, he strolled toward the black SUV and opened the door. "I thought maybe the sheets got stuck to you."

"Good morning," I said. "We have time. I just had to make sure Emilia didn't get any crazy ideas."

"Hmmm." He shut the door and climbed in the driver seat. "She had a cool head on her shoulders when I first met her. I think you're messing with her wits."

"Save it. She already made it clear she doesn't want to get involved."

Vic met my gaze in the rearview mirror as the car rolled forward. "You're both already involved."

"You're chatty this morning."

He shrugged and grabbed a file off the passenger seat. "Here's what I have on Levi."

"Anything I should know. Am I walking into a trap?"

"Nah. I think you're walking into a job interview."

I barked out a laugh and threw his file on the seat next to me. "He couldn't possibly."

"Respected lawyers are hard to come by. I hope he offers you a lot of money. I need a raise." Vic checked both side mirrors and merged onto the 101 heading south.

"I don't need any more money." I rubbed my clean-shaven cheek. Of all days, today I needed to look like a respected lawyer, one without a past. One that couldn't be bought.

"What's the plan, Dom?"

"Go in, hear him out."

"Where do you need me?"

"Right at the front door. Anything other than that would definitely raise some red flags."

"Front doors make me nervous. Too many blind spots."

"I know. Forty minutes...tops. Then you know what to do."

Vic scratched the back of his head. "'Kay."

I should've brought a gun with me, but normal lawyers didn't carry weapons to client meetings. As far as Levi was concerned, I was a lawyer with a reputable firm, meeting with an upstanding citizen of the community.

Vic pulled up to a building in the outskirts of downtown Phoenix with a big sign that read LS Real Estate and Associates. Creative front, I had to give him that. He could've gone with a dry cleaner or a nightclub, but he chose differently. He wanted to be regarded as a decent man. Did that influence come from Emilia's family? I filed that bit away as Levi's potential Achilles' heel.

"Good morning, Mr. Moretti." A tall woman in an expensive pantsuit met me at the door and ushered me to the elevator bay.

His office, with floor-to-ceiling windows, took up most of the top floor. Expensive art covered every wall. On the far right, two sofas faced each other over a Persian rug. The marble coffee table added to the lavish decor. It was as if he'd told his designer to make the room look extra-expensive.

"Mr. Smith will be with you shortly," the woman said with a small curtsy before she left.

Lots of money, lots of theatrics. Vic was right. This was an interview. Levi left me alone in his office to take a look around and size him up. Fine. I played along...no doubt he was watching. I strolled to the painting on my left. An original. The next piece was more or less the same. Big and colorful. To my right, his oversized desk sat in the corner with a big monitor only taking up a small section of it.

As usual, anything related to Emilia left me dizzy with questions. Why the effort to turn this room into something so specifically rich? Yesterday, Emilia's mom had said Levi wanted to be just like her husband. Could it be that this was Emilia's Dad's old office? Was he the one who had the idea to use a real estate firm as a front instead of the cliché nightclub? Was this building their feeble attempt at a normal life? A life that Levi ended in a matter of minutes when he decided he wanted it all for himself.

Emilia, I'm sorry you had to go through this on your own.

In school, we had our chance to lessen the load for each other, but I supposed we were too proud to ask for help then. This time around, it was different. It had to be.

The door creaked open and Levi strolled in, a smile plastered on his too-pretty face. The more I knew about him, the more I couldn't stomach that ridiculous grin. He closed the space between us, extending his hand a few steps before he reached me. The brotherly act was worse than his fake smirk.

"Mr. Moretti. Thank you for meeting me here." He sauntered around the massive desk to sit at his throne. He enjoyed playing the part of a top executive. My friend, Cole, was the real deal. This clown had no clue what he was doing. For Levi, this gig was about more than money. He wanted respect and status.

"Mr. Smith."

"Please. It's Levi." He hadn't asked me to use his first name the last few times we met. I didn't bother to offer the same. We weren't friends. "Please, have a seat. Anything to drink?"

"I'm fine, thanks." I lowered myself onto the chair he offered and unbuttoned my jacket. "You asked to see me. How can I help you?

He put up his finger and hit the pager button on his desk phone. "Could you get us a couple of..." he glanced at me, "couple of whiskeys."

I peered at the clock on the wall. It was fifteen minutes past eight. Must be tough to live with so many dead people on your conscience, but I didn't give a shit about his drinking problem. I'd grown tired of his *look how much money I have* display.

"Levi, how can I help?"

"My wife tells me she's having second thoughts about this silly affair. She called, and I think from now on things are going to work out between us. She seemed more amiable."

A woman came in with our drinks. She placed one in my hand and the other in front of Levi before she left again.

"I'm happy with the results. It was as I was promised. Expedient positive results."

What the hell was he talking about? He hadn't seen shit as far as results, expedient or otherwise. "My office is not aware of any changes."

"I'm sure my wife's lawyer will get to it sometime today. I don't know how you did it, but I'm glad it's over. Divorce is what ails our society these days. Families should work hard to stay together. Don't you agree?"

"I do. Family is everything."

He raised his glass. "To family."

"Yeah." I pressed the glass to my lips. He'd poured my favorite brand of whiskey. The asshole knew my drink.

I glanced at the clock again. Thirty past the hour. In ten minutes, Vic would barge through the door and end this tiresome civility. Why was Levi wasting my time? Unless...

"Anyway, I know you're a busy man. I wanted to thank you personally." He sipped from his glass before he stood. "If you ever decide you're ready for your own practice, let me know. I'm well known in the community, I could return the favor."

No, asshole. We were *not* exchanging favors. "I'm happy where I am."

Levi leaned on the edge of his desk and met my gaze with a smile that I was sure most women found charming. Why the charade? The door burst open and he jerked to attention, arms out. "Here we are. You're more than welcome to stay if you want."

Vic had been right about this being a job interview. I glanced over my shoulder to the two guys dragging a barely alive man between them. They dropped him at Levi's feet and stepped back.

I swallowed, glaring at the too familiar scene. I could fake astonishment and leave, but obviously, Levi knew a lot more about me than he first let on. He hadn't asked for me because he'd heard I was good. He'd come looking for me because he had an opening within his crew. Oddly enough, that was the good news. I could turn him down and be done with him. The bad news was that he was certain I'd say yes. Where the fuck did he get that idea? This criminal life wasn't what I wanted anymore.

The loud groan of the guy on the floor brought me back. I texted Vic to let him know I was on my way. "Just so we're clear. I'm not and will not ever be of a mind to start my own firm. What I'm curious about is what led you to believe that I would be?"

He furrowed his brows and gestured for his two men to cease beating on the punching bag now lying unconscious on the floor. "After you handled the divorce case so brilliantly, I figured you were trying to impress me." He smiled. "Shooting up the lady lawyer to send her running with her tail between her

legs was a great initiative. It's the kind of smarts I appreciate."
He slapped my arm.

My stomach churned. The asshole thought we were the
same. What was worse was he thought I wanted to impress him.

"I have to get back to the office." I had about a minute to
meet Vic downstairs.

"Of course. We'll be in touch." Levi crossed his arms and
nodded to his men to resume the beating.

I fisted my hands and forced myself to leave his office. If I
got involved, it wasn't just my livelihood on the line, Emilia
would suffer too because as fucked-up as this entire meeting had
been, I learned one important fact—Levi didn't send those men
to shoot at Emilia.

The same woman who'd greeted me earlier met me at the
elevator bay and walked me outside. Vic had the car running
when I climbed inside, and he hit the accelerator the second I
slammed the door shut. He was as anxious as I was to get the
hell away from this place.

"So how did it go? Am I getting a raise?"

"No. Though you did call it."

"Something happen?"

"Yeah. Swing by Emilia's office. I have some files I need to
get for her."

"You're the boss." He turned at the next street and drove
past Emilia's building. Old habits die hard.

"Levi didn't send anyone to scare off Emilia. Did you?"

"No." The question didn't offend him. He'd proven his
loyalty to me time and time again. However, in this business, it
never hurt to ensure the status quo hadn't changed.

"Right. So if Levi didn't, and you didn't, who else wants to
see Emilia dead? What did she forget to tell me?"

11

HOW IS THIS BEING BACK TO NORMAL?

Emilia

Dom let the door shut behind him. Yeah, the man could wear a suit. I rubbed both my arms to get me to snap out of it. Staying put like a good girl had never worked out for me. I needed to come up with a plan or at the very least a next step. A solid one that would put me back on track. I had every intention of keeping my promise to Dom, mostly because he was right. I wasn't a killer, but Levi was. I had to prepare for that and put him away before he decided to finish what he had started ten years ago.

I swigged the last of my coffee and poured another cup. What would make Jess call my office to shut down the divorce proceedings? She was safe with Mom. Why back down now that we had everything to lose? She wasn't alone. Surely she knew that.

Could it be a trap like Dom had said? A shiver went down my spine. If Levi had the ability to pull off something like that, to get my office to feed me information, to get me to leave my hideout, I was already dead. Something had changed, and I had to find out what. Not exactly a plan, but it was a start. I sat in front of my laptop, logged onto my company's secured network, and sent Jack an email to ask him to authorize the release of the files I asked Dom to pick up.

My fingers hovered over the keyboard. If Mom and Jess hadn't made it to the safe house, I would know by now. Mom and I had planned this getaway since the first day we got here. After years of being on the run, she was a pro at it. Calling them now would only compromise our plan. And if that happened, Mom had yet another escape plan to make it back to New York, which would be the worst-case scenario for me.

Back in New York, I had no way of bringing Levi down. I closed my eyes, and the gory images of Dad's dead body came rushing back. With a deep, calming breath, I focused on replacing Dad's face with Levi's. A little exercise I figured out early on to help me calm the storm that swirled in my chest every time I thought of Levi.

The idea popped in my head and in a matter of seconds, it became my plan. I couldn't call Mom and risk having our call intercepted like Vic did when I ordered a pizza. If I drove instead, I could make sure I wasn't being followed. I closed my laptop and went back to my bedroom. I couldn't wear a suit on my trip to Sedona. I flipped open my suitcase and pulled out a pair of jeans, a T-shirt, and a pair of boots.

Last night, after the make-out session with Dom and then dinner, I didn't get a chance to unpack. Probably a good thing. I didn't want to waste time packing a small bag. Sedona was two hours away. If I hurried, I could get to the safe house, talk to Mom and Jess, and make it back before Dom returned this afternoon, but I needed to leave now. I shut the suitcase and yanked it off the bed.

At the valet podium, I asked the attendant to call me a cab. Sometimes old school was the way to go. I climbed into the taxi and gave the driver directions to where I'd left my car yesterday. Every other day, Mom's driver would pick me up, or I would leave my car in a garage a few blocks down and walk the rest of the way.

The idea was to do something different every day, not to fall into a routine because once I did, I'd get comfortable and miss the little details or let my guard down. Just like I'd done in Dom's hotel. I closed my eyes and let my head fall back on the headrest. This hiding and sneaking around would be over soon.

When we reached the garage in downtown Phoenix, the driver switched my suitcase to my SUV. I handed him a couple of twenties, and he took off without another word. I did my usual inspection of the car, checking under the carriage, in the back seat, and the nooks and crannies in the trunk. I climbed in and followed the signs to I-17 North. Within minutes, I'd merged onto the interstate and was headed to Mom's safe house in Sedona.

Our cabin was a few miles from the town square, down by Oak Creek. As much as Mom had let go of the past the minute we left Phoenix all those years ago, she still allowed herself a few moments of weakness. Sedona had been the place where Mom and Dad had had their first date. In all the years they were married, they never got to return, though they always talked about it. She picked this place because, for her, this was where it all had started, but also where she felt safe.

The cedar-scented cool air greeted me as soon as I opened the car door. I leaned against the warm side of the SUV and let out a breath. Were we really safer here? Or was the quiet trickling of the stream behind the cabin and the chirping of birds just an illusion that we were in a remote and hidden place? All that drug money Dad had set aside for us kept us comfortable all these years. Too bad it couldn't also buy us peace of mind.

Twigs and small rocks crushed under my boots as I trudged up the driveway. I knocked on the door, counted to five, and then did a double knock.

Mom swung the door open and pulled me into a bear hug.

"Did anyone follow you?" she asked like she'd been waiting for me, craning her neck to look at the car behind me.

"No. I made sure," I said as she ushered me inside. The place smelled of pancakes and bacon.

"Are you hungry?"

"No. I ate before coming here." A lie, but I didn't have much time. "Where's Jess?"

"She's with Izzy. The poor girl didn't sleep much last night. She misses her bedroom. Sit." She poured coffee for me. I wrapped my hands around the mug and let my cold fingers catch the warmth. "You're here because Jess called off the divorce."

I sat back. "So she did call?"

Mom nodded. "I made her."

"Why?"

"Jess is just like her mother. Easily impressed and easy to manipulate. I loved my sister..." Mom made a quick sign of the cross for her deceased sister, "but it's the truth."

"What happened?"

"After we left, she tried to escape, which didn't make sense to me. Why go back to the man who's been making her life a living hell all these years? Especially if he knew you and I were still alive and that Jess knew. Anyway, afterward, I sat her down and asked her a few questions."

I rubbed my temple. I seriously doubted all the Dragon Lady did was ask Jess a few questions.

"What did you find out?"

"She lied to us. She never told Levi about you. Her plan had been to scare you off because she knew you wouldn't let her back down from the divorce. Apparently, Levi found out she was pregnant and was being extra nice to her. They're having a boy." Mom rolled her eyes. "Of course, Levi is all over that."

"Why did you make her call it off?"

"Because that plan of yours was a suicide mission. Don't you get it? We have a second chance to walk away. He doesn't know about us. And now he gets his wife back and everything can go back to normal."

I jerked to my feet. "Mom. We're in a safe house. How is this being back to normal?"

"I have a private jet scheduled. We can be in New York tonight. Emilia, we never should've left. Don't you get it?"

"You just undid everything I worked so hard for in the last three months. Why?"

"Because this need for revenge is going to get you killed. I've been worried sick. I never should've let you go after him. I panicked when Jess told me Levi knew about us. I wasn't thinking."

"Mom—"

"No, Emilia, you have to let it go. How do you think I've survived all this time? I forgave Levi for what he did so I could have a happy life with you. This anger, this obsession to make Levi pay, is no way to live. I thought that if I let you come here and get your revenge, you would finally get closure. What good would closure do if you're..." Her voice quavered and tears rimmed her eyes.

"Mom." I reached for her hand. Mom hadn't turned to stone when we left, she'd forgiven Levi? Was that even possible? My chest tightened. I had no forgiveness for him. "He stole everything from us."

"He did, but we rebuilt. Don't throw away everything for something that won't bring your dad back."

Nothing could bring Dad back, but I hated that Levi was still out there, free and respected by all. "You can't possibly want your only niece to go back to that monster."

"She's coming with us."

"I thought you said Levi was getting his wife back. Isn't Levi looking for her now?"

"He's not. She called him and told him she'd be home in a few days. He was fine with that. All he cared about was that the divorce was off and that his daughter was coming home."

"Eventually, he'll figure out she's not coming. What then?"

"Well, I haven't figured that part out yet. Jess is determined to go back with him. Honestly, I'm done trying to figure what kind of birds she's got in her head."

"We're not children anymore. You can't decide for us."

"I know that, but both of you are acting like children with little regard for your lives. This isn't like you. In New York, you were focused on your career and staying alive."

"My career was a means to an end, and you know that. I'm still focused on staying alive, but this time I'm also intent on living a life, maybe..."

"Ah. Your lawyer friend, the Adonis in a suit."

"What?"

"I'm not that old. And I have eyes."

I groaned and dropped my head into my hands. Was Mom right? Would I be so intent on getting my life back if Dom wasn't part of the equation?

"He handled himself well at the house. It's obvious he's interested in you. Where did you meet him?"

"Law school."

She gave me a knowing smile and arranged tresses away from my face.

"If you wanted to, you could make a real go of it."

"Not like this. I couldn't go through that again." *Losing someone I love.*

She blinked, and tears rolled down her cheeks. "Okay. You're right, but you can't put all your eggs in Jess's basket. Between her daughter and the pregnancy, she can't be trusted. She has to think of her kids, not just herself."

"Exactly. Does she really think her kids will be safe with Levi?"

"She says he's a good dad."

"And you believe that?"

"Sweetie, your dad killed people—bad people—for a living for many years before he decided to quit for us. However, in all those years, he was still a good dad to you."

"Hard as he might try, Levi isn't Dad."

If there was anything this whole mess with Jess taught me was that the divorce case wasn't the way to put Levi away for good. Jess and her family were safe for now, and that was a big win but definitely not the end goal here.

What other recourse did I have? I met Mom's gaze. Thanks to her, I knew for sure we still had the upper hand. Levi didn't know we were still alive, and that gave us a huge advantage.

"I have to head back."

Mom rose and hugged me. "I'm sorry about before. I panicked and let anger get the best of me."

She meant the fleeting moment when we both agreed the only way to end this nightmare was for me to kill Levi. I still believed that, but Mom didn't need to know that. Just like she didn't need to know that I'd been shot at more than once in the last forty-eight hours.

"Don't say you're sorry. None of this is our fault. Will you stay here?"

"Yes. At least until Jess figures out what to do." She let out a breath and smiled. "Would you stay for breakfast?"

"I can't. I have work to do."

"There is no way you left Phoenix without your computer. I know you have it. How about I make French toast and you can eat and catch up on work? You need to eat. You're getting so skinny," she called from the pantry. "I made pancakes for Jess, it's only fair I make something for you."

I chuckled. "Mom, I don't care if you cook breakfast for Jess. God knows she needs family right now."

"She needs you. Every time she talks to you, her resolve strengthens, and she seems full of hope. Stay and talk with her."

"I guess I can stay for a bit. It's pretty up here."

I pushed myself off the chair and trod to the SUV to get my computer. The fresh air filled my lungs. Instead of heading to the car, I followed the sounds of streaming water. As soon as I reached the side of the cabin, the creek dotted with pine trees came into view. I strolled to the edge of the rocky path and let out a breath.

Mom was back to her old self now that the situation with Levi had been diffused. What would she think if she knew about the shooting at the bar? This whole time, I'd assumed Levi's men were responsible for it, but now I wasn't so sure. The shooting at our house could've also been Levi trying to scare off Jess's new lawyer, but I had no proof.

Random shootings were not the kind of thing that happened in that part of town. Not to mention, the shooters had silencers and seemed organized when they entered the house. The way only trained men can be. On the screens, they'd looked like they were on a mission.

Thinking about that night made my skin prickle. Suddenly, I got the sense I was being watched, and all my senses spiked to high alert. What the hell? A large hand clamped down on my mouth and muffled my scream. I kicked hard as a second hand snaked around my waist and pressed me against a wide chest. Tears stung my eyes. How could I tell Mom and Jess to get out of here? A heavy weight settled in the bottom of my stomach.

My gaze darted between the house and my car where I saw something move. Were there more men out there? Shit. How many? My heart thrashed in my ears as I kicked, hoping to hurt the man holding me in place.

He tightened his grip around me. "Fuck, Emilia. Calm down."

12

WHAT DO WE DO NOW?

Dom

She rammed her boots into my shin again. "I'm going to let you go. Promise me you won't run."

Her body went limp against mine. I removed my hand from her mouth but didn't let her go. She stood still, her breath ragged. When her legs stiffened next to mine, she shoved away from me, spun and slapped me across the face. Yeah, I deserved that for sneaking up on her, but why the fuck did she leave the hotel?

"What the hell are you doing here?" She stomped her foot, her eyes brimming with tears. "You scared the bejeezus out of me."

"You left. I didn't know what to think. Why did you leave?"

When I'd returned to the suite with her files and didn't find her there, I thought the worst. The clothes she'd worn to breakfast were strewn all over the room, her suitcase and computer gone. It looked like a snatch job. The kind that would make anyone believe the victim had simply left in a hurry.

"You first. How did you find me?" She tightened her trembling fingers on her hips.

"I'm sorry. I didn't mean to scare you." Shit, this was definitely the wrong reaction. This was why I didn't do relationships. I wasn't the boyfriend type. Trouble followed wherever I went. And trust? I still had to figure that one out. "Vic tracked your computer."

She glanced upward. This looked bad for me, but when it came to Emilia's safety, her privacy was the last thing on my mind. With a deep sigh, she met my gaze. "Okay. We'll talk about my computer later. You came here because you thought I'd been what? Kidnapped?"

"Exactly."

"I'm sorry. I should've left a note."

I glanced down at my muddy dress shoes. "That would've been fucking helpful."

"I thought I had more time before you got back. I needed to talk to Mom. It wasn't a trap. Jess did call off the divorce."

"*What?* Why?"

"Mom saw an opportunity to get me out of this mess with Levi and she took it. So now I'm back to square one. Levi doesn't know we're still alive."

I braced my hands on my knees and blew out air. Now Emilia could go back to her old life, where danger didn't lurk at every turn. My chest hurt at the thought of not seeing her again, but it had to be done. This mission of hers was pure madness, and it was bound to get her killed. This next part I was good at. I could help Emilia and her family disappear again to New York or some beach. Anywhere as long as it was far away from Levi.

"Okay. This is good news. I can help you find a new place to live." I paced the length of the creek. The soothing trickling of the water rushing through rocks cleared my mind. Every step ahead of me was clear. "We can leave tonight."

Emilia chuckled, running both hands through her hair. "The hell I'm leaving. I'm back to square one, yes, but I'll come up with a new plan. You're going to help me, or are you backing out on your word?"

"Emilia—"

"If you are, tell me now." Her gaze dared me to say it. To break my promise to her and prove I was a coward, which I wasn't, but when it came to her, so much more was at stake.

"Of course, I will help you. I never break a promise."

"Good." She smiled, and that feeling of wanting to be everything she thought I was spewed across my chest again. What was more important? Impress Emilia Prado or keep her alive.

"I will help you with your Levi problem, except we're doing this my way now. That's non-negotiable." I pressed my lips together and stared back at her. An intimidating look that sent most people running for the hills, but not Emilia. She considered my offer, her gaze darting between me and the house, trying to find a more logical solution. At least I had that going for me. I was her best shot.

"Levi wasn't behind the shooting at the bar," I blurted out. No reason to sugarcoat it.

Her eyes fluttered, and she looked away. For an entire day, she thought her worst nightmare had become a reality. Now she'd been given a second chance. It scared the heck out of her. I wrapped my fingers around her elbow and pulled her toward me. She whimpered and buried her face in my chest.

"You were right." I held her tight, kissing the top of her head. "Levi has had a taste of power and loves it. There is no way in hell he's going to let that go. If he ever finds out you and your mom are still alive, he won't hesitate."

"So you understand?" She glanced up at me, her pretty eyes and cheeks wet with tears. "I can't just walk away."

"I understand." I ran my thumb over her jaw and plump lips. I wanted to kiss her, make her feel safe, make this threat hanging over her go away, but kissing always led to so much more, far more dangerous than sex.

"He scares me." She bit her lip, ran her hand up my chest, and cradled my face, pulling me to her. Damn, who could ever say no to this woman?

"I'm here. For whatever you need." I bent down and pressed my mouth to hers, letting her guide me to what she wanted because if it were up to me, she would be on the ground right now, and I would be buried deep inside her.

Her tongue coaxed me to part my lips and taste her. I took that much from her. Truth be told, at this point, I would take whatever crumbs she'd be willing to give. I walked her back. Small rocks rolled down into the creek as I caged her against a pine tree. Cold water splattered against my legs, but I didn't care.

Emilia's kiss was all that mattered to me at that moment. I pressed my body against her, and she sighed, running her hands up my back. My nerve endings stirred when she tugged at my dress shirt and ran her nails up my bare back. I gave into the hot blood coursing through me and deepened the kiss.

"I can't stand the thought of you getting hurt," I whispered between kisses. The usual drift I felt whenever Emilia was close pulled at me and muted everything around us. "Today, it was all I could do not to squeeze Levi's neck with my bare hands. Squeeze until he took his last breath."

"Wait, what?" She shoved me away, lips parted, her breasts straining against her T-shirt as she tried to catch her breath. "You saw him today? Why didn't you tell me?"

"Because I didn't know what he wanted. And..."

"And you thought I was crazy enough to follow you and try to shoot him?"

Yeah, the thought crossed my mind. "No. I wanted to feel him out first."

She peered at me, pursing her lips. I hated to see Emilia's anger directed at me, but maybe this was for the better. The side of Emilia that wanted me was so much more difficult to deal with. She made my brain get all fucked up and out of touch between right and what could get us both killed.

"What did he want? Is that how you knew he didn't send those men to scare me off?"

I nodded, opting for the truth. We were in this together now, whether I liked it or not. "Turns out he wanted to feel *me* out. He sort of offered me a job."

"You didn't..."

"Of course not. I've been done with all that for a while. No way in hell am I going back." She let out a breath and glanced down at her hands. I tipped her chin up. "What are you thinking?"

"If he didn't send those men to the house, then who did?"

I stuffed my hands in the pockets of my dress pants. "Good question."

"You know who, don't you?" She cocked her eyebrow. I swore it was like she could read my thoughts. More than that, I wanted to be honest with her. I was tired of secrets, tired of hiding my past, and trying to hang on to my present.

"At first, I thought you had some other scheme going on.

That you made enemies somewhere else. After I went to the hotel suite and realized you were gone, I finally got my head out of my ass and looked at the situation for what it was."

She shifted her body and pressed her lips to my shoulder. "Who?"

"Mickey."

She wrapped her arms around my chest. "I'm sorry."

"It's not your fault. Don't you see? This is all on me."

"Are you sure it was him?"

"Do I have proof, you mean? No. But this kind of mind game, that's Mickey's MO."

"What do you think he wants after all this time?"

"I have a couple of guesses. It's exactly as you said...no one ever leaves." I shook my head to clear my thoughts. She couldn't have this much control over me.

I stood staring at the precipice that was Mickey and everything that came along with it, and all I could think of was that if Emilia jumped with me, it wouldn't be so bad. I couldn't let her be a part of this. Mickey was much worse than Levi. Mickey hadn't replaced anyone like Levi. His place at the head of the table was his birthright.

"Don't look at me like that." She faced me. "Don't shut me out. Together we can come up with a plan. If Mickey is trying to get your attention, find out why."

"You know how it goes. He'll ask for one favor then pay it back and maybe do a little extra. Again and again, until somehow, I not only owe him but need him to stay alive. I won't go back."

She wrapped her arms around my waist. For the first time in a long time, I wasn't alone in this, and neither was she. I brushed her cheek with the back of my hand.

"So what do we do now?"

"Nothing is ever a coincidence. How did you come to be my cousin's husband's lawyer?"

"He asked for me."

She raised both eyebrows. "When was the last time you showed real interest in a girl? I know you came by the bar a few times before you talked to me."

I'd never had any trouble getting women, but somehow when it came to Emilia things felt different. I visited her bar at least three times before I plucked up the courage to talk to her. To my surprise, she'd shown interest.

I racked my brain to find the details of that night. All I could come up with was Emilia's tits hovering over her leather corset and her sexy-as-hell smile when she agreed to meet me at midnight. I'd gone home soon after with an idiotic grin on my face, inundated with thoughts of all the things I wanted to do to her later. Not once did I think to check if I was being followed. Not that night or any of the other nights I was there.

Vic didn't even know where I'd gone. I'd been in such a hurry to get ready for our date, I'd forgotten to warn Vic. He'd been pissed the next day and now I understood why. I'd left the door open. If Mickey had been waiting all this time to find a chink in my armor, he'd found it. Losing Emilia would kill me.

"Fuck. He's using you to get to me."

"Possibly." She glanced back at the house. "I wonder how much Jess knows. If Levi has had any dealings with Mickey, she would know."

I let her pull me toward the house. "You think he would actually tell her?"

"No, but Jess isn't the defenseless victim she likes everyone to believe. She's afraid of Levi, but she's also smart."

We trudged through the threshold. The cabin, if I could call this huge house that, smelled of pastries and syrup. As bad as Emilia had it all these years, she at least had this. She had a family—a home.

"I was getting ready to come looking for you." Her mom gave a slanted glance at Emilia's cousin, who sat on the other side of the table. "It's good to see you again." She smiled at me.

"Same here, Mrs. Prado." I shook her extended hand.

"Please. Sofia is fine. I'm not that old. Can I get you a coffee?"

"Yes, please."

"No." Emilia gave me her *this isn't a social call* look. She craned her neck to get a better look of the hallway beyond the kitchen and then turned to her cousin. "We need Jess to tell us how long Levi has been involved with the Italian mob."

"What?" Jess dropped her fork. Her gaze darted between Emilia and her mom. "Auntie?"

"Actually, no. First, tell me how you found us. And don't lie."

"At first, I thought you were a ghost." Jess placed her hand over her mouth. "I saw you at the cemetery where Uncle Emiliano is buried."

"Why were you there?" Emilia stepped toward Jess, her gaze dark with determination. In her haste to get even with Levi, Emilia didn't think to ask Jess the simple questions. Like how Jess managed to find Emilia and her mom after ten years of them being dead.

"I go there every Sunday after church. Sometimes Levi comes with us. The day I saw you I had to pretend I was ill to get him to leave before he saw you."

"You went to see him after I asked you not to?" Sofia narrowed her eyes at Emilia. One mistake was all it took.

"I had to see him, Mom." Emilia wiped her eyes several times before the tears stopped. "So what then? You followed me?"

Jess shook her head. "Levi took me straight home. After that day, things changed for me. Knowing I wasn't alone, that I had family still, gave me hope."

"How did you find me?"

"I hired someone. It took him just a few days to come up with an address."

Emilia's face went pale. Coming back to Phoenix had been a mistake. If Jess could find Emilia in a matter of days so could Levi.

Emilia ran her trembling hands through her curls. "Skip to the next thing. What do you know about Levi's connection to the Italian mob?"

Sofia blinked slowly. "Tell her everything you know."

"I don't know what I know." Jess was terrified of Levi. How did she manage to live with this fear all these years? Because of her daughter? "He's a good dad." She wiped her nose, and sniffled. "Levi asked me to bring Izzy over. He wanted to see her, and she wanted to see him. So I did. Before we left, a man came to the house. I was surprised because Levi never takes meetings at home. That's it. I don't even know if that means anything. I only mentioned it to Aunt Sofia because I found it odd. Levi looked worried. I wanted to know what she thought of it. I feel like I'm losing my mind. I promise I don't know him. I just want my kids to be safe." She rubbed her belly. Sofia put her arm around Jess and shook her head at Emilia.

Emilia turned to me. Jess was a dead end. Did she really not know Mickey?

"What did he look like?" I asked.

Jess's head snapped up at me, eyes wide as if she hadn't noticed I was in the room. "Balding. Maybe. Um, wide shoulders, maybe as tall as Emilia."

Jersey was riddled with balding, stocky, average height men but none of them had a reason to visit a drug lord in Arizona. Especially not one that was married to Emilia's cousin—Emilia, the woman I'd been pining over for more than five years.

The reality of the situation washed over me like a bucket of ice water. I'd started all this mess the minute I returned to the bar to look for Emilia. Mickey had come for me because, in his mind, I was still part of his family, and because he thought that now I had something—or rather *someone*—he could take away if I didn't do as he asked and play the good *son* again.

13

I'D LIKE TO GIVE THAT A TRY

Emilia

What happened to you, Jess?

Before Jess met Levi, she was full of dreams and all kinds of crazy plans, but after she fell for him, her entire life began to rotate around what he wanted. In spite of all that, she wasn't weak. The fire in her eyes, her strength, were still there. I could see it whenever Izzy walked in the room. I couldn't blame her for all the damage she'd caused...she didn't do any of it for herself. She did it for her daughter.

"I'm sorry." I sat in the chair adjacent to hers and squeezed her hand. "I haven't forgotten my promise to you. Levi will soon be no more than a bad dream."

She smiled. "It's rare, but when he's good, life is easy. I keep wishing it was that way all the time."

"It can't be because when it's there, it isn't the real him. Do you understand that?" I brushed the hair away from her face and hugged her. Feelings had a way of clouding the mind. This was why I never let myself get involved with anyone.

"I know. I'm sorry I ruined your plans, but Aunt Sofia made a good case for it."

"We'll find another way." I glanced at Dom. His quick nod made my words feel truer than I knew them to be.

After breakfast, Mom talked Jess into going out for a walk with Izzy and her. "There's a flamenco show in the city center later today." Mom smiled at Dom before she added. "Now that he's here, I can see you're not in such a hurry to get back. A bit of fresh air might do you both good." She pressed her hand to my cheek and strolled out with Jess and Izzy.

The door shut behind them and left us in an awkward silence. I opened my laptop and checked my email. Maybe some work would help me refocus on what I had to do next. *What do we do now?* Dom had asked. I had many ideas, but I was sure he wouldn't like any of them.

He sat across from me at the end of the table, his long legs in front of him, elbows braced on the armrest, gaze focused on the fruit bowl in the middle of the table. What was he not saying? When Jess had mentioned the mystery man who visited Levi, Dom had shut down as if he knew exactly whom Jess had seen. My money was on Mickey.

The minute hand on the clock seemed to be on fast forward. Any time spent with Dom always felt that way—rushed and short. We never had enough of it. When I checked the time again it was late in the afternoon and neither one of us had moved. Maybe we were both afraid that if we spoke, we'd have to talk about the elephant in the room. What did Mickey want from Dom?

"Flamenco dancing sounds like fun," I said.

His gaze snapped up at me. Heat rose to my cheeks when he surveyed my face, like he wanted to memorize every minor detail. Why did this feel like a goodbye? As much as it would hurt to see him leave again, I had no right to stop him. Promise or no promise, he didn't owe me anything. I couldn't ask him to risk his livelihood for me. My heart squeezed at the idea that this would be the last time I saw him.

"You should go." I beat him to it. "I'll be safe here."

He furrowed his brows. Sooner or later, he had to realize that staying with me was bad for his health. A bad idea all around. He rose to his feet, and I did the same to walk him out. Heart thrumming, I swung the door open and waved in the general direction of his car.

I swallowed my tears when he shuffled toward the door. *Don't look back. Just go.* He braced his hand on the door, biting the inside of his lip. His blue gaze burned with the same intensity it had the day he showed me his scars.

I wanted to shove him out and get this goddamn goodbye over quick. I wanted to scream at him and tell him to go already, but if I opened my mouth, I knew I'd beg him to stay instead. These last few days had been less lonely with him in them. Hope had seeped into my head that maybe one day I could have a normal life with someone.

He slammed the door shut and gripped my waist, caging me against the wall. "They can't tell us how to live our lives." His mouth found mine in a desperate kiss that sent a shot of adrenaline through my body. He sucked on my bottom lip gently before his tongue pushed past my parted lips. I melted into him, kneading every hard plane on his torso and chest. "I want you. And I refuse to give you up again," he whispered between ragged breaths. "I won't."

I threw my arms around his neck. "Stay."

"I'm being selfish. You don't care?" He brushed the back of his fingers over my temple and cheek.

"No. I'm being selfish too. I'm tired of being afraid. I keep wondering what we could've been if I hadn't been so scared to let you in when we were in law school."

"Me too." He stuffed his hands in the pockets of his dress pants and cocked his head. "Would you like to have a coffee with me?"

I touched my fingers to my lips to hide a smile. That had been the question he'd meant to ask when he barged into the library and told me I should get a coffee. Not in a million years would I have guessed he'd be nervous to talk to me, or that he would want me.

"It's almost five. How about a drink instead?"

"Am I overdressed for an afternoon of flamenco dancers?" He relaxed his stance.

Getting him out of that suit was a real shame, but he would stand out dressed like a city lawyer. "I'm sure we can find you something to wear."

A date with Dom Moretti turned out to be as normal as I had hoped for. He craved normalcy as much as I did. We drove into town and stopped at one of the shops to buy him a change of clothes. As soon as we strolled in, the woman behind the register stood at attention. Her smile turned into a wide grin when Dom greeted her in a low, gentle tone. Why did he do that? Why did he assume women would be afraid of him? From where I stood, the store clerk looked like Christmas had come early. I rolled my eyes and grabbed a couple of jeans and a Henley shirt for him to try on.

"Fitting rooms are over there." I shoved the clothes in his hands.

"Come with me. I need help getting out of these pants." He snaked his arm around my waist, kissing my neck. Heat fluttered at my core. If I went in there with him, we would both end up in the county jail for indecent exposure.

"I'll wait out here."

"You thought about it." He grinned.

"Yeah, I did."

"Let's have our date and then we'll see where that takes us." He kissed my cheek and went in the dressing room.

In minutes, Dom had changed out of his suit and into a pair of jeans that clung to his backside and muscular thighs like they'd been custom-made for him. The sleeves of his T-shirt stretched around his biceps as he threw his clothes into the bag the shop attendant had given him. I stood there watching him, pretending I didn't have this jittery energy swirling in my chest. He took my hand and we strolled the rest of the way to the city center, where a live band played a slow drum beat that filled the air while fire dancers ambled to the middle of the square.

"Looks like they're getting ready to start," he said.

"There's a wine tasting room over there. I bet we'll have a good view from there."

"Okay." He flashed me his signature panty-melting smile. He could tell I was a nervous wreck. And why wouldn't I be? Less than an hour ago, he'd almost left for good.

In the restaurant patio, he ushered me to the far end. The landscape to the right of our table looked like the painted back-drop of a western movie, complete with a pink and lilac sky adorned with puffy white clouds and a bright sun setting behind the Sedona Red Rocks. Was Sedona this majestic or did the hot blood rushing through me have anything to do with how colorful the desert marigolds looked? Or how slow they swayed in the cool breeze?

I plopped myself on the iron chair Dom offered me and waited with a schoolgirl grin while he rearranged his seat to face mine. When he sat, his knee burned the inside of my thigh. In spite of the raw charge between us, sitting here like this felt normal and familiar.

The beat of the drums echoed against my chest as the fire dancers created rings of fire with their torches in my peripheral vision, casting shadows on Dom's chiseled jaw and full lips. He slipped his hand into mine and let me feel his warmth for a few seconds before he ran his hand up my bare arm. My pulse fell in step with the steady rhythm of the percussion, and I was over-whelmed by how much I wanted him. What I felt for Dom had always had this raw edge to it, fierce and unwavering. My eyes fluttered closed, and I surrendered to his touch with a shudder.

"Don't be nervous." He pressed my hand to his chest and smiled. "What do you usually do on dates?"

"I've never been on a date."

He let go of my hand and swigged his wine. "Are you...?"

"What? A virgin? Ohmigod, no."

A round of applause broke around us. Back in the square center, the fire dancers finished their act by extinguishing the torches with their mouths, leaving everyone in complete dark-ness until the porch lights in the wine bar came on.

"So, you just didn't want to?"

"Dates can get tricky. And I've never had time for complicated."

Why bother with getting to know someone if I knew at the end of the night or weekend, I'd have to leave and never see that person again. It was the same with all my relationships. For the most part, I'd managed to stay away from everyone, but every now and then loneliness would win over.

For many years, I told myself a quick tumble in the bathroom of some dive bar was all I needed, and maybe for a while it was, but then I started to feel resentful about the whole thing, especially when the occasional nice guy wanted to see me again the next day. I ran a finger along Dom's jaw. I couldn't remember the last time someone looked at me with this much interest.

"So, your *number*, are we talking several?" He braced his arms on his knees, holding my hands loosely in his.

"Does it matter?"

"No. Just trying to figure out how much you can handle."

The usual electric rush flickered in my belly and rushed down to my toes. What did he have in mind? I leaned forward and pressed my forehead to his.

"I'm not afraid of you. A part of me says I should be. That I should run like I always do but an even bigger part of me wants to be with you. All of you."

He lowered his gaze. "We probably should've gone back to Phoenix."

"And miss out on our first date?" I ignored the mental picture forming in my mind of all the things we could be doing right now if we hadn't stayed in Sedona. "You know, this is where Mom and Dad had their first date too."

"Yeah? How did they meet?"

"Dad was very young when he started with the cartel. By the time he was twenty-two, he had enough money to buy a house. Mom sold him his first house."

"And your mom, she didn't care what he did for a living?"

I shook my head. "He was honest with her from the begin-

ning. She said she could see there was good in him. I saw it too."
I shrugged. "He was my dad."

He cradled my neck and kissed my lips. "I've never had a
girlfriend before."

"Never? I seem to remember seeing a lot of women hanging
around you in law school."

He shook his head. "I always thought that if I showed too
much interest, Mickey would try to use them against me. Turns
out I was right."

"He doesn't own you."

"I know. Problem is, he seems to have forgotten that."

"I've been thinking about that. What would it take for Levi
and Mickey to back down? How do we convince them we're not
a threat to them?"

"As long as you leave Levi's family alone and don't threaten
to expose him, I think you'll be fine. I wouldn't be opposed to
moving back to New York. With you."

Was Mom right in thinking the only way to move on with
our lives was to forgive Levi? Before Dom, all I could think of
was retribution. I still wanted that for Dad, but ever since Dom
waltzed back into my life, the price of revenge had doubled. If
we moved back to New York, we'd have a chance at a happy life,
a home, a family.

"I'd like to give that a try. I mean, we were fine before I
dragged Mom back to Phoenix to look for Levi."

"You came back to Phoenix for revenge and didn't even have
a plan?" He sat back in his chair. A cool breeze brushed
between us.

"I guess not, but I came up with one fairly quickly after Jess
found me. I almost didn't recognize her when she showed up at
the house."

"What were you doing at the cemetery?"

Going to the cemetery that day to see Dad had been child-ish. Mom had warned me against it saying it was too dangerous. I missed him too much.

"I'd never seen his grave before. I wanted to make sure he'd gotten a real resting place."

"And Jess just happened to be there?"

"I believe her. He was like a father to her too. You should've seen her. She was a hot mess. I had no reason to doubt her. She made me see how we needed each other. She didn't think we could get Levi for murder, but she thought we had a shot at proving he was dealing."

He linked his hands and placed them on the top of his head, staring at the rock formations in the distance where the sun had disappeared just a few minutes ago. "Emilia, there is no such thing as coincidences."

"What do you mean? Do you think Jess was following me?"

"I think she was sent to talk to you."

"Let's ask her." I placed my palm on his thigh.

"No. We're done trying to get her to tell the truth. It's obvious she only has one thing she cares about. And I don't think it's her daughter."

"You're being too hard on her. I know my cousin has her flaws. Her fear of Levi and her love for her children got her wires all crossed. I do believe she's trying to do the right thing."

Why did he always end up here? Jess would do anything to keep her daughter safe. I knew that without a shadow of a doubt. If she stayed with us, she'd never have to worry about having a roof over her head. She'd have all the money she would need or want if that was important to her.

"Jess knows Mom and I are the only ones who can help her."

"Unless Mickey made her a better offer."

"I don't know. What could Jess possibly want that she doesn't already have with us? We're her family. We're all she has left."

Thing was, no matter how hard she tried, Jess was still afraid of her husband.

14

WE'RE IN THIS MESS TOGETHER

Dom

After a nightcap in the living room, Emilia's mom talked me into spending the night. She showed me to a room, and in a non-subtle way mentioned Emilia would be sleeping in the bedroom next to mine.

Going against what every fiber in my being told me to do, I agreed to stay. I shifted my weight on the too soft and too empty mattress. I tossed and turned for hours before I sat up. I swore I could still hear the sensual drumming of percussion.

Despite the cool air in the place, sweat beaded on my back. Did I do the right thing by staying? I supposed at this point I had no choice. The lawyer in me wanted physical proof Mickey was behind the shootings and Jess's mood swings when it came to her husband.

The other side of me, the part that ran around with Mickey for over ten years, didn't need the message fully spelled out. Mickey knew about Emilia. He knew I'd do anything to keep her safe. Anything.

I kicked the covers and swung my legs over the side of the bed. Pacing the length of the room and feeling like a caged animal, I stared at the connecting door to Emilia's room.

Sofia was on my side, and it gave me hope that maybe this thing with Emilia might work out in the end. I padded over to the door and placed my ear against it. Great. Now I was stalking her in her own home. I stomped back to the bed and climbed in. If Emilia had wanted to spend the night with me, she'd be in my room by now.

The next morning, I woke up feeling like I'd only slept a handful of minutes, aching and tired. I tried to get comfortable in the bed to rest a little longer, but it was no use. I had to get up and drive back to Phoenix. I walked over to the bathroom and found a tray lined with toiletries. I showered and brushed my teeth. For clothes, my options were the suit I wore yesterday or the jeans Emilia had picked out for me. I opted for the latter and headed downstairs.

Emilia was already at the table drinking coffee. She wore her hair up in the usual ballerina bun that matched her clean-cut pantsuit perfectly, but not the other side of Emilia I'd had the fortune to meet. Her suitcase and laptop bag laid on the floor by the door. At least she had agreed to come back with me. Whatever waited for us in Phoenix, we'd face it together.

"Where's your mom?" I asked.

"Out. She doesn't like goodbyes."

"Ready?"

"No." She laughed. "You?"

"No." I cradled her face and kissed her.

She wrapped her fingers around my wrist and met my gaze. "You didn't run out in the middle of the night. Thought for sure you'd be gone before dawn."

"Is that why you didn't come to my room last night?"

"Maybe."

"Whether you like it or not, we're in this together."

I ushered her to the door and grabbed her things. Out on the gravel driveway, Vic waited for us in Emilia's car. I nodded to him. He started the SUV and followed closely behind us. By the time I merged onto I-17, Emilia relaxed her shoulders and laid back against the headrest.

Her instinct had been spot on. Out of fear for her, I'd held her back the day we thought Levi had come after her. Would we still be here if I'd helped her kill Levi at her Scottsdale home? Would Mickey still feel he had something to hold over my head if Emilia was free? Probably. Levi and Mickey were two mutually exclusive problems. Even if Mickey had somehow figured out a way to incentivize Levi.

Within the half hour, we left the Sedona cool air behind. The pine trees and red rock formations were replaced by brown and pale green shrubbery. The sun beat down on the asphalt and everything else with an intense heat I'd never felt anywhere else. How could anything survive out here? Amazing how all living things could not only adjust to the harshest conditions but also thrive.

"Are we lawyers or not?" Emilia's voice brought me back.

"What?"

"All we have now is speculation. I need proof Mickey is behind this."

"What do you have in mind?" I'd never been the type to lay back and take it, and neither was Emilia. This was the main problem. We had to stop playing nice.

"Screw Jess. I'm her attorney. Until I say otherwise, her

divorce is still on. I'm texting Mom. She can't let Jess near the phone or email again."

"What do you need?"

"Can you schedule a follow-up deposition?" She faced me, a dead serious look in her eyes.

"You can't possibly—"

She cut me off. "I am. I want Levi to know I'm alive. I want him scared. I want him to know he's about to lose everything he holds dear."

"Okay. So we're back to the suicide mission plan. How do you know that's how he'll feel? What if he goes for a more murderous mood?"

"Yes. We're back to the suicide mission. Or my original plan." She tucked her ankle under her leg and shifted her body toward me. "I should've never strayed from it."

"Except now, we have good reason to believe that *your* original plan was orchestrated by Mickey. To lure you out. And me."

"That seems like a long shot to me. Why now? Why is Mickey all of a sudden dead set on getting you back?"

Yeah, why now? Maybe he thought I'd been gone long enough. Maybe he'd guessed I would do anything to keep Emilia safe.

"You know what? It doesn't matter because now I know Levi wants more than what he already has. How else did Mickey get to him? I want in on that. When he sees me again, I'll know if he knew I was alive, or if he was just acting under your old boss's orders."

"I don't like it."

"I'd rather have you with me when I go in, but you're certainly not required to be there."

"Fuck, Emilia. Of course, I'll be there. When do you want to see him?"

"Today. Can you make that happen? If we have the element of surprise still on our side, I'd like to cash in that chip as soon as possible."

I didn't like this new-again plan of hers, but it was all we had. When I spoke with Levi before, he seemed relieved that the divorce situation had gone away. Was he really a family man? Or was there more to it? Maybe he'd been happy to be done with his so-called favor to Mickey.

I gave Emilia a slanted look. The Emilia from the bar was back, full of plans and unrealistic hope. I couldn't help but want her even more, which scared the hell out of me. There wasn't anything I wouldn't do for her. If she asked, I didn't know if I'd be able to plea for Levi's life again. I'd probably finish him off myself.

I clutched the steering wheel and counted to ten over and over until the feeling subsided. That part of me died a long time ago. I couldn't let it take over again. I wasn't a killer. I fished my phone from the cup holder and called the office.

"Mr. Moretti. How can I help you?" My assistant answered after the second ring.

"Could you set up an appointment with Mr. Smith for this afternoon? I need him to sign some papers."

"Of course. Right away."

"Thanks. Text me when it's done." I hung up.

"You forgot to say please." Emilia smiled at me.

"Fuck." I grabbed the phone again and texted a quick *Thank you for handling this.* "I feel bad she got stuck with me. She's always so jumpy around me."

"You kind of used to have that same effect on me too." She chuckled, squeezing my hand. "Trust me, there are worse things than a boss who doesn't say please. I'm sure she enjoys the eye candy every morning."

"I can't tell if you're trying to get in my pants or trying to make me feel better."

"Maybe both."

"Are you sure? Last time I asked, you made it sound like sex with me would get us both killed."

"I think that possibility is on the table regardless. So, yeah, I'm sure."

My heartbeat shot into overdrive. I darted my gaze from her face to the road, and then the highway sign that read *Phoenix 30 miles*. Emilia bit her lip and glanced away toward the desert landscape zooming by. I kissed her hand and took several calming breaths. It would've been nice for her to come to this conclusion last night when we had two whole rooms all to ourselves.

Driving into Phoenix at ten in the morning meant little traffic. We whizzed through the interstate and made it back to the hotel a full ten minutes before the time the navigation app had given us. As we entered the resort, Vic drove in front of us. I followed closely behind to the back entrance, parked the car by the loading dock, and climbed out to get Emilia's bags. When I reached her door, Vic had already helped her out. Was the old man finally coming around?

We entered through the industrial laundry room. Several people walked past us pushing carts or hauling dirty linens, pretending we weren't there. I forced my gait to match Emilia's. As long as her stride was, I still had to slow down for her.

Though all I wanted to do was throw her over my shoulder and rush her to the suite.

"I've seen you walk way faster than this and in higher heels," I said against her temple, gripping her waist while we waited for the elevator. "Are you having second thoughts?"

"No, I just didn't want to assume."

The elevator doors slid open at the end of the hallway, and we got on. I hit the button for our floor, dropped her bags and pinned her body against the mirror.

"Assume away," I whispered on her lips before I covered them with mine.

She tunneled her fingers through my hair and pulled as I coaxed her lips to part for me. I got lost in our kiss, tasting her, until I realized if I stopped now we could do way more in our room. I broke the kiss first, and she rewarded me with a long sigh.

"I have a big bed waiting for us. Come on."

She picked up her laptop bag and I grabbed her big suitcase. When the doors opened, I put my arm out to stop her. Her smile died on her lips as she followed my line of sight and found the door to our suite cracked open. Out of habit, I reached behind me and cursed when I didn't feel my handgun. I guess it was time to stop playing the civilian. I gripped her suitcase, the only weapon I had on me, with both hands.

"Stay close," I whispered.

She nodded, her eyes wide.

We padded down the corridor, staying flush against the wall. I peered through the gap in the door and pushed it open when I didn't see any movement inside. I stepped into the living area and picked my way toward Emilia's bedroom then mine.

We were alone. A normal person would call the cops, or at

the very least, call the front desk to complain, but we weren't the normal type.

"What do you think they were looking for?" Emilia shut the door behind her and threw the bolt. "Or did they just leave a mess as a warning? To tell us they knew."

"Don't know." I followed her movements around the suite. Like a couple of nights ago at the bar, she had that cool composure about her, methodically taking in every detail that was out of place in the room...the papers on the floor, the ripped sofa pillows, and my clothes strewn across the room.

"They raided your minibar." She pointed at the knocked-over bottles on the butler's pantry.

She was a total turn-on. If I didn't want to hurt Mickey before, I wanted to now. Once again, my plans to spend the day naked with Emilia were shot to hell. I sat on the sofa and fished my phone from my back pocket. I had a text from my assistant saying we were all set for noon. Emilia plopped herself next to me, her hand on my shoulder.

"We stick to our plan."

I let out a long breath. "Which one?"

"One monster at a time." She kissed my shoulder, a knowing smile on her lips.

"Right." I chuckled. "Let's just hope they wait their turn."

"This was Mickey, wasn't it? You said mind games were his thing."

I nodded. He was great at pitting people against their fears and shortcomings. His little display here was meant to remind me that Emilia wasn't safe, no matter how hard I tried, but if his men were able to get in, it was because Vic and I hadn't been here. I didn't have time to analyze this to death. We had an appointment with Levi, and our focus had to stay on that.

I sent Vic a text: *He was here.*

He responded right away: *Need new room, less flash.*

I sent him a thumbs-up before I turned to Emilia. "Don't unpack. Vic is getting us a new room. We'll leave some of our stuff here and sleep in the new room tonight."

Heat rushed to her cheeks and my cock stood at attention. "Just to clarify, the sleeping arrangements are for your own safety. We don't have to do anything you don't want."

"I want to stay with you tonight." Her words sounded like a long-awaited promise.

"How are you okay with all this?" I asked. "I'm sorry I brought this on you."

"Same as you. I've waited for this for a long time. Also, I think it's fair to say I kind of started this too."

"Why? Because you agreed to see me again at the bar? That's bullshit."

"No, because I decided to move back to Phoenix. If I had stayed in New York, I wouldn't be in this mess."

"We. Why is that so hard for you to remember? We're in this mess together."

"I've never been in a mess together with someone. Other than my mom, of course. You know what I mean."

I tilted her chin up and kissed her lips. "Me neither. How about we each take credit for our share?"

"Works for me." She rested her head on my shoulder. "Did we get an appointment with Levi?"

"Noon."

She glanced at her watch and sighed. "I guess we should get going."

"Yeah. I need to change clothes." I fell back on the sofa and pulled her with me.

She didn't fight it. Instead, she cuddled in the nook of my arm. After today, everything would change for her. Whatever was coming our way, it would be better than spending the rest of our lives cowering in some dark corner of the country. Emilia deserved to have her life back.

15

YOUR POUND OF FLESH

Emilia

I'd imagined this moment many times in the past ten years. When we'd first left Phoenix, every time I thought of Levi finding us I felt trepidation. As time went by, he became the monster under the bed. The thing that made me lock every door at night and check every window. A person could only live for so long with this kind of dread in her soul. Now, seeing Levi standing in the conference room at the end of the hallway made me feel a kind of peace. A certain calm before the shit storm I was about to walk into.

"Join us when you're ready." Dom squeezed my hand and sauntered toward the double glass doors ahead of us.

When I'm ready?

Was I ready? I stood frozen. My legs didn't respond because I couldn't command them to move. Words eluded me. Instead, the memories of the last time I saw him face-to-face flickered in my mind like the previews of some horror movie.

Jess had been the one who'd told him where we were. I

blamed her for everything for many years. Yet in a way, she'd been the one to save our lives too. The scars on my back tingled as they did every time I saw him in my head standing over us, striking my back over and over until I finally uttered the words that made him stop.

She's pregnant.

What happened after was a blur. His words sounded muffled as he picked up Jess from under me and shoved her out the door. He returned to shoot me twice before he left us for dead.

Mom had kept us alive all this time. She'd done her part until I was ready to end our story with Levi. Hot blood rushed through my body and the urge to kill him returned. I pictured Dad lying on the marble floor—cold and so still. I let out a breath and replaced Dad's face with Levi's. I knew there was a better way to end him, but for the life of me, I couldn't think of one. All I wanted was to see him dead. Tears stung my eyes, and everything in front of me turned blurry. My feet shuffled back toward the elevator and the room swayed out of focus.

A small hand pressed against my back. "Mr. Moretti asked me to get you some coffee."

Dom's assistant's timid words made the room stop spinning. I took the mug from her. The side of it read *Harvard. Just kidding.* I chuckled, and the tears spilled down my cheeks. "Thank you."

"Can I get you anything else? I have ginger gum."

"I'm fine, thank you. The coffee is all I need." I wrapped my fingers around the mug, and the pressure on my chest let up. Dad wasn't here to see what I'd become. He'd die all over again if he came back to find out I'd become a killer. The choices that led him to his demise, he'd made for this very reason. He wanted something different for me. I sipped the coffee.

Time to face the monster under the bed.

I put one foot in front of me and then the other. By the time I reached the door, my legs were strong again. I entered the room. Dom's cheeks turned a little red. The only tell he was worried sick for me. I smiled at him. He responded with a curt nod as a proper opposing counsel would do. This prompted Levi to turn in his chair. I stood a few inches taller when all the color drained from his face. Was I more than someone he killed a long time ago? Or had I become the ghost that haunted him at night?

The adrenaline rush that filled me when I first walked in spiked again. He really didn't know I was alive, which meant Jess had been telling the truth. She hadn't told him about Mom and me. I looked at Dom. Here was proof that Mickey was behind the shootings, and maybe even behind Jess's sudden urge to make amends with her family and divorce her husband. If Dom had come to the same conclusion as me, he didn't show it.

Levi's knuckles turned white as he tightened the grip on the armrest. Why did I think he'd take out a gun and shoot me the second he saw me? He blinked fast as he recovered from the initial shock and swiveled his chair to face Dom.

"What the fuck is this?"

I strolled around the long table and set my folio and mug on it. My movements were slow and calculated. I wanted him to see that I was real and that I was no longer afraid. A smile pulled at my lips because it was true. He was a spineless coward not a monster. All these years, I made him to be bigger and scarier than he really was. If Dom weren't sitting next to him, I was sure he would've fled already. Not so scary without a gun in his hand and cronies to back him up.

"I didn't think we'd need introductions." I pulled the chair out and sat. "We haven't changed that much."

His gaze darted between Dom and me. "Where's Jess?"

"Safe."

"She put you up to this?" He turned to Dom.

The jerk was actually surprised and offended. I'd expected more, a reason to shoot him and be done with it, but this was Levi...he had to let me down one more time.

"I asked for the meeting, yes," Dom said.

"What do you want? Jess wants to stay with me. What's this?"

"You mean, how am I still alive?"

"I don't know what that means."

So he was willing to admit he knew me. It would've been hard for him to pretend otherwise given his initial reaction. He was definitely going for amnesia. Suddenly, he couldn't remember if I was supposed to be dead. Fine.

"Except you do, but let's put that aside for a moment. Let's talk about you. What do you want, Levi?"

"I want my family back."

"Okay. For whatever reason, Jess wants that too. Is that it? I walk out of here, and you'll move on and keep pretending I'm still dead."

His head snapped up at Dom. "I'm always happy to see my wife's family."

"Cut the bullshit. You left me for dead ten years ago. I'm done hiding. I want my life back."

A slow burn swirled in my belly. I would've preferred he'd come at me with guns blazing. This wasn't how I'd pictured this would go. I'd come here for a fight, not this gaslighting bullshit. I racked my brain for something to say, to cut him deep and get a rise out of him, but I didn't know Levi at all. Even back when I thought I did, I really didn't. What was the one thing he cared about?

"Mom has Jess and Izzy. They won't come back to you until you convince me that we're through."

His lips turned a pale white. So Jess and his kids were the only things he cared about. Could've fooled me.

"What do you want?" he asked.

"A guarantee that you won't come after me and Mom."

"Okay. Let Jessie go."

"Okay? No, asshole, it's not okay." I pushed my chair back and jerked to my feet. I wanted to hurt him. This thing with him wasn't over. I knew it wasn't. "You don't get to betray your own family and then say *okay* to me."

The idea of offering a kind word or a sorry didn't even cross his mind because he wasn't sorry. And for a moment, I wondered if maybe he really had forgotten what he did to Dad. How else could he just sit there, with surprise yes, but then not beg me for forgiveness and not cry his eyes out for the horrible thing he did to us. I was in the way of something he wanted so he agreed to my one demand.

I pressed my lips together and turned to Dom. The crease between his eyes got tighter as his chest rose and fell. He shook his head once. Was that his apology? An apology for not being able to give me the release I needed. Levi met Dom's gaze as if seeing him for the first time. When he switched his attention to me that usual greedy tint to his eyes had returned.

"You want to kill me? You can't. Unless you want every headhunter in the city to come knocking at your door." He stood, bracing his hands on his hips. His eyes bored into mine. How could he be so sure I wouldn't kill him in his sleep?

Because he thought I didn't have it in me? Because he didn't think he deserved it?

"Is that what Mickey offered?" Dom finally broke his silence.

"No." He wiped his nose with the back of his hand. The mention of Mickey's name made him step back.

"I know he's been to see you. Mickey doesn't leave home. Ever. If he came, it's because he thought it'd be worth his time and effort. What did he ask for?" Dom asked in his lawyer voice. There was no threat in his tone. If someone were to walk in on us now, they'd see this as any other deposition. Except for the fact that Dom was interrogating his own client.

Levi swallowed. "He did me a favor, that's all."

"What kind of favor?"

"He came to warn me that someone was hell-bent on doing me harm." He shook his head as if he was disappointed to find out it was me who'd been wishing him dead.

"Wait, Mickey knew I came back to Phoenix?" I turned my attention to Dom.

"I'm sure he keeps tabs on everyone around me. He never really let me go." Dom shook his head, glaring at Levi. "He didn't ask for anything in return?"

"No. He only mentioned that if I ever needed a good lawyer, I should call you."

"Jesus, so Mickey knew Jess and I were going to file for divorce?" For Mickey to know about our plans, he had to have set up some kind of surveillance at our house. A cold shiver ran through me. This was a new level of creepy.

"He left me your card." Levi's gaze darted between Dom and me.

"That's it? A stranger comes to your home, warns you about

a plot against you, leaves you my card, and you just let him walk away?"

"I had no choice." He bit the inside of his cheek. "I had him followed. He didn't like it."

"No, I can't imagine he did." Dom sat back on his chair. Somehow Levi's response satisfied him. Was he just glad to have been right about Mickey? Or was this something else?

"I get it. You've come for your pound of flesh." Levi waved his hands in my general direction. "I'm not an idiot. You come at me, and I will burn your house to the ground."

Was Levi afraid of *me?*

"I'll make this easy." Dom stood, and Levi's shoulders tensed. "Your initial response was the right one. As far as you know, your wife has no family left. Amnesia is the best medicine for whatever ails your soul. No one is coming for you, and all you have to do is do nothing." Dom's voice reverberated in my chest.

His calm demeanor made the hair on the nape of my neck stand. He advanced on Levi the way a predator would approach its prey—slow and calm at first. Dom's leering eyes pinned Levi in place. This wasn't Dom, *the lawyer.* This version of him was someone he'd fought hard to leave behind. I knew that now. I hated I was the one who brought it out of him, but I couldn't bring myself to ask him to back down. I squeezed my fists, biting my tongue because what I wanted to ask of Dom wasn't fair. Yeah, Levi deserved to be shot dead. However, this wasn't Dom's problem. It wasn't his job to rid me of Levi.

Levi peered at him, memorizing every detail of Dom's beautiful features. Levi had to recognize they weren't the same. Dom was the big bad wolf looking at Levi like he was something to eat. Dom was bigger, deadlier.

Concession fluttered in Levi's eyes. He knocked on the table twice, swung the door open with a forceful pull and sauntered out of the room. And all I could do was stare as the monster who'd hunted me for years walked away from me, leaving me full of anger and confusion.

"What the hell just happened?" I rushed to the conference room door.

"Your Levi problem is gone."

"You know that's not true. Was it just me? Or did he think I had the ability to..."

Dom nodded. "He's afraid."

"This isn't how I thought this day would go."

"Me neither. I thought Mickey had asked Levi to talk me into working for him. You know. Get me back into the fold."

"Mickey didn't ask Levi for anything. Mickey isn't the humanitarian type is he?"

"No. He isn't." Dom shook his head. "Good news is Levi is off your back."

"For now. Until I know what made him back off, I won't be safe. I need to make sure the status quo doesn't change and put a target on my back again."

"You're right about that. I promise you, I will do anything I can to keep it that way. Anything." Dom rubbed his cheek, trying to keep himself in check. When he met my gaze, he smiled. "You're free."

"Yeah, for now."

"You're still free. Take what you've got and don't look back, Emilia. We're both here. Let's make the most of it."

He relaxed his stance and strolled toward me, his eyes soft and full of longing. The old Dom was back. He wrapped his arm around my waist and cradled my neck.

"Forget about Levi. He's gone. Let's go home," he whispered on my lips, and I melted into him.

Home.

The word spilled from his lips like some sort of promise of a dream I hadn't considered I could have with him. Could we really give into whatever this thing was? I'd expected this hole in my chest to shrink some after today, yet the void was still there, no matter how hard I tried to push it away.

"Hey." Dom held me tighter to keep me from sinking further into my dark place.

I slid my arms up his chest and into his hair. I met his gaze—full of want, intense and focused. Was he right? Was I really free? I hated that Levi got to walk away—unscathed.

In all my fantasies of how this would end with him, I always envisioned the paramedics taking his body away. I always thought I'd be standing over him, filled with satisfaction and the feeling of true freedom. I didn't feel light at all, instead, I felt like something heavier had landed on my chest. I didn't see Dad at the end of the table, smiling at me and nodding in approval. I still wanted revenge. This wasn't enough. Not by a long shot.

16

PEOPLE LIKE US

Dom

"Cancel my appointments for the rest of the afternoon," I said to my assistant as I ushered Emilia into the waiting elevator.

"Okay. Text if you need anything," she called into the gap of the closing doors.

All I needed right now was to go home and leave the outside world behind for a few hours. Emilia leaned against the mirrored wall. How was it possible that even though Levi agreed to let her be, it still felt like nothing had been resolved for her? Why was this still hanging over her head? Revenge wasn't the answer to anything. She should know that by now.

Emilia turned to me. The anguish I found in her eyes made my stomach churn. I knew she had wanted this to go way different, to end differently. Her hand trembled, and I squeezed her fingers. No doubt if she'd had a weapon with her, she would've shot the asshole. Wasn't that why I stopped carrying one? To ensure I was never tempted to take justice into my own hands.

"This can't be it." Her gaze bounced around the confined

space of the elevator car as if the answer she needed was hidden in some dark corner of it.

"Emilia, shooting him would've been doing him a favor. He's scared shitless. And honestly, I don't blame him. Mickey is not someone you want to get in bed with. Now Levi owes him a favor. And I guarantee you, Mickey will come to collect soon. He's no longer your problem. Let them go at each other all they want."

"I'm trying." Her voice trembled. Tears streamed down her face as she labored to catch her breath. I ran the pad of my thumb across her cheek to wipe them off. Her lips brushed my fingers as she turned away from me. "I'm trying to let go, but I can't. This thirst for revenge has a tight grip around my chest. Every time I try to push it away, it latches on tighter, and I can't breathe."

I wrapped my arms around her. What could I say to that? Other than I knew exactly how she felt. I knew how it felt to be wronged, to have to swallow your anger and walk away for the sake of your own health and sanity. "I'm here for as long as you need me. For whatever you need."

She snuggled her head in the nook of my neck and shoulder, fitting perfectly against my body. Yeah, I was here for whatever she wanted. The crying stopped by the time we reached the lobby. When she glanced up at me, something different shone in her eyes.

"I need *you*," she whispered.

Vic drove us back to the hotel. He'd arranged a new room for us without asking if we'd need a king size or two queens. I'd like to think that Vic was an incredibly perceptive man and not that I was blatantly obvious in how I wanted my relationship with

Emilia to evolve. A relationship? Could people like us aspire to such a thing?

Emilia dropped her laptop bag on the sofa, doing a quick turn to take in the junior suite. The space was cozy, with a breakfast table in the corner and a sitting area but no separate bedrooms. A bed and Emilia in the same room made my whole body stand at attention. She'd had such an insane day already between her mom's non-goodbye and Levi's non-apology. I couldn't add more to it.

"You should lie down." I sat on the sofa armrest.

"Oh yeah?" She cocked an eyebrow.

"To sleep. I think you should sleep." I rubbed my cheek, a slow heat fanning through me. This was a bad idea. "I'll stay until you're settled in. I'll be on the floor above you."

She nodded and licked her bottom lip. Pushing her away would be so much easier if she were afraid of me. If I had to make an effort to appear less threatening, like I had to do with most people. But Emilia wasn't like most people. Her strength and her complete disregard for her safety were a byproduct of the life she had to live. Those particular qualities were a complete turn-on for me. Hadn't we already established that going down this road with Emilia could not end well? It would kill me if I were the one to cause her any more pain. She'd had enough of it.

I had to stop pretending to be something I wasn't. I wanted her to see the real me, see that whatever romanticized ideal she'd made up about me couldn't be real and that I would sooner or later disappoint her. I let every raw fantasy I'd ever had about her flutter in my mind. Every bite, every kiss, every touch, letting it show on my face. She needed to know my intentions were far from noble.

"I don't know how to be gentle."

She met my gaze. "I'm not afraid of you."

"I know that." I pushed off the sofa.

My pulse picked up the pace when she bent over and removed her pumps. Her jacket came off next, followed by her pants and silky top. She stood tall on her tippy toes and let out a breath. The effort tightened her midsection. Proud tits and defined abs—what a fucking lethal combination.

With a slow prowl, I closed the space between us. She kept her eyes on mine, daring me, as I reached for her black lacy bra and the taut nipples peeking through the fabric. To my surprise, she slapped my hand away. Hard. The sting on my skin lingered for a few seconds before it subsided.

I flashed her a toothy grin. For the first time in a long time, I had no clue what I was doing. Though I knew exactly what I wanted from this incredibly beautiful woman, who for some fucked-up reason couldn't find a reason to fear me.

"You're hurting right now. I shouldn't be here."

"Take off your clothes." Her voice was low and raspy.

Of all the bad ideas...

I unbuttoned my jacket and shrugged it off. Cool air brushed against my hot skin when I removed my dress shirt and undershirt. A drumbeat hammered in my chest as Emilia ran a hand over my bullet scars and the ink across my stomach.

I ran my fingers up her arm, but she slapped them away. "Shoes."

"I don't do games." I toed off my shoes and bent over to pull off my socks.

"I know." Her gaze bounced from my mouth, down to my chest, and settled on my prominent crotch. As always, Emilia looked calm and collected, unaffected, but the red in her cheeks and the blast of her flowery perfume gave her away. She was aroused, and I loved that I was the reason for it.

She unbuckled my belt, undid the button, and my pants dropped to the floor. I stepped out of them, and she backed away, her eyes caressing every inch of my bare skin. I fought the urge to pin her against the wall and take her already because now that we were finally here, I didn't want to scare her off.

A part of me wanted her to know the real me, yes, but there was also the side of me that had fantasized about being with Emilia for so long that I was willing to do just about anything to make sure she didn't leave me. I wanted to bury my hands in her hair and kiss her tanned skin that glowed even under the dimmed lights of the room. Did she not feel the same turmoil I felt? How could she stand there looking like a fucking goddess and not let me touch her...taste her?

"You want this. What's holding you back?" I asked.

Her head snapped up at me. "You're a force of nature. I can feel myself drowning in your energy. I'm not scared. I just don't know what will happen if I let go."

"I know."

She was torn up about it as much as I was. Emilia and I were logical creatures and getting physically involved defied reason. I could feel myself falling. By all accounts, that was a terrible idea. Wasn't that why Emilia had her battery-operated Dom?

Back in law school, she'd found a quick way to replace me and keep all this complication out of her already messed-up life. Now we'd come this far, and it was impossible to stay away anymore. A target had already been placed on both our backs, and it happened the day I went back to the bar to see her. That was the day Mickey realized Emilia meant more to me than I let on.

"You had a plan before. What was it?" I reached for her hand and placed it over my heart. When she tried to pull away, I pressed my hand over hers to keep her there. "Tell me what you want."

She stared at her trapped hand, breath ragged and cheeks tinted with a deep red. Heat swirled over my chest where her skin touched mine and shot down to my erection. Emilia standing in front of me, hot as all hell in a matching lace bra and thong was a dream come true.

I shuffled into the circle of her personal space until the lace of her bra brushed my arm. She pressed her breasts against me, and her eyes fluttered closed.

"I want to touch you." The soft whisper left her lips and buried itself deep inside me.

Who could say no to that? She walked me backward, her smooth and toned legs entangled with mine, making the hair there stand on end. The back of my knees touched the edge of the bed, and I lowered myself onto the mattress. I used my hands to slide back and kept my gaze on her, ready to pull her toward me if she broke our contact.

"Hands behind your head."

I did as she ordered, biting the inside of my cheek. Dark curls spilled on my chest as she straddled me. I couldn't tell if we were in her fantasy or mine. My chest tightened like a vacuum, sucking in all the desire I felt for her.

Her fingers slid from my biceps down to my side. When she reached my obliques, she dug in her nails gently, thumbing my V line. The cool comforter felt wet from my sweat, and my cock throbbed in my boxer briefs. I didn't know how much more of her game I'd be able to handle, but I wanted to give her as much time as I could.

She glided down my torso. Lace and smooth skin rubbed against me. Holy fuck. I wanted to touch her and see more of her. I hooked my finger under the strap of her bra and slid it over her shoulder. She slapped my hand again and put it back behind my head. With a sexy grin on her face, she kissed my lips and slipped her fingers inside my briefs.

"Fuck, Emilia." I gritted my teeth as she gripped my cock that was now hard as stone. "Tell me you're almost done."

A mischievous giggle filled the room while she continued her exploration. This time she used her mouth, lapping one of my nipples and then the other on her way down to my abs. Her kisses followed a familiar pattern. When I glanced down, her wet tongue traced the wings inked below my chest. She sucked hard, and I welcomed the pain, though it did nothing to defuse the urge coursing through me.

"I've wanted to do this for a long time. To see your naked body, see you subdued under my touch."

"I'm here." My wrists over my head weren't tied, but I couldn't move. "And I'm most definitely subdued."

"I'm almost done."

My hips bucked when she wrapped her mouth around my erection. Hot blood rushed to my ears and muffled the guttural moan that escaped. This entire encounter was beyond anything I would've expected from Emilia. Little Miss Proper who always acted like she was too good to even be in the same room as me, who more than once refused to give me the time of day.

Her taut nipples rubbed against the inside of my thigh as she worked me. The fierceness in her eyes told me she wouldn't let go until I gave in. She came up for air, silently asking the question. I conceded with a nod, and a wicked smile spread across her face. She made me wait a few more seconds, letting the frigid air-conditioner breeze blow across my wet cock. I sunk deeper into the pillow as her warm lips covered me, and she began her sweet torture of me all over again.

This time I didn't fight it. I surrendered to her as an orgasm tore through me, fast and hard. Drumbeats pulsed in my chest, echoing in the far corner of our hotel room before all sounds got muted. I shut my eyes and fell into a dark oblivion.

When I woke, the sun had ceased its relentless beating on the window, though the sleepy heat of the afternoon remained. Emilia broke the silence first, her cheek resting on my navel, her hand still cupping me.

"That was close to what I thought it would be," she mumbled.

I barked out a laugh. Close? The woman had rocked my world. What else was there? "I have to ask...what was missing?"

"Trust me, nothing was missing. You are more beautiful than I thought." She kissed my belly and braced her elbow on my hip bone. "I thought you'd fight me more. You know, try to do me instead. I'm glad you didn't."

"I wanted to, but I couldn't move." And that was the truth. My want for her had paralyzed me. I'd been too afraid she'd walk away. "There's nothing I wouldn't do for you." I cradled her cheek, pulled her toward me, and kissed her mouth.

She thrust her tongue past my lips, no hesitation like before when she thought sex with me would get us both killed. Maybe she was right in her assumption, but if she needed me, I needed *her* a thousand times more. Yeah, we'd crossed the line.

And now there was no going back.

I sat up and adjusted her hips on top of me. We fit perfectly kissing like this. She nibbled my ear, and the soft spot behind it.

Her hands slid down to my crotch. I gripped her wrists and shook my head when she pulled back to look at me.

"I need to touch you. See you." I pressed her fingers to my lips.

A crease fluttered across her forehead. Was that it? She wanted my surrender, but she was afraid to give me hers. Desire unfurled below my navel and rushed into my erection. I rubbed it against her wet core. Her head fell back, and those perfect globes rose up into my face. I pressed against her again, letting her feel the length of me.

Because now it was my turn.

17

HE SAVED ME

Emilia

I licked my lips to ease the bruising from Dom's kiss. He held both my wrists in one hand, then held me tighter as I struggled to free myself. I wanted to touch him again, run my lips over his salty skin.

He shook his head again, his signature panty-melting grin on. "My turn, doll."

His erection ground against me, and my mouth watered. This was the point where all my fantasies about Dom ended. Mainly because I had no real point of reference. I had never been with someone like him. I wanted to memorize every inch of him. The feel of his hard muscles under soft skin, his taste, his smell...

If he left tomorrow, I wanted to keep this moment.

He ran his hands up my waist and cupped my breasts, crushing them together to suck on both nipples. *Jesus.* Every time Dom touched me, I felt myself drifting. I couldn't fight it anymore. He was here, and I wanted him.

I needed him.

Dom treated me to another blast of that testosterone cocktail of his. This time he served it with a side of *I want you now*. He reached behind me and unhooked my bra with one hand while the other one reached inside my panties. His fingers on my aching bud reminded me of how long it'd been since I had any kind of male contact. Too long. His lips on mine were pure ecstasy, full, soft, and so demanding.

I melted into him, out of ideas as to why we shouldn't do this. Why this was bad for the both of us. When I opened my eyes, Dom had both hands on my butt cheeks, supporting my weight as he walked me past the sofa and sat me on the breakfast table. His hot blue eyes explored every inch of my body as his hands followed closely behind, leaving a trail of goosebumps.

"What—"

He pressed his lips to mine and kissed me hard before he pushed me to lie back on the table like some sort of feast. "I said I needed to see you. Are you telling me you don't want this?" he asked out of breath.

I let my weight fall back on the cool wooden table, and he yanked my thong off with a loud rip. A shot of adrenaline rushed through my body and then settled hot and heavy at my core.

"Let me in, Emilia." His warm breath fanned the heat building between my legs.

Up until now, all my relationships had been void of emotion because it was safe to keep it that way. I'd held onto the idea of Dom because no one ever compared to him. With him as the measuring stick, it was easy to never fall for anyone else. Never in a million years did I consider that Dom might want me. How could I let him in without falling myself? If there was something I knew for certain when it came to Dom it was that if I ever let him in, I'd fall. Hard. I also knew that, one way or another, he'd break my heart.

My trembling thighs fell to the sides. He hooked his arms under my knees, gripped my hips, and plunged his tongue into me. I moved my fingers through his hair, soft and wet in my hand. I arched my back, and time slowed way down. Like in those moments before a car crash when the body braces for the inevitable. Dom had crashed into my life in a similar way. Up until now, I had managed to avoid this collision but lying here on a breakfast table of a hotel room, I couldn't stop it anymore. Worst part was, I didn't want to.

Dom pressed his large hand on my stomach and fastened my leg over his shoulder. He tasted every part of me with a reverence that made my cheeks blush. I had not expected this from the guy who said he didn't do nice.

He cradled the nape of my neck and brought me in for a kiss, his mouth warm and wet. "I want to see you come."

He buried his fingers inside me, and as if my body obeyed only him, I orgasmed on his palm. It sprung from my core and unfurled with a burst into my chest. My heart thrashed in my ears and made everything go quiet and dark.

"Christ," Dom whispered on my cheek as he set my legs down.

With two long strides, he picked his pants off the floor and fished his wallet from the front pocket. His gaze met mine across the room as he ripped open a black packet and unrolled a condom over his erection. Those blue eyes made all kinds of promises as he stroked himself. My hands itched to touch him, to feel his warmth on my skin again.

I squeezed my legs together before I let my feet drop to the floor. The A/C came back on again and blasted cold air around us. His chest hitched as I strolled over to him and snaked my hands around his waist, kneading every plane and hard angle up his torso.

"I don't need nice tonight. I need you," I said against his lips, my breath ragged. I hated that my words sounded like a plea.

"Good. Because I can't hold back anymore." He wrapped my legs around him.

His fingers dug into my butt cheeks as he carried me past the bed and slammed my body against the wall. He adjusted his hips, rubbing his cock against me right before he entered me.

"Ohmigod." My head hit the wall while a string of incoherent words spilled from my lips along with gasps of air. An electric hum tottered deep inside me with every one of his thrusts. I clenched around him and the feeling intensified. "I'm so close."

"I know. I can feel every inch of you." He seized both my wrists with his hand and raised them over my head while he clasped my ass to keep the pace he'd set for us. "Do you have any idea how long I've been dreaming about doing you against the wall? On the bed, the couch, and every other fucking place in between?"

I gasped when he plunged again, and the hum swirling at my core ripped through me. I buckled against him, meeting his hips until every last sensation was spent.

"Emilia." He buried his face in my neck, his mouth sucking on my skin as he found his own release.

We stood there, arms and legs tangled with each other, his heart drumming on my breasts, pumping as hard as mine. Sweat dripped from his face and down my arm as he held me pinned against the cool, silky wallpaper. Did I know how long he'd thought about this? If he dreamed of this the same way I had, then like me, he'd been waiting for this moment since the first day we met more than five years ago.

The A/C kicked in again, blowing frigid air in our faces and effectively defusing some of the heat still pulsing between us. I sighed, and he released my hands. My knees wobbled when my feet slipped to the floor. With a deep laugh, Dom caught me by the waist and walked me backward toward the bed. He regarded me as I pulled the covers back and climbed in.

"Don't go." I glanced up at him, drawing my knees in, suddenly feeling naked.

"I wasn't planning on it." He sauntered toward the bathroom. On the way back, he stopped by the mini bar and grabbed a couple of waters. "You need to stay hydrated." He shoved a bottle into my hand and climbed in next to me. His body heat touched my hip and spread through the rest of me like a tidal wave. He scooted down on the bed and pulled me toward him to snuggle in the nook of his arm. "And to think we could've been doing this while we were in law school."

I swigged my water. "Yeah. Although, if we had, I think I'd still be in school."

"You're probably right." He chuckled and let out a long breath. "I don't think I would've minded. Life made more sense when I was in school. I had a path to follow."

I traced a finger along the wings tattooed on his abs. "And now we have to make our own."

"Where do you go from here?" he asked.

"You say that like I'm done and I need to move on."

I'd been on the run for so long, I never considered that one day it would all stop. Though my anger and insatiable need for revenge were still there, the monsters under the bed had retreated for good. So why didn't I have an answer to his question? Deep down, I'd come to terms with the idea that I might not come out on top when it came to Levi, so I never allowed myself to make plans for the future.

"For starters, are you staying in Phoenix? He asks, heart in hand." He cocked his head to look me in the eye.

I smiled. "That's easy. This is my home. I can't imagine being anywhere else."

"I like it here too. I was thinking about maybe buying a house."

I sat up to face him. He picked up his knee, and I laid back on it. "What's wrong with this hotel? I like it here."

"I've never had a place of my own. The idea appeals to me. The suite life is getting old."

"I never pictured you with a wife and kids."

His eyebrows dipped into a tight V. "And why not? I could have me a wife." He sounded offended.

"Bikes and leather jackets don't exactly scream family man."

It screamed hot sex and wild, emotional rollercoaster ride. Somehow, I had landed on that side of Dom's life. I craved his body so much, I'd convinced myself I could handle getting this close, but that part of my life hadn't changed. Love made people weak. I couldn't afford to be weak. Not now, not ever.

"Hey." He pulled on a lock of my hair to bring me back. "This isn't a proposal. It was just a thing to say."

"I know."

"Are you sure? You went all pale."

"Family isn't what it's cracked up to be." I shrugged, hoping the cryptic response would send the conversation in a different direction.

"I know." He lowered his gaze.

My heart squeezed tight. I knew where he'd been before he

went to Columbia. I knew he'd left the crew he'd run around with in New Jersey, but I never considered what his life was like before Mickey.

I cupped his face to make him look at me. The usual intensity in his eyes dissolved as if a light had flickered off inside him. "How did your parents...?"

"Did my parents give me permission to join Mickey's crew?" He raised a brow and adjusted his weight to rest his shoulders on the upholstered headboard. "I never asked."

"You just left to go with Mickey."

He inhaled and pursed his lips. "No. They left."

"What?"

"I never knew my mother. She died when I was little. Dad passed when I was eleven. Mickey was Dad's friend. When they placed me in a foster home, I just moved in with him."

"And your foster parents didn't care?"

He gave me a bitter smirk. "Mickey took care of them."

I swallowed and covered my mouth.

"Oh, no. Not like that. He paid them off to let me stay with him. He knew social services would never approve him as a legal guardian, and he didn't want to bother with it, but he cared enough to make it so I could stay with him. He sent me to school and later even paid for me to go to college."

"He was like a dad to you."

"He was." Dom nodded. "He saved me."

What little I knew about Dom's life suddenly made sense. Why he had been allowed to leave. Why even at the age of twenty-two in law school, he'd had deep knowledge of all things illegal. Like me, he'd been practically born into the mob. Mickey's group was the only family he knew. One day, he was expected to take over. Was Mickey biding his time until the prodigal son decided to come home?

"He was crushed when I told him I was done."

"Why did you leave?"

His gaze drifted to the corner of the room. Under my hand on his chest, his heart beat fast. "He thought of me as his son but that didn't exempt me from his mind games and need to control everything. My senior year in college, he decided to put me through the wringer." Dom was family, and Mickey still felt the need to test his loyalty by forcing Dom to kill for him. He nodded as if reading my thoughts. "He was my friend."

The lump in my throat twisted until tears stung my eyes. "Dom, I'm so sorry."

"I knew what Mickey was from the beginning." He shook his head, rubbing his cheek. "The older I got, the more he realized he couldn't control me anymore. He hated it."

"But he let you go."

"Yeah. I didn't give him a choice. He knew the only way to stop me was to kill me. He was particularly pissed when Vic told him he was leaving with me."

"Vic? Pizza guy Vic?"

"Yeah. He was there when Mickey took me in. He didn't agree with Mickey's methods and decided to leave too. For months, I waited for Mickey's men to come for me. I became reckless and stupid because I honestly thought my days were numbered."

"But he didn't come for you."

"No. And I'm sure Vic had something to do with it. When I realized I was truly out, I decided to clean up my act and enrolled at Columbia. I figured if I helped people, I'd somehow atone for some of the damage I'd done when I was with Mickey." His eyes drifted from my face, down to my chest. That intense and focused look of his returned. He licked his lips and thumbed my nipple.

My eyes fluttered closed at his touch. I was familiar with the feeling of losing loved ones, be it to a gunshot wound or greed but no matter what, family was family. The hole they'd left behind was too deep to be filled with new people—strangers. Dom knew that. It was why he never had any real relationships in college. Whatever made him think I'd be different?

He cupped my face and brought me in for a kiss. His tongue desperately searched for mine, and I caved. I ran my hand up his muscled torso, over his puckered scars. His kiss deepened. A salty taste touched the tip of my tongue—my tears, or maybe they were his. I squeezed my eyes shut and swung my leg over him, feeling the length, the strength of his body under me.

He was wrong in thinking I could make his pain go away. No one could, but for now, even for a little while, it was nice to pretend we were whole.

18

LET ME DECIDE WHAT'S FAIR

Dom

My alarm went off at six in the morning. I reached over to the nightstand and tapped my phone. Of all days, today I didn't want to wake up from this erotic dream.

"You're a snoozer? I would've never guessed that about you." Her raspy morning voice startled me. Emilia slept curled up next to me. It hadn't been a dream.

We'd spent all afternoon and most of the night talking and having sex. After a while, I lost track of time and lost touch with reality. No way Emilia could be this much like me, so perfect for me. She knew my darkest secret and not only did she understand, but she also didn't judge me for it. She stirred next to me. The fullness of her breast pressed against my side, and just like that, I was ready for the next round.

"I'm not a snoozer, but today, I can't remember why I needed to get up this early." I kissed her lips, sliding my hand down to her hip and ass.

"Me neither." She trailed her fingers down my abs and my

thigh. Her touch felt cool against my burning skin. "At some point, I need to get back to the office."

I let out a breath. Of course, she wanted to get back to work. Was it safe? Levi had said he'd let her be, and I believed he meant it. Would he be able to keep his word if Mickey decided Emilia was more trouble than she was worth?

Until Vic found out if Mickey had been to Arizona, or if any of his men had been sniffing around, I couldn't let Emilia out of my sight. I would love nothing more than to spend the next six months with her in this room, naked, and catching up on all the things I'd dreamed about one day doing to her. I grabbed a handful of her perfect breast and bent down to suck her nipple.

"You probably shouldn't keep your clients waiting either." She sighed and let her head fall back onto the pillow to give me better access.

I hummed an affirmation before I switched to her other side. My phone beeped and the screen displayed my first appointment for the day.

"Are you up for a quick road trip?" I asked.

"I can't. I have to get to the office." She gripped my biceps. "I don't know how I'll get any work done, but I have to try."

I kissed her slender neck, running my teeth along her soft spot. "I have one appointment that can't wait. After that, I promise we can come back here and you can have your way with me again."

She slapped my shoulder and laughed. In the past few days, I'd become addicted to that sound. "You're not as good as you think you are."

"Then tell me." I applied pressure to her bud for a couple beats before I buried two fingers inside her.

Her moan sent a current of desire through me. "Where exactly are you going?"

"Paradise Creek." I shifted my weight to get a better angle. Her slick valleys sucked me farther in, and all I could process was that I didn't want to leave her. Like last night, she called my name when I reached the spot that made her tighten around me. "I don't want to spend the day without you. Come with me."

"Okay. Just don't stop doing what you're doing." She cupped my cheek and kissed me hard. I removed my fingers and toyed with her clit. I wanted to savor this moment, make it last somehow. She bit my bottom lip in frustration and pushed her pretty pussy into my hand. "Don't be cruel."

"I like having you like this." I did but denying Emilia what she wanted wasn't something I knew how to do. I slid my fingers from the top of her wet clit down to her entrance. A couple thrusts and her hips buckled as she found her release.

She rested her head on my shoulder, her breathing uneven. I knew sex with Emilia would be different, but I never imagined it would be this. That my need for her wouldn't subside after one night. Wasn't that how it usually went with all the women I slept with? A slow burn swirled in my chest. I couldn't stay here and forget about the world outside, forget about work and my past.

When I felt her relax against me, I nudged her a little. "Get in the shower. I'll bring your things from the suite upstairs."

"Okay." She kissed my shoulder in a way that was so Emilia, so intimate. With a loud sigh, she kicked the covers and got out of bed, treating me to a great view of her heart-shaped ass.

"You did that on purpose."

"Yes, I did." The running water muffled her words.

I jerked out of bed before my cock convinced me to send all to hell and join Emilia in the shower. Nikki's case couldn't wait.

While upstairs, I sent Vic a text to let him know we were going to Paradise Creek. To which he responded that he'd have the car ready for us. I started to type that I didn't need him to come with us, but I knew that would be useless. And for Emilia's sake, I could use the extra security.

After a quick shower, I went in the bedroom next to mine to get Emilia's clothes and toiletry bag. Did I feel like a peeping Tom going through her things? A little, but I still went through a few items until I ran across a shirt dress I liked.

When I finally made it back to the room, Emilia had already finished blow drying her hair and sat waiting for me on the bed. She jumped to her feet as soon as I opened the door. My heart sank. For a moment, fear registered on her face. She recovered quickly and greeted me with a smile.

"I just grabbed the first thing. I hope it's okay." I handed her the clothes.

"It's fine." She dropped the towel wrapped around her and gracefully put on her bra and panties before slipping into the dress. "If you keep looking at me like that, we may not make it out of here at all."

"Sorry." I turned my back to her.

"It's a little late for that, I'm already dressed." She strutted to the bathroom, grabbing her toiletry bag from me on her way there. "Let me do my makeup and then we can go."

"What's in Paradise Creek?" she asked as Vic merged onto the 101.

"Remember the cold case you helped me with the other day?"

"Yeah," she said with a frown. "The murder case?"

"That's the one. I got the results back. You were right. The wound in the picture is post-mortem. I wanted to tell Nikki in person."

"Why her and not your client?"

"Because her sister doesn't want to see me. She doesn't want to get out of jail on a technicality. She wants to prove she's innocent."

Emilia glanced at her hands. "An innocent spends half her life in prison for a crime she didn't commit while Levi roams free."

"Life isn't fair. I thought you knew that."

"I do. That doesn't mean I have to like it."

"Come here." I pulled her toward me. For one, the pain in her eyes said she needed comforting, but also I couldn't stand not having her in my arms. She unbuckled her seatbelt and scooted over to the middle, while her gaze darted to Vic's scolding eyes in the rearview mirror. "Don't worry about Vic. He hears and sees nothing."

"Don't believe that, Ms. Prado." His voice boomed in the car like he'd been waiting to be acknowledged to speak his piece.

"Vic." My pulse quickened. Yeah, technically Vic worked for me, but he was more than my right hand—he was family. And that meant I had no control over the things that came out of his mouth. Right now, it looked like he was about to unleash hell.

He switched lanes and made eye contact with Emilia for a second before he spoke again. "By the look on his face, I can see he finally got what he wanted," he said.

Emilia squirmed next to me.

"That's none of your business." I gripped her shoulder to keep her in my embrace.

"Except it is. My job is to keep you alive. Back when you were at Columbia, I didn't interfere because I could see Ms. Prado had a head on her shoulders. She did the right thing by staying away from you. But now? How do you think this looks? You getting involved with the girl you've been in love with for years?"

"That's enough, Vic. I mean it."

"You know I'm right."

Emilia cleared her throat and moved away from me. She kept her gaze on the window, her chest rising and falling with every breath. I reached for her hand, but she pulled it away. What could I say to her really? That I wasn't in love with her? I didn't even know if that was true. Falling in love meant making plans for the future. People like Emilia and me, we didn't have the luxury of a future. We lived in the moment. We survived.

"Please say something."

"He's right." She turned to look at me. "Me being here is messing with your head. With your priorities."

"You are my priority. I don't give a fuck what he thinks."

Vic threw his hands out as if saying *you just made my point.*

"Last night..." she lowered her voice and I leaned forward to catch the rest of her words, "was amazing. Beyond anything I ever thought being with you could be."

I leaned back for the inevitable *but.*

"But this...I mean...love?" She could hardly utter the word. Was it possible that the idea of love scared the hell out of her just like it did me?

"I'm not in love in with you. I mean, I do care what happens to you." I touched the pad of my fingers to her soft cheek, and her gaze dropped to her hands. No doubt she saw the truth in my eyes. I was in love with her. I'd been in love with her for a long while. I glared at Vic in the rearview mirror. Goddammit. He couldn't let me have this for one day.

"Vic. Please drop me off in the next town. I'll order a car from there," she said.

"No." I pointed a finger at Vic, and he conceded with a nod. At least we were in agreement on this. What Emilia was asking for was dangerous. "You're staying with me."

"I'm not your prisoner." She pursed her lips, peering at me.

"Stay with me, please. Or whatever else you want me to say, but I'm not letting you go off on your own."

A slow burn unfurled in my gut. The hot sex from last night and the avalanche of emotions that came with it were—possibly —messing with my ability to make sound decisions. Getting involved with Emilia was a bad idea. Regardless, we were here now, and I wasn't backing down.

No matter what, my gut told me she needed my protection. This deep desire I felt for her had nothing to do with it. Levi was out of the picture, but we still had to deal with Mickey. I cradled her face. I meant to tell her she was still in danger, but her eyes fluttered closed, and I kissed her instead. The feel of her mouth, full and soft made me wish for the possibility of a future, plans... love, if that was what she wanted from me.

"We're here," Vic announced. A second later the SUV jerked to a halt.

Emilia placed her hand on my chest and fuck me if the look in her eyes wasn't one that felt like a goodbye. I pressed her hand against my pecs, letting her feel my heart pounding. "I have to go be a lawyer and a friend. If I ask nicely would you promise to wait for me in the car?"

"I can't love you," she whispered and slid her hand out of mine. "Thank you for everything. I can take it from here." With one last nod to Vic, she climbed out of the car and slammed the door.

"You couldn't wait until we were alone to enlighten me with your fucked-up wisdom, could you?"

Vic shrugged at my words. "She needed to be reminded of what is at stake here. Hell. Seems you need to be reminded as well. What is it about her? It's not like you've never gotten ass before."

"Fuck off." I kicked the door open and unfolded my frame out of the car.

I looked to my right and didn't see Emilia. When I turned left, her bouncing curls caught my attention. Like a fucking eighteen-year-old, I chased after her.

She had no idea where she was going, but for some reason, she kept going straight toward the wreckage on Main Street and Nikki's hotel. The entire block was desolate and in ruins. What the hell happened here? No doubt Nikki had something to do with that. Another woman with a knack for attracting trouble, but I couldn't worry about her now. I meant it before. Emilia was my priority. Even if she didn't want my help anymore, she still needed me.

She reached the intersection, but before her high heel touched the asphalt, I snaked my arm around her waist and picked her up. She yelped and kicked as I carried her toward one of the abandoned buildings, some candy store that looked like it'd been closed for the season.

"Let me go."

"Hear me out first."

When I set her down, she fell backward on the red brick wall, her breath ragged, cheeks red. She glared up at me, but after a few beats, her eyes softened as they moved down to my lips. At least we still had this intense want for each other. I closed the space between us and covered her mouth with mine.

With a sigh, she ran her fingers through my hair the way she'd done last night when she let me taste her. I kissed her until the pressure in my chest subsided. Until I was sure she wouldn't leave me.

"Promise me you'll still be here when I get back."

"Vic is right. I'm just messing with your head. I'm making things worse for you, and it isn't fair."

"Let me decide what's fair or not for me." I thumbed her jaw as I got lost in her beautiful face, her high cheeks, those plump lips now red from kissing me, and her big brown eyes. "Promise me. If something happened to you, I'd never forgive myself."

She blew out air. "Fine. Go be a lawyer. I'll wait for you."

"Will I be pushing it if I asked you to wait in the car?"

"Yes."

I raked a hand through my hair. "Of course. Just make sure Vic can see you."

"Okay."

I pressed my lips to her forehead and headed toward Nikki's hotel. Vic met me halfway down the block and handed me my briefcase. His gaze darted between Emilia, who'd stayed in the shadow of the building behind me, and my face.

"If you have something to say, say it now."

"The day you decided to go back to the bar to see her, and then brought her home, you sealed her fate. Now you gotta think long and hard how you're gonna undo all this mess. Not just for her sake but for yours too."

Fuck. He wasn't wrong.

19

HELLO, COUSIN

Emilia

We should've stayed in our hotel room. I leaned against the brick wall, heart thrashing in my ears while Dom met Vic one block up. Why did I agree to wait for him? Oh yeah, I glared down at my trembling hands...his kiss. It was always the same feeling as if our touching could fix everything that was messed up in our lives. I knew it couldn't, but every time he was near, I couldn't help but hope that it was true, that love could conquer all.

Vic was right. This thing between us made us a target. I blew out a breath and waited for my need for him to dissolve inside me. Do I take off and let him be? I could meet up with Mom and Jess in Sedona and be out of his life before dinner. He wouldn't say it, but I was sure Mickey's change of heart had something to do with me. He thought he had the upper hand now. Dom had finally shown he had something to lose.

Me.

I braced my hands on my knees to catch my breath. Love? Dom Moretti loved me? How was that even possible? How could he even know? I squeezed my eyes shut and the wind got knocked out of me. Long, skinny arms pinned me to a body I didn't recognize while a dark flannel material was pulled over my head.

The Arizona heat and the heavy fabric had me gasping for air within seconds. I opened my mouth to scream, but no sound came out. When the initial shock wore off and the adrenaline kicked in, I swung my legs in the air hoping to kick anything I could. Instead, I got shoved into the back seat of a car.

My head hit a seatbelt buckle and I balled up my body. Until I figured out what to do, I needed to save my energy and focus on breathing through my nose. I'd spent the last ten years preparing for this moment. How to avoid it and what to do when the inevitable happened.

Levi or Mickey had me. Now I would find out what my life was worth, and what they wanted.

I breathed in through my nose and out my mouth. Flutters rushed around my belly. Once again, I'd let my guard down. The reason was simple. When Dom was around, I felt safe.

Now here I was...taken.

My hands weren't tied, which meant there were enough men in the car to keep me restrained. I tested the limit of my freedom by shifting my weight and sitting up. No one stopped me, so I let my feet fall to the car floor for additional support.

A bit of good news...they just wanted to talk. I moved my hand slowly, palm spread to show them I had no intention of fighting them. When I removed the ski mask, Levi's face came into view in the seat behind me. Through the back window, I saw Vic as he stood in the middle of the street with both hands on his hips watching the SUV drive away.

"Hello, cousin."

"Don't call me that." The scars on my back prickled. Images of the last time he called me that flickered in my mind. He proved to me that day we were not family. "Where are you taking me?"

"Just going for a drive. We need to talk."

"You had your chance for that yesterday. What else is there to say?" The driver made a left turn and hopped onto the 101 heading toward Phoenix.

"There were things I couldn't say in front of your boyfriend."

"You mean your lawyer?" I met Levi's gaze. He sat with slumped shoulders, arms resting on his thighs. The bodyguards on either side of him with their straight faces and angry eyes kept their attention on the road ahead and behind us. For someone at the top of his game, he looked tired and beaten.

"Is he really on your side?"

"What do you want, Levi?" The usual acid that spread in my stomach whenever I thought of him rushed in. I breathed through my nose again and tampered down my anger. "You want me dead? Go ahead. Let's just end this already."

"I never wanted you or Aunt Sofia dead."

I swallowed my tears. "That's where you and I are different because I do want you dead. One way or another, you'll pay for what you did to my dad."

"Why the hell did you come back? Your presence here puts everything I worked so hard for at risk."

"What...?" Red spots flashed in front of me. I launched for his neck, clawed, and punched at his face until the man sitting in the passenger seat pulled me back and shoved me into my corner again. "What you worked so hard for?"

I kicked the man trying to keep me in place. He gripped my wrists and wrapped his arms around me in a tight bear hug. I gasped for air as hot tears streamed down my cheeks. Levi had murdered Dad ten years ago, left us for dead in a pool of Dad's blood, and now he was here demanding to know why I was trying to ruin his life. What the fuck.

"You walked out like we were nothing, you animal."

"I gave you a way out. My orders were to kill all of you. If your dad hadn't fought me the minute I walked in the door, and if he had given me the chance to explain, all of you would've made it out of there alive."

My face blanched as blood rushed to my toes leaving me cold. I searched through my memories of that night. Yes, Dad had fought Levi, but he did it to protect us. "You showed up with guns blazing. What was he supposed to do?"

"How about trust me? We were family."

"Jess had already told us you had been sent to kill Dad so you could replace him."

"I could've killed her for saying that. For making it all that much more difficult for everyone. It didn't have to end that way, Emilia." He rubbed a hand on his cheek, sucking his bottom lip between his teeth.

Was he telling the truth? I sat back against the car door. The panel rubbed against my scars where the skin was almost numb. "She could've died. Lost the baby."

"I never said I was perfect. If you hadn't told me about the baby, I probably would've...I was that mad." He shifted his weight and braced his arm on his thigh. Was that pain in his eyes?

"Does Jess know all this?"

"No, of course not. I couldn't let her carry that burden. To know that her family was dead because of her. That she only heard part of my conversation with the boss. That even though I had been sent to kill all of you, it was never my intention to follow through. If it hadn't been for the baby, she never would've tried anything. Izzy made her strong."

I nodded. "Knowing she had a hand in all that would've killed her for sure." Poor Jess. If she'd known the mess she'd caused, she never would have asked for my help after she saw me at the cemetery the day I went looking for Dad's grave.

The car whizzed down the freeway. The sound of tires on the smooth asphalt filled in the silence between us. When he spoke again, his gaze was fixed on the desert landscape outside. He stared at it for so long, I thought he'd forgotten I was there.

"I wanted a family so bad. Jess is impulsive. She lets her emotions dictate her actions. By the time she thinks things through, it's usually too late. I know she ratted me out because she loved you. She thought she could save you. I was so angry at her that night. Because of her, I had to shoot the one person who believed in me, but I had no choice. It was him or me. I had a different plan for your family, but Jess ruined everything. I had but a second to decide, to choose. I chose family. *My* family." He met my gaze. "I did what I could to save you."

"You shot me in the back," I screamed at him.

"I made everyone believe you were dead." His deep voice reverberated inside me. The words flashing over and over in my head like an echo. "Why do you think the cartel never came looking for you all these years you were in New York? I kept them away from you. I kept your secret. Aunt Sofia's bodyguard was good. He did his job well, but he only succeeded because he had my help."

I'd always wondered how Mom's bodyguard had managed to get us out of the house and into the ambulance unnoticed. Why no one came looking for us at the hospital. So this was the reason why when I showed up to the deposition, Levi had been shocked but not really surprised. He'd known I was alive. He just never thought I'd ever had the courage to come back.

"Why are you telling me this now? Why not explain all this that night?"

"Because Jess got to you first. You didn't give me a chance to tell you I had a plan. Yeah, the cartel wanted Uncle Emilio dead. And they thought I was the right guy for the job. I accepted because I was the only one who could help you leave and start over somewhere else. When I got to your house, all hell broke loose. Instead of taking a few days to plan your escape, I had to make it happen in a matter of minutes. I saw the opportunity and I took it, hoping you'd be smart enough to do the rest. Which you did. Until now. You shouldn't've come back."

This conversation was surreal like something out of a nightmare. Everything I believed to be true was only a half-truth. Not once did I consider that Levi did what he did to fake our deaths. Somehow it all made sense. It all fit. We had someone helping us from inside the cartel. Levi had been helping us all this time. How else did we manage to hide from them for so long? The answer was simple. They didn't know they had to look for us. Levi kept our secret.

I sat frozen. Levi's lips kept moving, his hands in the air as he tried to explain why he did what he did, but I couldn't hear anymore. All these years, I'd been running away from a ghost, my own fears. All these years, I had an opportunity to lead a normal life. Instead, I spent it plotting my revenge.

"I came back to kill you."

"Seems I'm on everyone's To Do list."

"What does that mean?"

"The cartel isn't happy with me lately. They think I've gone too soft. Then you show up hell-bent on revenge. What do you think they'll do to me if they find out you're still alive? To top it all off, a guy who looks like he stepped out of a *Godfather* movie shows up at my door and demands my help. Guess what he'll do to me if I don't deliver you?"

A bark of a laugh escaped my lips. The sound boomed in the car, raw and coarse, I didn't recognize it as my own. "So you told me about how you never meant to hurt me or my family, only to tell me you're here to hurt me and my family? You really think you can just kidnap me and get away with it? What part of 'I came back to kill you' did you not understand?"

He made eye contact with his driver and smiled. "I always liked you, Emilia. Even now with the odds stacked against you, you still think you can win. I admire that. You've got some serious balls. Don't make the same mistake your dad did. I'm here to help you but let's be clear. You go against me or mine, I will shoot you. And this time I won't miss on purpose."

"As long as we're being clear, I'm not an idiot. You're not here to help me, no more than you're here because you love Jess and Izzy. You're here to save yourself."

Suddenly, I understood why Jess had managed to stay with him all this time. Why she felt like what she had with him was real and worth fighting for. Why one day she wanted to leave him and the next she wanted to stay and work things out regardless of the fear he instilled in her.

Levi was a master of bending the truth. Even now, with everything I knew him to be capable of, his words didn't feel like lies. Or maybe I needed to believe him. I was so tired of carrying this anger with me. Levi was offering me a way out. Being free meant I wouldn't have to send Dom away. If he loved me, why couldn't I love him too?

I stared out the window. The sunlight shined on my face, warm and bright. I'd lived in darkness for so long, I had lost hope that one day I could stand in the light again.

"I could blame all this on Jess's impulsiveness, on Uncle Emilio's inability to trust me." Levi's words sounded so far away and yet cut so deep. "Wasn't that the real reason why all my plans were shot to hell? Why I had to kill him?"

"Don't you dare put this on Dad. He didn't pull the trigger. You did. Don't make this about him."

"I'm not. That's not what I'm saying. The thing is, I wanted this life. I wanted a family and a way to provide for them. Really provide for them. That's what put me on this path. What led me to have to choose between my adopted family and a family of my own." He glanced at me, letting the truth touch his eyes. "I'm sorry I hurt you."

The hook that had been latched in the center of my heart for so long twisted as its sharp point slid off and left me breathless. My cheeks and ears turned a hot red. I believed him. I believed he was sorry. Flashes of the night he killed Dad played in my head again, but I pushed them away. The lightness I felt, the air filling my lungs was something I didn't want to lose again. Levi had released me with his apology. And for the first time in ten years, the idea of forgiveness didn't seem so alien to me. Love didn't seem so alien.

Maybe there was a way to move on, like Mom had done, and

make up for lost time. I had to figure out a way to forgive Levi. If I could do that, Dom and I would have a shot. That would be assuming Dom loved me and wanted to stay with me. He never said as much. As usual, I freaked out and ran off. I didn't want to do that anymore. I was done running.

"Why am I here?" I asked.

"Because you need to disappear again."

20

THEN YOU WERE ALSO TOLD I DON'T BLUFF

Dom

I let the front door to the hotel close behind me. Nikki had a shit load of problems to work through. Although there wasn't much I could do for her in that department. I had my own crap to deal with.

Vic waited at the end of the block. His somber look made my pulse quicken. What now?

"Spit it out. Fast." I glanced left and right. Emilia was nowhere to be found.

"Levi has her."

"And you're just telling me now?"

"You had business to take care of. I don't think he means her any harm." He pushed off the wall and headed toward the car.

"You don't think? Are you fucking kidding me?"

"If he wanted her dead, she'd be dead by now. Get in. They're on their way to Phoenix."

When Vic suggested we bug Emilia, I hesitated because it was an invasion of her privacy but as Vic had put it, she could forgive me for this. Getting killed on my behalf, not so much. I never imagined bugging her phone would serve us well this soon. I climbed in the back seat and let my head fall back.

Please. Not her.

Vic merged onto the 101. The engine shifted gears in succession as he pushed the SUV to speed up. He was going fast but not hauling ass like I needed him to.

"Where is she now?" I rubbed my face.

He looked at his laptop wedged in the passenger seat. "They're a few miles out of the city."

I took a deep breath. I had to consider this case the way I would any other. If I let my feelings for Emilia get in the way, she might not make it. My feelings...after all this time, Emilia finally knew the truth. She knew I was in love with her.

"Take me straight to her."

"Sure. And then what? At some point, you gotta get your head out of your ass and do the right thing."

"I am doing the right thing."

Did I make a mistake going back to the bar to see her? Yes. Would she be safer if I let her go now? Hell no. I didn't care what Vic or Mickey thought. Emilia belonged with me. Levi had no interest in harming her but like Mickey, Levi only wanted a bargaining chip.

I'd be an idiot if I didn't read between the lines. Vic had tried to warn me. Mickey was getting ready to make his move. I knew what the ultimatum would be too—return home or he'd make sure Emilia didn't get to see another sunrise. Of course, it would be more than that. He'd make her see it was all my fault. She would die knowing my love killed her. I had to find her.

When Vic whizzed past the exit to the hotel, I fisted my hands, forcing even breaths.

"Do you know where she is now?"

"Looks like he's taking Emilia to her office."

"Of course. He needs her to stop the proceedings of his divorce." Acid fluttered at the pit of my stomach. If he wanted her dead, she'd be dead already. I repeated that over and over in my head. I reached under the seat, retrieved my handgun, and checked the cartridge.

"You're packing now? I thought you were done with that." In the rearview mirror, his eyes wrinkled at the corners.

"Levi's left me no choice. If he's thinking of using Emilia as a bargaining chip with Mickey, he's got another thing coming. Emilia is coming with me today, one way or another."

For once, Vic didn't argue with me and instead hit the accelerator with more urgency than before. Even if Levi needed Emilia alive, he still wasn't one of the good guys. We reached the front of her building, but Emilia wasn't there. I'd expected to see one of Levi's cars, but the street was empty. I climbed out and ran inside to check with the security guard.

I forced a shorter gait and plastered on a smile when the guard made eye contact with me.

"How can I help you?" he asked.

"I'm here to see Ms. Prado. Could you let her know I'm here?"

"Certainly. Name?" He grabbed the phone. After looking for her extension, he dialed and waited.

"Dom Moretti."

"I have a Mr. Moretti here for Ms. Prado." He nodded a couple of times before he said a quick thank you and a goodbye.

"Ms. Prado hasn't come in yet. You're welcome to call her direct line and leave a message."

"Thank you. I'll do that." I spun and took long strides back to the car. "She's not here," I said to Vic when his eyebrows rose in question.

"I refreshed the application. This was her last location. Nothing else is coming up. Like we lost the signal or something."

"How long ago was that?" I asked.

"About forty minutes."

I slammed my hand on the hood of the car. Forty minutes was a long time. They could be anywhere. Goddammit. We should've stayed in our hotel room this morning. Where could she be? If they came here, Emilia never made it inside the building. The security guard had said she wasn't in yet, which meant she hadn't come in at all.

Vic hit a few keys on his laptop before he rebooted his system. "Maybe there's a glitch or something. Those chips can be buggy." He chuckled at his own joke, then he stopped when I glared at him.

"Wait. Could it be that she's somewhere where signal is limited? Like a garage?"

"You might be right." He pulled up a map of downtown and dropped a pin on all the nearby garages. "One of the garages where she parks her car is only half a mile away."

I climbed in the passenger seat. "Let's go check it out."

Hot blood pumped in my ears as we turned into the underground floors of the parking garage. We had no reason to assume that Levi brought Emilia here, but what did we have to lose? There was no other place for us to look except for the hotel.

"We'll do a quick drive through, and then we'll go back to the suite."

"Okay. I'm glad to see you're using your head again."

I had to focus on the task at hand because if I let my mind run wild, I would come up with a hundred and one ways to make Levi hurt for taking Emilia like this. Was she scared? Was she wondering where I was? If I knew how to get to her? I fisted my hand and slammed it against the car door.

On the last turn that led to the bottom floor of the garage, I spotted Emilia's long curls, bouncing all over the place. Vic let the car roll to a stop as all four of Levi's men turned to us. Squinting to see through the red spots in my vision, I hopped out of the car with a death grip on my gun behind my back.

One of the men held Emilia by the waist while Levi wiped away at his mouth. Whatever plans he had for Emilia, she was giving him hell. I'd expected no less. What I should also have expected was that I'd be outgunned in this scenario, but I didn't stop to measure our dicks. Before any of the men could react, I punched one in the throat and then the liver. While he recovered from the impact, I put him in a headlock and shot the next guy in the foot.

How about that? It was like riding a bike. In perfect synchronization, the last two men moved to protect Levi, using Emilia as a human shield, guns out. For a split second, I considered shooting the guy gripping Emilia by the waist. I had the angle and the aim. All I needed to do was pull the trigger.

I wanted to do it. I wanted to save her.

I didn't care that I'd spent the last five years of my life trying to forgive myself for the life I took. I didn't care that if I killed him, I'd become what Mickey wanted to me be, and everything I'd hated about me for so long. The look on Emilia's face made me take a second pause. Sweat ran down my back while my finger hovered over the trigger, stiff and numb.

The adrenaline coursed through me, giving me all the clarity I needed. In my peripheral vision, the guy I shot lay on the floor, slithering back toward his group. The man in my hold stood still, his heart pumping hard against his chest plate and my forearm.

I met Emilia's gaze and she shook her head once. "It's better if I go with him."

"No, it's not. You're coming with me."

"Dom. You can't go against the cartel."

She was right. I couldn't go against them except this had nothing to do with the cartel. Otherwise, Levi would have more than four bodyguards with him. No, this was a loose end Levi wanted to handle on his own.

"Let her go. She's not a threat to you."

"I know she's not, but your family insists she can be. I will not be made the fool with my boss."

So that was the big favor Mickey had offered Levi. If Levi played along, Mickey wouldn't tell the cartel that Emilia and her mom were still alive.

"No, I can't imagine Emilia turning up after you killed her would look good on your bad-guy resume. If you hurt her, you'll answer to me."

Levi's laugh echoed against the concrete walls. "I was told you'd say that."

"Then you were also told I don't bluff."

Levi's gaze darted from Vic sitting in the SUV behind me, and Emilia, who couldn't take her eyes off me. If she was pissed at me for showing up to get her or thankful, I couldn't tell. And honestly, I didn't care. I just wanted her to leave this place alive.

After what felt like a lifetime, Levi nodded, and the man holding Emilia loosened his grip.

"Walk," he ordered.

"Get in the car, Emilia." I kept my eyes on Levi and my gun on the man who a few minutes ago I almost shot dead. Icy fingers gripped my heart. I'd come to the conclusion that he needed to die way too easily. Solving the problem, pulling the trigger...it all had come to me way too easy. Was this what Vic had been afraid would happen if Emilia stayed?

Emilia held my gaze for a moment. With one last backward glance at Levi, she rushed to the car. The adrenaline pumping through me dissipated and left me covered in cold sweat.

"Stand down," Levi said to his men before he met my gaze. "Make sure she stays away. And if I were you, I'd keep your dog on a shorter leash."

"Forget about Emilia and her family." I released his man and stepped back toward the car.

"I've been trying to. So how about you tell your dad to forget about her," he called after me.

I slammed the door and shut Levi's words out as his form became smaller in front of us. Vic didn't bother to turn the car around. He reversed his way out until we were two floors up. I replaced my gun under the car seat and leaned back, rubbing my cold hands on my cheeks.

Next to me, Emilia stared at the side of my face. I couldn't look at her. If she feared me after that display, I didn't know what I'd do. After a long while, she settled on the side of her seat and glanced out the window as Vic merged onto the freeway.

I wanted to tell her we were going home, but what place would that be? The hotel? Her mom's cabin in Sedona? New York? My insides twisted at the idea of her leaving for good. I wasn't ready to let her go. There had to be another way out. A way that didn't include us being apart. The big assumption here was that Emilia wanted the same thing.

I exhaled and turned to look at her. She kept her attention on the buildings alongside the freeway for a moment before she turned to me. Something unfurled in my chest when her eyes didn't show fear or even anger. The softness I found there was something entirely different. I fought the urge to hold her and kiss her. If I did that, I wouldn't be able to stop myself. I gave a quick glance at Vic, who only shook his head.

"Thank you," Emilia whispered.

"I shouldn't've left you alone." I reached for her hand, but she pulled back and shifted her weight in the seat.

"I let my guard down. It was stupid. I should've seen it coming."

"Don't say that. I should've been there for you." I searched her face.

Even after the ordeal she'd gone through, she wasn't crumbling in fear. There were no tears in her eyes. Though I could tell she'd been crying, she wasn't full of rage like before when Levi left my office. This time it was different. She seemed at peace. What the hell happened to her in the two hours she was gone? If Levi wanted something from her, why didn't he ask when Emilia confronted him?

"Would you come back to the hotel with me?" I blurted out. I couldn't stand the silence. I couldn't stand the thought that Levi convinced her I was the monster she should be afraid of. I rubbed my hands on my pants. Had she finally figured out that I was the reason her Levi problem kept coming back? That she had it right when we were in college. She was better off staying away from me. I needed to let her go before I hurt her.

"I kind of have to." She placed a warm hand on my cheek, a ghost of a smile on her lips. "All my things are there."

"You know what I mean." *Stay with me.* I gripped her fingers on my face and brought them down to my mouth. I kissed the tips as the usual desire fluttered below my navel.

She leaned toward me, her eyes soft and serene. She exhaled the way she'd done the night before and this morning right before she gave into me. Except this time, she pulled her hand away.

"I know what you mean, but we need to talk."

And there it was, the proverbial *but*.

FORGIVE, HOME, LOVE

Emilia

The suite door clicked open, and Dom held it at arm's length to let me in. I kept my gaze on him, searching his face for the obsidian look in his eyes that showed up when Levi's men had me in a tight hold. All I could think at that moment was that Dom had found me.

A million butterflies had fluttered in my chest when his SUV turned the bend and came to a screeching halt a few feet from me. Dom moved so fast, I wasn't sure what'd happened until one of the bodyguards dropped to the floor. In the same beat, the guy standing next to me hooked his arm around my neck and knocked the wind out of me.

That was the moment when I saw it. Dom's handgun aimed a few inches from my temple, while Dom had his human shield in a vice grip. For a long second, I was sure he would pull the trigger. He'd shot the other man so easily. Every move had been smooth and controlled as if he'd done it a million times before. I'd fought back tears because the last thing he needed was a hysterical woman but inside I wept for him. How many times did he have to fight like that for the muscle memory to set in?

He let out a long breath, shut the door, and threw the bolt. "You never have to fear me."

I shuffled back to take a better look at him, his whole frame. His eyes showed something different. There was a softness in them. A passion that felt familiar because I felt it too.

"Seems to me you're the one who's afraid."

"Not anymore." He closed the space between us and captured my mouth.

We had so much to talk about but the resolve I'd found in the car to stay away from him until we had talked this through went out the window the minute his lips touched mine.

"I can't think when you're near," I said in between breaths.

"We can think later. Right now, I need you."

With deft fingers, he unbuttoned the top of my dress before he pulled it down and let it drop to my feet. He reached around and unhooked my bra. He kneaded both breasts, sucking one and then the other. This morning and the time we'd spent together seemed like a lifetime ago. I'd missed him, his scent, his strength, his body.

"Take it off." I slid my hands under his suit coat and pushed it off his shoulders.

Gripping my hips, he walked me backward until he had me pinned against the wall, his teeth grazing the soft spot behind my ear while he removed his dress shirt, and then his undershirt. The shiny leather of his belt in contrast with his tanned and muscled torso sent a blast of adrenaline to the aching spot between my legs. I ran my hands from his chest down to the V line peeking out from the waistband of his pants. Gosh, the man was beautiful.

A wicked smile pulled at his lips. He leaned in to whisper in my ear, "I know I said you could have your way with me, but right now I need to be inside you."

I sighed, and he turned me to face the wall. His belt clinked playfully, cold and hard against my bare skin as he unbuckled it with urgency to free his erection. The soft grooves on the silky wallpaper brushed against my nipples and face, but I didn't dare move. I stayed right where he wanted me. I'd do anything to get him to finish what he'd started. He cupped and kneaded my butt cheeks while he rubbed his cock on the lace of my underwear. The only thing separating me from him.

I couldn't take any more of that. "Now, Dom."

His touch fell away. I couldn't move. Instead, I waited with a patience I didn't feel as he ripped open the condom wrapper. "You're so fucking gorgeous." He slid his forearm up my back and moved my hair out of the way, letting it cascade on my right side. His cool mouth brushed up my spine and over my scars. He removed my panties, and then he entered me with a force that made me gasp his name. A couple thrusts was all it took for me. I clenched around him, feeling how hard he was for me. I let out a breath and waited for my release.

"Not yet." He panted, his breath hot and heavy on my shoulder. After a long second, he gripped my hip with one hand to still me while the other slid from my lower back up to the center where he drew small circles along the puckered skin etched across my back. He followed his fingers with wet kisses, nibbling and sucking as he went along. "Our skin shows where we've been, but it can't tell us who we choose to be."

"I think I understand that now." I licked the sweat off my upper lip and moaned when he rocked his hips into me. The heat lingering inside me almost hurt. I shuddered against his warm skin and surrendered to him.

The tenderness of his touch, the heat of his skin, the slick of his tongue on my scars...it all screamed a single word in my head. *Forgive.* Once again, the idea of forgiving, forgetting the past, and moving on with my life felt easy. It felt like the only answer.

"I love you," he said, and my body tensed. My own muscle memory. He snaked an arm around my waist while he caged me against the wall with the other. "Don't run off again. Please."

"I'm not. Just not what I was expecting you to say right about now." I took a deep breath, taking in his scent, feeling his strength around me and his hard cock inside me. The urge to take flight slowly dissolved, and I relaxed in his arms again.

He buried his face in the nook between my neck and shoulder and thrust into me again. This time he didn't hold anything back. With my palms pressed against the wall, I rested my forehead on my wrists and allowed myself to imagine a life, a future with this incredibly beautiful man, who not two hours ago had risked his life to rescue me because he loved me.

"Dom," I sighed, repeating his name.

"I'm right here." He brushed his sweaty cheek against mine and kissed the corner of my lip. His hips continued their synchronized dance. With every pump, he reached deeper inside me, past the spot that made me want to scream his name. He placed a large hand over my heart, and I leaned into it, giving in, turning into a puddle of want in his arms.

The pressure at my core built and I gave in to that too, letting Dom take over. I didn't want to run anymore. I wanted this. I wanted him. My heartbeat spiked, hard and fast. It drowned Dom's string of curses and mine as we both found our release. The heat from his body, or maybe it was my own, spread from my ears all the way down to my toes. After a few more beats, the A/C unit took pity on us and finally cranked on, blowing cold air in our faces. Dom released me. I spun to face him, but instead, I slowly slid down the wall, all the way to the floor.

"I can't feel my legs."

With a husky chuckle, he bent over and gathered me into his arms. "Come on, the bed is more comfortable."

"Maybe next time we start there?"

"I can work on that." He maneuvered through the living area and laid me on my side of the bed. Shaking his head with a wide grin on his face, he reached down to take off my high heels. I hadn't even thought of taking them off before. Yeah, my head got cloudy whenever he kissed me like I was the last person on earth. "If you don't take these shoes off, we may not get to have that talk you promised."

"Right." I scooted up the bed and got under the covers. Now that the afterglow of sex had subsided, the A/C air was too much for me. Or maybe the shivers had more to do with nerves than low body temperature. "I'm going to need a minute to gather my thoughts here."

"Take your time." He sauntered around the bed. The mattress dipped under his weight as he sat to take off his shoes and socks. When he stood, he unzipped his pants, let them drop to the floor, and climbed in bed with me. It didn't matter that it was still daylight out. Just like him, I didn't want to leave this room or this bed.

"We should get something to eat." He picked up the receiver. "What are you in the mood for? Sushi?"

"Sounds good." I rolled on my side and ran my hand up his

stomach as he placed an order with the concierge. "You can't expect them to drop everything to bring you food." I laughed.

"They have people for that." He dropped the phone on its base and shifted his body to face me. "Are you okay? I mean, do you want to talk about what happened?"

I swallowed the lump in my throat. "He apologized."

"Really?" His mouth fell open. "What did he say?"

"Just that he was sorry he hurt me." Hearing myself say the words aloud released yet another part that'd been dormant inside me. "I want to forgive him."

"That's a good start." He cupped my face and flashed me an amused smile. "But if he apologized, why were you giving him hell when Vic and I showed?"

"I lost my temper."

"Yeah, I got that. But why?" He sat up on the bed, brows furrowed.

Heat rose to my cheeks. For ten years, I'd spent my life doing the right thing, letting Mom tell me what to do because that was the only way to stay alive. Just when I thought I was getting my life back, Levi informed me I needed to disappear again.

"I can't keep running. I won't."

"I know. I promise you, you don't have to hide anymore."

"That's exactly what Levi wants me to do. If I want him out of my life for good, I have to return to New York."

"I see." He rubbed the sexy stubble on his cheek. "It's bad for business when the people you were asked to kill turn up at your doorstep alive."

"That's exactly what he said."

"It's not a bad idea. New York can be home for you."

I bit my lip and stared at him. Did he really not get it? *This* was my home. Levi was the one who should be hiding and running from the cartel, not me. I'd been back only a few months, but somehow I feel like I never left. I had a house, a job. And Dom was here.

"So you'd be okay if I skipped town?"

"Of course not. I meant what I said before. I love you. I don't expect you to feel the same way. All I'm asking is that you don't run away from me. As crazy as it sounds, I'd like to maybe...I don't know."

"Make plans?"

"Yeah." He grinned. "I'd like to make plans with you if that's what you want."

"I want that very much."

He leaned in and kissed me. Desire unfurled in my belly and down to my core. I pushed him away. We needed to do some thinking now. This thing with Levi had left me feeling lost. I needed a plan to ground myself again.

"New York is not an option."

"Same here." He sat back and leaned against the headboard, his gaze on the bedroom ceiling. "I can't go back there. Too many memories. Too many...temptations." He pressed the palm of his hand to his eye. "Not like you. The bad kind."

"The situation in the parking garage brought back memories for you, didn't it?"

He shook his head. "It was more than that. Once I was able to put aside the fact that it was you, your life on the line, the job was easy. I could see what I had to do. And how."

He raised an eyebrow at me, his gaze intense and focused on mine as if trying to read my thoughts or to see if my next words were the truth. The look in his eyes when he almost shot Levi's bodyguard was a shock to me but not really a surprise. I understood well what went through his mind because I'd seen Dad do the same many times. If Mickey raised him and trained him to be his right hand, it was normal for him to revert to what he knew when faced with a similar scenario.

I wasn't an idiot. Dom's trained-assassin reaction was exactly what got us out of that mess today. Some things were hard to unlearn. Should I be afraid of him? Absolutely. Every fiber in me said I should. But was I?

Not one bit.

"I know. You came for me." I placed a hand on his cheek. I smiled, and the pressure in my chest let up.

"Always. There isn't much I wouldn't do for you. I hope you know that."

"I know that."

"I would never do anything to hurt you."

"I know that too." And that was the truth. I exhaled, and he did too. "So we're both already here and we want to stay. Why do we have to be the ones that leave? Just because Levi doesn't have the balls to tell his boss what he did. Or didn't do ten years ago?" My logic was, at best, childish but Levi owed me this.

"I know. It's not fair that after all this time, you should be the one to leave again. I'll think of something. You deserve to go home."

Home.

"Hmmm...home...I like the sound of that." I removed the covers off me and flushed my body against his.

"If we're done talking..." he licked his lips and scooted down to capture my mouth, "I think we should give that sex-on-a-bed idea of yours a try."

I let out a laugh. "I don't know what I was thinking before. Anywhere is fine with me. As long as it's with you." I kissed him, pushing my tongue past his lips, tasting him. He rubbed his erection on the outside of my thigh, and a shiver coursed through me.

With a chuckle, he twisted his body to reach his pants on the floor and grabbed a condom out of his wallet. Every muscle in his torso flexed and cut under his skin as he fumbled with his clothes. When he returned to me, our mouths connected again, our kiss urgent and desperate.

Love.

His lips on mine whispered the word over and over, though Dom never uttered a single word.

22
THE MEETING WE'RE CRASHING.
THAT'S TONIGHT?

Dom

I toweled dried my hair, admiring Emilia's long legs sticking out from under the sheets and her hair sprawled on my pillow. These were the details I always wondered about when we were in college. When I thought she hated my guts. I lay awake too many nights trying to picture this very scene. Did she sleep naked? On her side or on her belly? What was her favorite drink? And why the hell was she so distrusting? I knew all that about her now...and so much more. I traced the outline of her hip under the sheets, and she hugged her pillow tighter.

A knock on the door broke my focus on her. Dammit. I'd like to go a few minutes without interruptions or ghosts from our previous lives rearing their ugly heads, where we could just spend the entire day in bed. I tossed the towel on the chair and grabbed a pair of sweatpants from the drawer. Last night, they'd delivered our sushi dinner to the grand suite, so we decided to move back in. Vic stayed in the room across the hall and had security tight. For now, we were safe here. One day soon, this sense of security would become permanent.

"Room service," a male voice called from the other side of the door.

I sauntered out into the living room, past the sofa where Emilia and I had watched a movie and made out before we found our way back into my bedroom. With a smile, I peeked through the peephole. A man stood there in the hotel uniform guarding our breakfast. I swung the door open and let him in.

While he set up the buffet in the kitchen, I sat at the head of the table and fired up my laptop. I had cases that couldn't wait any longer, but old habits died hard. I fished my burner mobile out of my computer bag, ran the scramble app, and plugged it into my laptop. The last time I checked the ads on the deep web was the day I figured out Emilia was in trouble with the local cartel. Out of habit, I'd placed a sniffer on the ads that had to do with her.

"Would that be it, Mr. Moretti?" The attendant handed me the check. "I hope the flowers are to your liking. Peonies are hard to find this time of year."

"You're a good man." I added an extra amount to the tip for his trouble and handed him the check. "Thank you."

The second he closed the front door, Emilia came out of the bedroom. "I heard voices."

"Breakfast is ready."

"Oh, good. I'm starving." She padded out of the room, wrapped in a terry bathroom robe, bare feet, wet hair.

She was a vision.

She went straight for the coffee carafe and poured two mugs, adding cream to mine and sugar to hers.

"You remembered," I said when she set the coffee on the

table. She went to sit on the chair adjacent to mine, but I pulled her toward me to sit on my lap. "You smell good."

"So do you." She wrapped her arm around my back, her gaze dropping to my chest. She was good for my ego. I squeezed her thigh and kissed her lips.

My phone beeped with a new message. I looked around to make sure I'd heard right. And there it was, a new message from Nikki.

"There's no escaping the real world is there?" She stood. "Are those for me?"

My face and ears turned hot. Getting her flowers had felt like the thing to do. Now I wasn't so sure. Was I trying too hard? "Yeah. I know peonies are your favorite."

Her eyes softened. "Thank you. They're amazing. How did you know that?"

"I sat behind you in ethics class, remember? I could always tell when you were bored with the material. You'd sit there and draw peonies. You even had a pink pen to color them in."

"That's right." She brushed her fingers over one of the flowers and brought it to her nose. "I didn't think you had noticed."

"I noticed everything about you. Mostly the way your shapely ass would turn into a perfect inverted heart every time you leaned forward on your seat." That earned me a laugh. A sweet sound I didn't mind being hooked on.

"You're impossible." She inspected every dish the server had laid out for us. "Wow, how many people are coming over for breakfast."

"I didn't know what you liked. You didn't eat anything last time."

"I mostly stick to protein, but this French toast is making

eyes at me." She picked the sticky toast with her fingers and dropped it on a plate. On her way back to the table, she licked her fingers and my cock twitched.

My phone beeped again. Jeez. I glanced away from Emilia and opened the messages app to read Nikki's message. She needed to talk to me.

"Do you mind if I return this call?" I asked Emilia, who regarded me with anticipation. No doubt she thought this was about her. One day, she wouldn't have to have her guard up all the time. That was a promise. "It's work."

"Sure. I need to get caffeinated before I can function." With her usual grace, she placed a napkin on her lap and sipped on her coffee.

I tore my gaze away from her and dialed Nikki's number. She picked up on the first ring.

"Dom. Thank you."

"I haven't done anything yet, doll." I chuckled. "How's the new beau doing?"

"I can't even." Air rustled on the speaker. "I'm sorry to keep calling, but I really need your help."

"No worries. What do you need?" I glanced at Emilia, who, for whatever reason, had a hard time cutting her French toast. Was she jealous? Oh yeah, this woman was good for my ego.

Nikki spoke fast, the way she always did, giving every detail of what was going on with her. Apparently, she'd found a witness that could get her sister out of jail. She just sort of misplaced her, and she needed my help finding her. An easy job. If only Emilia's situation were this easy.

"I'll see what I can find on my end. I'll keep in touch." I pressed the end button and dropped the phone on the table before I turned my attention to Emilia. "She did my friend Cole a solid. We owe her. Plus, she's a friend."

"This Nikki girl sounds like she's a magnet for trouble." She took a bite of her eggs.

"Remind you of anyone?" I rose to my feet and went to fix myself a plate. After last night's workout, I needed a big meal.

"You mean me?"

"Yeah. You." I set my plate down and turned my laptop screen toward her.

"What's this?"

"Trouble."

She dabbed her lips with her napkin and brought my laptop closer to her. Of course, she knew her way around the websites I had tagged. The news was bad. Her eyes showed a good dose of fear, but she kept her composure as usual.

"A handful of bounty hunters answered the ad."

"Yes but only one received a ping back." I pointed at the link. "Now we can find out who's after you."

"How?"

"I'm going to crash their meeting." I plugged the details in my phone and texted them to Vic. "The first time I saw this, I assumed right away Levi had put a price on your head."

"Yeah, me too. But now we know who did, don't we?"

I nodded. "I'm certain it was Mickey. And I can't keep lying to myself or you. He's doing all this to send me a message."

"Yesterday, Levi was in a rush to send me back to New York. Now Mickey has hired a bounty hunter. Sounds like he's done playing games with you."

"I'm done too."

"I'm coming with you."

"No."

"You're cute. That wasn't a question. I'm not going to stay in here like some damsel in distress. Mickey doesn't own you. He needs to understand I'm not a pawn."

In a way, she was right. If someone wanted me dead, I'd want to face the asshole too. I just wished I wasn't so afraid for her. I couldn't lose her. "Fine, but we'll drive separate cars. You go with Vic."

"Okay." She sat back, fisting her shaking hands.

"What are you doing for dinner tonight?" I reached across the table and unraveled her fingers.

"Are we making plans?" She smiled at me.

"We're making plans. Actually, I have a missing person case. I thought you could join me."

"Am I your date or your hostage?"

"I didn't mean—"

"I get it. You have to do your lawyer thing, and you don't want to leave me alone." She wiggled in her seat. "Where are we going?"

"A Different Point of View."

"Fancy." Her wide grin twisted something in my chest. She knew every detail of my life, and she wasn't scared. This woman didn't attract trouble. She was in love with it.

"Dinner is at six p.m. sharp."

Later that night, I got to see yet another side of Emilia when she stepped out of her room wearing a silky white dress that hugged her tits just right. The only thing holding the dress in place was a criss-cross of black satin ribbon going down on either side past her hip bone. She sauntered into the room and sat on the sofa to put on her killer stiletto shoes.

"The concierge desk only sent two options. It was this or a

black number." She peeked at me through long eyelashes, her cheeks a pretty pink.

"You look beyond beautiful." I leaned against the sofa and ran my hand down her back where a zipper should be but wasn't. She strutted around and walked straight into my arms. The mix of soft skin and satin was a huge turn on for me. "Are you trying to help me with the case or give me a heart attack?"

"You like the dress?"

"Yes." That was a huge understatement.

"Let's go. If I had to guess, I bet that's Vic sending you a million texts because we're two seconds late."

I fished my phone out of my suit coat. Sure enough, I had ten texts from Vic letting me know what he thought of women and their total disregard for time.

"He says he's waiting."

She laughed, grabbed her clutch, and followed me to the door. "I'm sure those were his exact words."

"That was the gist of it."

Downstairs, outside the lobby, Vic waited by the SUV. His jaw dropped to the floor when he spotted Emilia in her hot-as-all-hell dress. I put my arm around her and thumbed her bare skin. She leaned into me. I loved how familiar our bodies had become. When I met Vic's gaze, he gave the same disapproval look. Beautiful or not, Emilia was a liability.

We climbed in the back seat, and he drove the short distance to the restaurant. Despite Vic's colorful texts, we arrived thirty minutes before our reservation time. That was all the time I needed to talk to the bartender and see what he knew about Nikki's mystery person. We sat at the bar, and Emilia ordered a glass of champagne. Not her drink. Maybe just the drink that went with the dress and this charade that we were on a real date.

I took her hand and kissed her fingers. Maybe one day our plans would include another real date. But for now, this was enough. We were finally together.

"What makes you think the bartender knows something." She sipped from her glass.

"Nothing in particular. Nikki has reason to believe the person she's looking for was here a few days ago. If she was here, whoever was working the bar that night would have seen her."

She drank from her glass again. Every time she did, she scanned the room. Same as me.

"Can I get you another round?" the bartender asked.

"Please. Also, if you don't mind, I'd like to ask you a few questions."

He swallowed, and his gaze darted toward the door. I hadn't asked a damn thing and the guy had already incriminated himself. Whatever he was guilty of, I didn't care. I pulled out my phone and showed him a picture of Tessa Cavalier, the woman who could help Nikki's sister. Next to me, Emilia shook her head. She was right, this guy knew a lot.

"She was here a few days ago. Did you see her?"

"She looks familiar."

I placed a one hundred dollar bill under my empty glass and pushed it toward him. "And now?"

"I didn't work the bar last week. I'll have to ask my friend."

I added another bill to the pile. "Does your friend have a name? Maybe he knows the guy who works the cameras? I'd like to know for sure she was here."

"I'll see what I can do. You got a number?"

I gave him my card, and he stuffed it in the back pocket of his jeans. I swigged from my fresh drink and draped my arm over Emilia's chair. She shifted her body toward me and treated me to a sexy stare.

"This isn't the only reason we're here is it?" She kissed my cheek. "I can handle it. Please don't hide things from me. We're in this together."

"We're in this together." I repeated her words mostly as a reminder to me. No more lies. I pressed my mouth to her glossy lips before I waved the bartender over again. He tossed a raggedy towel in the sink and strolled over to us. "Another round?"

"Yes." I paid him two hundred dollars this time. I needed a straight-up answer. "I was told Scott would be around today."

"He's busy working at another bar tonight."

"Which one?"

He grabbed the bills off the counter and said over his shoulder, "I've got your number."

"Are you hungry?" I turned to Emilia. She arched her eyebrow, her eyes bouncing between mine, trying to read the truth in them. Lying to her had been a mistake. If she wasn't pissed at me now, it was because she understood me. I loved that about her, how she knew me and accepted me.

"This won't be over until I meet with him. Face to face."

She ran her hand up my leg and leaned closer to whisper in my ear. "The meeting we're crashing. That's tonight?"

"Yes."

"Except we're not crashing a meeting. Mickey set this up?"

"Yes, he did. I was one of the bounty hunters who answered the ad. He replied only to me. I was supposed to come here tonight and ask for Scott."

Mickey had been biding his time. Ever since I moved to Phoenix, he'd kept a close watch on me—and Emilia. He'd been wrong to assume I had come here for her. But in the end, his patience had paid off. Just as Vic had said. I sealed our fates the day I went back to the bar to look for Emilia.

The ad on the deep web was a warning, a way of saying *I've got my eye on you and her. I'm in control as always.*

He was done waiting.

23

HOME IS WHERE THE HEART IS

Emilia

"Thank you for dinner." I took the hand Dom offered to help me down the stone steps that led to the valet podium.

"My pleasure." He pulled me into his arms and kissed me. A long, searing kiss that I was now utterly hooked on. This hadn't been a date at all, but it sure felt like it. He held my hand while we waited for Vic. We still had that Mickey meeting we needed to tend to, but for the next few minutes, I wanted to pretend this thing with Dom was real.

"I think tomorrow I'd like to pay Mom a visit in Sedona," I said. "Maybe you can join me?"

"Making plans again? Okay." He flashed me one of his smiles. "I would love to join you. Vic can take you. I can meet you up there after work."

"I don't need a chaperone."

He glanced upward. "I know, but—" His words were muffled by the loud roar of a truck engine. The driver pulled up in front of us, left his keys with a disgruntled valet attendant, and headed up to the bar upstairs.

"Someone's having a bad night," I said.

"I think I know him. He's Nikki's guy."

"Guy?"

"Boyfriend. I don't know. At first, I thought he was another mark, but I think she cares about this one."

"Do you think he's here about your mystery woman?"

He nodded, his gaze focused on the stairs. "I think so. Do you mind if I go talk to him? I don't want the bartender to get the wrong idea. I don't want Henry to end up on Mickey's radar."

"That would be bad." The last thing Dom needed was yet another person Mickey could use against him. "Go. I'll wait for you."

He shook his head and gripped my waist. He didn't have to say it. The last time I waited for him, I ended up in the back seat of Levi's car, possibly headed for New York.

"I promise I will wait in the car." Right on cue, Vic pulled up at the curb. "See? There's my chariot now."

"Okay." He ushered me to toward the car and held the door open. "I gotta go back inside. You're in charge."

"Okay." Vic's voice rumbled from the driver seat.

"I was talking to her." Dom winked at me and then shut the door.

I leaned back on the seat, my gaze focused on Dom's long stride. The man could wear a suit. I touched my lips and caught Vic staring at me in the rearview mirror. Was the guy ever happy? He certainly wasn't whenever I was around. I smiled back at him and the way he frowned, wrinkling his nose at the same time, reminded me of someone I couldn't place.

Most of the time Vic came and went almost unnoticed, like a

spy. I glanced up again and caught his eye. And then I realized where I'd seen him before.

"You're like one of those agents in spy movies," I said.

He snorted and looked away.

"I bet people never see you coming."

"What is it, Ms. Prado?"

"You came to the bar several times. I was undercover, but you knew who I was."

"Dom wanted me to." He kept his attention on the valet attendant as he grabbed a ticket from a patron and tried to manage the crowd. All of a sudden, Vic didn't feel like staring at me through the rearview mirror.

"He would've told me about that. So, who sent you?" I already knew the answer, but I wanted him to say it. All this stuff Dom's foster dad had done sounded so impossible. If I hadn't grown up with Dad and his dealings with the cartel, I would've thought Dom was crazy, scared of a ghost, someone who couldn't be real.

"Mickey has Dom's best interest at heart."

A shock of adrenaline rushed through me. "Dom trusts you."

"And he has no reason to stop doing that, Ms. Prado. I agree that Dom would be better off with his kind, but that doesn't mean he needs to be forced into it. In that regard, Mickey and I don't see eye to eye. Dom knows this."

"So you were spying on me just for fun?"

"I wanted to be prepared for this moment. I needed to know who you were. Obviously, I misjudged you. You should've stayed away. Now Dom has a difficult choice to make."

"He made that choice when he decided to talk to me at the bar."

Vic shook his head. "No, Ms. Prado. That day he simply

forced Mickey's hand."

"How so?"

"When Mickey sees an opportunity, he never hesitates. Even when it comes to his own son."

"Dom is not his son."

"Not this Dom." He held my gaze in the mirror.

The old man's beef with me was that I was part of a world Dom had envisioned for himself. A different one than the one Mickey wanted for him. One where he got to make his own choices about what kind of man he wanted to be. The kind who would go out of his way to help those who needed him, like Nikki. Dom wasn't a trained assassin. He didn't want to be. I rubbed my temple and thought of Dad. If this wasn't the definition of irony, I didn't know what would be.

Why was this such a difficult concept for Vic and Mickey to understand? One way or another, Mickey needed to get it through his thick head that his prodigal son wasn't coming home.

"He deserves to be happy."

"Yes, he does, Ms. Prado."

What an infuriating man, disagreeing with me by agreeing with me. When I turned my attention back to the window, Dom appeared in my line of sight. My pulse quickened, and I couldn't catch my breath. I kicked the door open and slid down the seat to meet him.

His body tensed when he saw me. I looked to his right and spotted Nikki's friend. He swallowed, his mouth slightly open before he turned to Dom. It was too late for me to turn around and pretend I wasn't with Dom. Not that it mattered, this guy appeared to be a friend.

"Hi. Emilia Prado." I offered him my hand, and he shook it.

"Henry Cavalier. I'm a...friend...of Nikki's."

Next to him, Dom shook his head. "Well, friend of Nikki's, we gotta go." Dom wrapped his fingers around my arm and ushered me back to the SUV, where Vic stood leaning against the driver door.

"She's coming with us?" Henry followed closely behind.

"Yes. She's one of my clients. Very important." A wrinkle appeared in the corner of his eye when he turned to me with a smile. He opened the door and gestured for me to get in. "Ms. Prado."

I slapped his hand away and climbed into the car. What the hell was this? Now we were all going on some kind of field trip.

"Explain," I whispered when Dom sat next to me in the back seat.

"He needs a ride and a second."

"Don't lie to me."

"That's the truth. Also, it seems we're headed to the same place. Scott, the guy Mickey said I should ask for to take me to our meeting place is also the guy who has information on Nikki's missing person."

"How is that even possible?"

"Mickey's way of telling me he knows my every move." Dom waited until Henry settled in the passenger seat. "Vic, this is Henry. Henry, Vic. Got an address," Dom said to Vic, and he nodded.

I had a million questions going through my head, but Vic just did as he was told. He didn't even give Dom one of his *I don't agree* looks. I sat back and crossed my arms. Dom and Henry continued whatever conversation they had going on back at the bar. He was mad at Nikki, or she was mad at him. This guy was in bad shape. He looked like he hadn't slept in days, broken. He needed help. I glanced at Dom and he smiled at me. Yeah, this was the kind of person Dom wanted to be. And I very much wanted to be part of that.

After almost an hour, the car finally rolled to a stop at some dive bar in a dark and shady part of town. When Henry unbuckled his seatbelt, Dom placed his hand on Henry's shoulder.

"Let me go in and see what I can find out. You're too tense."

Dom unfolded his frame out of the car and went inside. Henry climbed out too and leaned on the hood of the car, fuming when a Tesla pulled up next to us.

"What's going on?" I asked Dom when he returned.

"Mickey isn't here."

"More games."

"I don't know. This Scott guy, though. He's in way over his head. There she goes."

"Who's that?" I craned my neck to get a better view of the blonde bombshell walking into the bar, sticking out like a sore thumb.

"That's Nikki." He smiled the way a proud brother would do. "Something doesn't smell right here, but we're already here. We might as well try to get some answers."

After what felt like hours, Nikki left the bar with some guy hanging all over her. "Is that our guy?" I sat back to hide behind the tinted window of the car. Nikki glared our way and then talked the guy into letting her drive.

"Yep." Dom tapped Vic on the shoulder. "Don't lose them."

A beat later, Henry hopped in, hands fisted on his thighs. "She's leaving with that asshole."

"Got 'em." Vic pulled out of the parking lot and followed at a distance.

Nikki had taken a big risk leaving the bar with that guy. I regarded Henry's profile. Something told me she'd done this for him. A couple of miles down the road, Nikki pulled into the parking lot of an abandoned building, high beams on.

"We have to get her out of there. Don't slow down."

Gravel crunched under our tires as Vic pulled up several feet away from Nikki's car. Before we'd come to a complete stop, Henry sprung out.

"This is what happens when you let feelings get in the way. Your friend is lucky that guy wasn't packing." Vic watched as Henry yanked the other man out of the car.

"Gun's under the seat." Dom kissed my temple and climbed out.

Vic shifted his weight so he could get a better view of the situation going on outside. Henry beat the crap out of the guy, while Nikki stood there watching not at all perturbed by the scene in front of her. Obviously, not her first time. I reached under the seat and checked the cartridge on the handgun.

I turned my attention back to Vic. "So, you and Dom, you do this a lot? You drive him places so he can do his mobster thing."

That got a chuckle out of him. "I guess you can say that. He's good at what he does."

"I can see that." The trunk door opened, and Dom shoved a guy in the back like he was yesterday's trash. When he closed it, the guy sprung to life, trying to hook a leg over the back seat. "Hey there." I dug my gun into his crotch. It was dark, and I had no other way to make my point.

He blew out air that smelled of rancid liquor and day-old fast food. After a few seconds of what I was sure him considering his non-options, he plopped himself down.

Dom scooted into the seat, a big grin on his face. "Good

girl."

Vic didn't wait for Dom's orders. He put the car in gear and careened out of the parking lot. No doubt his main concern was meeting more of Scott's friends. As we got back onto the main road, Dom turned to the guy in the trunk, half passed-out and with a busted lip. "We had a meeting today, and the other guy didn't show. Did he leave you a message for me?"

He nodded. "He said home is where the heart is. Or some bullshit like that."

Dom rubbed his cheek and caught my eye. "Pull over, Vic."

Vic slowed down the car. The tires pumped and screeched on the asphalt grooves. He pushed the button to open the back door and slammed on the brakes. When he accelerated again, Scott went flying out and landed on the side of the road with a loud thud. Calm as could be, Vic put on his turn signal and merged onto the traffic again.

I checked the safety latch on the gun and replaced it under the seat. "Is this a new game of his?" I rested my head on Dom's shoulder, and he wrapped his arms around me. He held me tight, making me feel safe.

"No, it's the same goddamn game. He controls everything. He knows about you, about Nikki and all her problems. It's why he chose Scott to deliver his message."

"His message." My heart raced. I didn't like the idea of being hunted like this.

"I'm glad you came tonight."

"Is he at the suite?"

He cradled my face and kissed me hard, his lips bruising mine. "It's where you are. So yeah, that's where I would call home." His hot breath brushed my cheek. This pressure in my chest, this taste of fear, it had never felt like this. Like it could crush my chest plate if I didn't push it down. Tears stung my eyes. Dom cocked his head to catch my gaze. "Hey. He won't hurt me. That's not what he wants. I think it would be best if you stayed with your mom tonight, though. Vic will drive you."

"You trust him?"

"Who? Vic? Yeah, why do you ask?"

"He spied on me when I was undercover at the bar. Before you even knew I was there."

Dom pursed his lips and turned to Vic. "You knew where she was, and you didn't think to tell me?"

"You didn't ask." He shrugged. "I went back because if I found her, it meant Mickey was already on her track. Him and I, we think the same. He knew, same as me, that if you ran into her again, you wouldn't let her be. You were a mess when she turned you down the first time."

Dom trusted Vic blindly, and this was why. The old man knew him better than he knew himself. And in his own way, he loved Dom. Vic kept his eyes on the road. I regarded his face, and something inside me told me I could trust him too.

"I'll go with Vic." I kept my eyes on him and spotted a ghost of a smile on his face. I wouldn't say this meant I was growing on him, but at least he didn't hate me like I'd first thought.

"As soon as I'm done with Mickey, I'll come meet you."

I pressed my forehead against his. I hated goodbyes. "Maybe we could do brunch tomorrow. There's a..." I swallowed my tears. "Mom says there's a cute French restaurant with the best brunch in town. You can sit by Oak Creek and..."

"You like making plans with me?" He relaxed against the seat and tilted my chin up with his finger.

I glanced up and met his hot blue eyes as my heart drummed fast in every part of my body. "Yes. I really do."

24

ONLY WHISKEY AND CIGARS

Dom

I had Vic drop me off at the front entrance. No sense in going through the laundry room anymore. That had only given us a false sense of security. This was more my speed. Out in the open with balls on the table.

Emilia squeezed my hand when the valet opened the door. Her eyes showed a kind of fear I'd never seen registered there. She was afraid for me in a way that she'd never been afraid for herself. How about that? Little Miss Proper was in love with me.

"I love you," I whispered on her lips before I kissed her goodbye. "I'll see you later. Okay?"

"Okay." She nodded.

I glanced over to Vic. "Don't let her talk you into anything crazy. Go straight to her mom's."

"Get on with it. And tell that old man I said to fuck off."

I chuckled. "I will make sure to deliver your message."

With one last kiss, I climbed out and shut the door. Emilia's nerves were putting me on edge, and I didn't like it. Female intuition was like dark magic to me. I didn't understand it.

As soon as I crossed the threshold, Mickey's guys met up with me.

"Mr. Moretti, this way."

"I know where my suite is." I rolled my eyes but let them have their moment. This kind of mind game I could handle. Messing with people's livelihoods, that was a different deal. We got on the elevator car and rode in silence to the top floor. At the end of the hallway, two other guys guarded the door to the grand suite.

I'd be lying if I said I didn't care to see Mickey again. For many years, the formative years, he was like a father to me, incapable of doing me harm. I believed that everything he did, he did for our family.

I stepped into the room, and my gaze zeroed in on his form. He sat at the head of the table, a big steak in front of him, drinking a glass of Valpolicella. A lump churned in my stomach. That was Emilia's wine. I breathed out and forced myself to let this minor detail go. That had always been my relationship with Mickey—letting go of the minor details. Details that over time became a huge deal to me.

"Dom, my boy. I thought you'd skip our meeting."

"You're in my suite. It would've been hard to miss."

"Come here." He stood and hugged me. His bald head barely reached my shoulders. To his credit, the hug felt real. "Join me. I ordered your favorite. Steak Florentine. Wait 'til you taste these potatoes. It's like they filled them up with cheese or something."

I played along. Well, sort of. Instead of sitting to his right where Emilia used to sit, I took the chair on the other end of the table. After a few breaths, he nodded to the server, who sprung to life to move the place setting and my steak over to me. It was like he used to say 'The devil is in the details.'

"I need a whiskey first," I said to the server before he placed my covered plate in front of me. He nodded and scurried to the kitchen to make my drink.

Mickey braced his elbow on the table and shook a big steak knife at me. "Whiskey. A man knows his drink." He regarded me with curiosity. If he'd been keeping a close watch on me all these years, he only knew of my comings and goings, not the minor details. He took the time now to really see me.

After the server placed my whiskey on the table, Mickey raised his wine glass. "To family."

I shrugged and swigged from my glass. "What do you want?" Like I'd said, balls on the table.

"That's what I like about you, Dom. Even as a kid when your dad passed, you wanted facts—a plan for the future. Remember that day when you came to me? Begged me to let you join my crew?" He eagerly cut the big chunk of meat on his plate and placed a bite in his mouth.

"Yes, I remember."

"Thought you might." He washed down the florentine with his wine.

I'd gotten so used to Emilia's graceful movements. How well she fit in this space, in my new life. I glanced around the room at the four oversized men who looked like they were one nose scratch away from knocking over a side table or the sofa. They were out of place. They didn't fit in my life, no more than I fit in theirs. Neither did Mickey. Even if in my previous incarnation, I'd begged him to take me in.

"How about that lady lawyer? Where is she? I had hoped to

meet her in person today." He glanced over at his bodyguard and pressed his lips together when he didn't get confirmation she was on her way here. Vic knew what he was doing. I trusted him. "She's very pretty. A little too brainy for my taste, but I can see why you like her."

I knocked back the rest of my whiskey. Bringing up my past hadn't gotten him the reaction he wanted, so now he was trying his luck with Emilia. Vic had warned me about this. No doubt it took Mickey two seconds to figure out she was a way to get to me.

"You crossed the line when you went after her." I signaled for the waiter to bring my dinner. No idea how I was going to scarf down this food.

"Dear boy, you crossed the line when you left. And so, now we find ourselves in this unpleasant situation."

"You don't own me."

"What?" His entire face puckered into a frown. "This isn't about me. This is about family and what's good for you, for all of us."

I cut through my steak and took a bite. Eating served as a distraction. If I kept focused on my plate, I wouldn't have to worry about Emilia. At this point, I was certain his men were out there looking for her. Would they know to go as far as Sedona?

"I agreed to meet you because we never got to finish our conversation five years ago."

"No, we didn't. Did we?" He pushed his plate forward. When the server reached over to pick it up, he asked for dessert. "Another surprise for you. These cannoli arrived today. Just for the occasion."

The server cleared the table and brought a tray of treats big enough to feed twenty people. He prepared new drinks for us. Sambucas with three coffee beans floating in the clear liquid. How long did it take for Mickey's people to organize this feast? This wasn't something he could just get the concierge to do. I fisted my hands. How long had he known we'd meet tonight—in my suite?

I glared at his guys again. They'd changed their stance, not relaxed but not frigid like before. A pressure gripped my chest. I grabbed my phone from the inside pocket of my suit coat and sent Vic a text.

Are we good?

I waited for his response as the spike lodged in my ribs twisted deeper, cutting the air to my lungs. Fuck me. How long did it take to type a *yes?*

Yeah, we're good. I'm staying.

I sent a quick thanks and dropped my phone back in my pocket. This conversation needed to end soon. I missed her. Two hours was a long time to wait to see her again.

"Joey's mom sends her regards." He bit into the cannoli, catching the excess vanilla cream with his finger and licking it off.

"What?"

"You know what." He chuckled and turned to the server. "Let's get some whiskey and cigars in here. Why don't you boys join us?" He waved at his crew as if he'd suddenly gotten some good news.

His guys gathered around the table while the server helped Mickey light up his cigar. To hell with the no smoking signs. That was how Mickey lived. Life on his own terms with little regard to the people around him or all the damaged he caused.

"The day you left." He puffed out smoke. "You didn't give

me a chance to explain. To tell you that your friend's family would be taken care of. I made that promise to him, and I've kept it ever since. She's wanted for nothing."

"Do you realize how insane that sounds? Maybe you didn't pull the trigger, but you're sure as fuck the reason her son died."

"Are you saying I should just throw her out?"

"That's not what I said. Definitely not what I want you to do."

He leaned back, taking a couple short drags from his Cuban cigar. "So what do you want me to do? To say that I went too far? That I misjudged you and your ability to prove your loyalty to me? Because if that's what it would take, you got it."

Was that a fucking apology? If it was, it didn't sound like one. Not that I cared. Why in the hell did he think this cluster-fuck of a dinner would make me change my mind about him, about the kind of person I'd managed to become without him?

"What do you want, Mickey?"

He peeked at his men over his cigar and furrowed his brow. "Dom, we're here to take you home. Don't you think it's about time you do that?"

The pain in his eyes made my stomach churn. I drank from my glass until it was empty. The server refilled it, and I reached for it again but stopped midway as memories of my childhood played in my head. I pushed them away, buried them, but it didn't make the familiar feeling go away. I hadn't forgotten that not long ago I craved Mickey's approval. Like any child trying to gain his parent's favor, I aimed to please him. That kind of embedded behavior was hard to shake.

I ran a finger over the rim of my glass and thought of Emilia. Her laugh and the way her eyebrows shot up whenever I did something that impressed her. Like this suite, like me. She had a lot of power over me, but she never used it for her own gain or to control me. She'd said she couldn't love me, but she showed me what love really was.

"No."

"I'm sorry, boy?"

"I'm not coming with you, Mickey." I sat back in my chair. "So what are we going to do about that?"

He looked at his bodyguard, and the guy shook his hand once. Mickey had gone through his entire arsenal to try to change my mind, but I could see it in his eyes now, the realization that Emilia was the key. So Vic had been right, no matter how hard I tried to ignore his warnings. What he'd said would come to pass was here, staring me in the face. Mickey was planning to use Emilia to get me to go back.

I didn't think I'd ever stop being grateful for what Mickey did for me. He was there when I needed him the most. This bullshit of using Emilia to get me to jump through hoops for him, that I couldn't stand. I wasn't his fucking puppy.

"Are you really this selfish?"

"Family doesn't make you do things you don't want to do."

"I'm talking about Emilia Prado, the cartel princess who's been on the run for the last ten years. I gave your girlfriend her life back, and now you're going to throw it away because you're sweet on her ass. I thought I'd raised you better with family morals and to do for others."

Cold sweat covered my body. The answer to his question lingered in the front of my mind before I pushed it away. Emilia wanted to be with me. She loved me. Me.

"You're her only way out. Everything she ever wanted in life, she can have now."

My head snapped up at him. I swallowed my tears. How

could I have been so selfish? Was this the reason for the fear I saw in Emilia's eyes when we said goodbye? Did she know this would be Mickey's offer? Her life for mine.

Mickey had wanted Emilia here so he could give me a live demonstration of what would happen to her if I didn't agree to return home. However, the picture in my mind was more powerful than whatever physical damage his crew was capable of.

I imagined Emilia in a new house. No panic rooms and no secret tunnels. She'd get up in the morning and go to work, save women like her cousin, children, and just be the lawyer she always wanted to be. I saw her walking to the store or the park, holding hands with someone who deserved her love. Someone incapable of hurting people. Someone who could give her the luxury of a future together. She, more than anyone I knew, deserved that life.

If I left the room now, Mickey would make sure the cartel found out Emilia was alive. Levi would be forced to tie up loose ends. He wouldn't even have to do it himself. Mickey would already have a guy lined up for the job.

"Do this for her. You'll be like her dark angel, her secret protector. She will always be safe because of you."

My heartbeat spiked. Wasn't that what I wanted for her since the beginning. How all this got started? The desperate need to keep her alive kept me from walking away. I rubbed the angel wings tattooed on my torso, feeling Emilia's lips on me as she traced every line with her kisses.

I braced my elbow on the armrest and dropped my head into my hand. The warmth of her skin and her scent assaulted my senses as if she were here in front of me.

If I believed in wishes, I would've wished for more time with her.

I took in a deep, calming breath and forced my pulse back to a normal beat. I focused on my toes, letting the numbness take hold there before I dragged it up my leg, my core, and straight into my chest. I let it swallow me until her hands on me turned to wisps of smoke and I couldn't feel her anymore. Until the air no longer smelled of vanilla, only whiskey and cigars.

When I met Mickey's gaze, he smiled. A genuine gesture that showed he was pleased. Yeah, Mickey should be pleased to see me do "the right thing."

"How soon can you move back home?" he asked.

"Give me two weeks." No point in dragging it out.

"I promise you. We will watch over her as if she were family."

Yeah, we would, because she was.

25

STOP SAYING THIS IS A CHOICE

Emilia

"Hey, baby." I hugged Izzy when she slid off Jess's knee to hop onto mine.

In a handful of days, Jess had made great progress in detoxing herself of Levi. No, she wasn't over him because that would require way more time—years even. But for now, she'd stopped defending him and begun to be honest about all the emotional abuse she suffered while they were together.

Izzy didn't seem to mind her new living arrangements in Sedona. Although soon she would no doubt start asking what happened to her dad. A pang of nerves twisted in my belly. I brushed her cheek and hugged her. Dom had been right all along. Whatever made me think I had the right to take another's life? To deny Izzy the right to grow up with her dad.

She hugged me tightly, choking me until she decided she had enough and jumped off.

"Why are kids always so bouncy?" I laughed.

"It's all the cookies and hot chocolate your mom has been

feeding her." Jess sat back in her chair, her hand resting on her stomach.

"How are you doing?" I asked.

"I'm fine. I'm good at being pregnant." She chuckled. "Hmm. My one skill."

"Don't say that. You have plenty of skills."

"And you? Are you going to be okay with Levi's lawyer?"

"His name is Dom."

I hadn't exactly explained to Jess and Mom the extent of my relationship with Dom. As far as they knew, he was just a hot guy from law school that would be a good distraction for me. At least that was what Mom had said.

Jess rose to her feet. "I should get the munchkin back to bed. Oh, wait." She went back to the kitchen and grabbed a wooden spoon. "I almost forgot my monster swatter. Those pesky things camp out under her bed unless we show up fully armed." She waved the spoon like a lightsaber.

"Need any help?" I chuckled.

"No. I'm fine."

Jess ambled down the hallway, rubbing her small bump. What did Dom think of babies? The thought crept into my head out of nowhere. I smiled at my wine glass. Babies were a plan I hadn't considered until now. The idea had seemed so foreign before...

The grandfather clock over the mantel struck midnight, and I jerked in my seat. *Jesus.* How did it get to be this late? And where the hell was Dom? I sauntered to the window and peeked out into the driveway. My chest tightened. I tried not to think of what Dom's delay could mean.

Vic flashed his headlights. Did he want me away from the

windows? The guy's heart was in the right place, but he was going a bit overboard with his Jason Bourne tactics.

I grabbed my sweater off the chair and headed outside. The nanosecond I opened the front door, he jumped out of the car.

"It's better if you stay indoors."

"Is there something you're not telling me?"

"Isn't it obvious? Dom wanted you out of the city because he was afraid Mickey might try to grab you. Best way to twist his arm. I agree."

And now I felt like an idiot for not asking the question before. Vic wasn't into sugarcoating bad news.

"Shouldn't he be back by now? I mean, how long does it take to tell Mickey to fuck off?"

"I can see why he likes you." He chuckled. "I didn't think he'd make it here tonight."

"You're right. He may not want to risk being followed."

"That's not what I meant, Ms. Prado." He raised both eyebrows. "You don't know Mickey like I do. Think about it a minute. What does your gut tell you?"

The crushing pain that gripped my chest when Dom crossed the lobby doors rushed back. How would Mickey convince him to go back to him? By threatening my life? If I'd survived Levi, we could survive Mickey. Didn't Dom know that? I met Vic's gaze. No, Dom wouldn't know that we could make this work because ever since we reconnected, all I could talk about was how much I wanted to be free. To live without fear.

"That's right. Against his better judgment, that boy loves you. Dom may be a lot of things, but he's never been selfish. As long as he's with Mickey, you'll be safe. Just so Mickey doesn't get any ideas, I'll be staying with you."

"I can't accept this. You need to go back and talk to Dom. Tell him I'll go anywhere with him."

"His orders for me were to stay with you. Until he says otherwise, that's what I'm gonna do." He shrugged and climbed back into his SUV.

If this man had been responsible for raising Dom, I could see why Dom was as stubborn as he was. I stomped back into the house and headed straight to Jess's room.

"What are you doing?" Jess closed the door behind her.

"Looking for something to wear. Do you have a pair of jeans I can borrow?"

"Take anything you want. I've been living in yoga pants lately. The rubber band hack isn't doing the trick anymore." She laughed, rubbing her belly. "Is something wrong?"

"No. Why?" I pulled on the satin ribbon on the side of the dress and let it fall to the floor before I hopped into Jess's skinny jeans.

"No reason, other than my well-trained gut. What's going on with your hot lawyer?" She sat on the bed and fixed her gaze on mine. The look in her eyes reminded me that Jess had been raised by the same woman as me. Our guts were never wrong. She knew. I couldn't lie to her.

"Dom is in trouble. He thinks I need a knight in shining armor."

"Oh, that's sweet."

"You know it isn't. It's dangerous. God knows what his foster dad has planned for him." I donned one of Jess's T-shirts. Since I left the hotel, I'd had this hum in my chest. Because of Dom, I ignored it, but now I knew I was wrong to let Dom's feelings for me lull my senses. We should've stuck together. I should've told him I loved him.

"Foster dad?"

"It's a long story. For now, I need to get out of here." I tossed my dress on the bench by the bed and headed out.

"Emilia, stop." She gripped my wrists outside her door. For a preggers lady, she sure was fast. "Think about what you're doing. From the beginning, I got the feeling Dom wasn't your average lawyer. He might be one of the good ones, but that doesn't mean that you can butt into his business. It never ends well. And you know that."

"He needs my help. It's my fault he's stuck with Mickey. He doesn't want to be there. He should be here. With me."

"He made his choice."

"It's the wrong choice." I yanked free and darted toward the kitchen to grab my purse. How the hell was I going to get past Vic? Out in the living room, Mom sat in the recliner near the window, with her hands folded on her lap. Crap. Vic got to her already.

"You can't keep me here."

"Vic explained what happened tonight. Don't you think you have enough troubles of your own?"

"What did Vic say?"

"That we're free."

"What?"

"Dom worked out a deal with Mickey. Vic says that as long as Dom stays with his family, you and I are free to do whatever we want. Levi is no longer a threat to us. Emilia, this is what we've been waiting for all these years. To finally be able to live our lives without fear."

Yes, this was what we'd wished for year after year. I never once thought about the price I'd have to pay. "I don't want this life without him."

"Oh, sweetie. I believe you, but do think that's what Dom would want for you? He's giving up everything so you can have what you always wanted. Don't be ungrateful and throw it all away."

"You're okay with this? We walk free while he's stuck in his worst nightmare. Mom, don't you get it? Dom spent years trying to stay away from that place. Now because of me, he's trapped."

"It was his choice."

There was that word again. Dom had no *choice* at all. What the hell are they thinking? "It was the wrong choice." I turned on my heel and swung the door open. Vic stood on the other side, leaning on the doorframe. He met my gaze, both eyebrows raised as if asking *where are you going?*

"Lovely. Twenty-eight years old, and I'm still being told what to do."

"This isn't just about you, Ms. Prado." Vic stuck his hands in the pockets of his jacket. "Let the boy be."

"Is that it? It is, isn't it? This whole time you've been biding your time waiting for Dom to come home."

"Dom has a talent that, in my humble opinion, he was wasting as a lawyer but that choice was always his."

"Choice? How in all that is holy is this a choice? All of you." I spun in place to find Jess standing behind me. "Stop staying this is a choice. It isn't. Far from it. This is nothing more than another one of Mickey's fucked-up mind games. Remember? That's why Dom left to begin with." I faced Vic.

"We can stand here until we're both blue in the face, but two things will not change. Dom is with his family now. And you're not leaving this place." He reached inside and closed the door.

I ran both hands through my hair and glared at Mom. Of

course, she and Jess would jump at the opportunity to get their lives back. In all honesty, I'd be doing the same if it weren't for the small fact that an innocent had to pay for our sins. Wasn't that how it always went? I didn't appreciate being on the giving end. This wasn't who I was.

"Are you two ready to make a home here in Sedona?"

"Home is wherever you are, Emilia. As long as you're alive. I won't ask for anything more." Mom sat back in her chair and exchanged a meaningful look with Jess.

"I have to think of the kids." Jess rubbed her belly again.

What was I supposed to say to that?

My gaze flitted between Jess and Mom. This wasn't how I was going to make them see reason. Or rather, this wasn't the way to help Dom. I strolled past Jess standing in the middle of the hallway and went into the room where Dom had stayed just last week. No one had bothered to change the sheets or make the bed. The room stood exactly how Dom had left it with the covers rumpled on the footboard.

I lay on the bed and buried my face on his pillow and screamed. His scent had vanished. It'd been too many days for it to still be here. Four hours and I was already missing him like crazy. I missed the way he filled the room and all the empty spaces in my life.

So this was it? I was finally free from Levi. The shadow the cartel had cast over our lives for the past ten years was no longer there. I'd pictured this day so many times. Not once did I imagine I'd feel worse than before.

Dammit, Dom. Why did you have to sacrifice yourself for me?

It wasn't fair for him. It wasn't fair that I didn't get more time with him.

I turned on my side and brought the covers over my shoulder. Bringing my knees up toward my chest, I balled my body tight, shivering under the cool sheets. My eyes fluttered closed and all I could see was Dom's beautiful body, the ink on his chest and the intense blue of his eyes. *Not fair.* The words floated in my mind. *Not fair.*

Mom deserved to finally live without fear. Jess had her kids. I had no right to expect them to understand or help Dom. Vic was right. This was Dom's choice. Here was the thing, though. Dom didn't have all the facts when he made that choice. He'd assumed I would want a life without him. And for a long time, I'd assumed the same, but now that he'd left, now that I had a whole life without him staring me in the face, I couldn't fathom spending my days with someone else—someone who wasn't Dom.

The anxiety crushing my chest finally let up. Hot blood rushed to my toes and fingers, warming me from the inside out. I unfurled my body with a loud sigh as I threw the covers aside. What the hell was I doing? Since when did I wait for anyone to come rescue me? Since when did I start doing as I was told?

Dom had another thing coming if he thought he could just take off, tell me to stay put, and what? Sit still and be pretty? Mickey, Vic, and Levi could all go to hell. Dom belonged with me. I padded across the room and fished my phone out of my purse. I could text Dom and tell him I loved him, that he'd made a mistake submitting to Mickey's will, but I already knew what his answer would be. He was doing this for my own good.

No, I needed to call someone who would want to help Dom. I racked my brain to think of whom Dom could trust. Truth be told as much as Dom and I had in common, along with a deep connection, I didn't know much about his life outside of our hotel suite. I knew he worked at a firm where he was almost partner because of a big account he brought with him.

I squeezed my phone in my hand, trying to think of what account that was. Was it a communications company that his friend from college owned? He told me about that once when I asked why he'd moved to Phoenix.

Pacing the room, I pictured Dom's office and the many files he had on his desk. Wasn't it based in Tucson? I tapped on the search engine on my phone and typed "communication companies in Tucson." Several entries came back, but only one name stood out to me because I heard Dom mention it on one of his calls. *Cole.* I clicked on CCI and followed the links to the contacts page where I found a phone a number.

The next morning, my heart beat fast when I dialed the number and ring after ring buzzed in my ear. On the fourth ring, a woman answered. "CCI, Derek Cole's office. I can help you."

"Hi. I'm calling on behalf of Dom Moretti. Could I speak with Mr. Cole, please?" I had no idea what I'd say or how Derek Cole could help, but desperate times called for desperate measures.

"Of course, I'll transfer you." The speaker went silent. She hadn't asked anything else, which meant she knew Dom.

"This is Derek Cole," a voice boomed in my ear.

THE VORTEX

Dom

"There's really nothing I can say to change your mind," Cole said.

It wasn't a question. He knew me almost as well as Vic, minus the one little detail about my life. The part I had spent the last five years pretending wasn't real. He sat in the uphol-stered chair in the living room of my hotel suite, ankle braced on his knee and his fingers stuffed in his blond hair. His gaze darted across the room as if the one word that could make me stay was written on the walls or the furniture.

His gut was right. There wasn't anything he could say or do to make me choose differently. Mostly because the choice hadn't been mine. Or rather, this was no choice at all—Emilia's life in exchange for mine.

Yeah, no choice at all.

"I'll continue to manage your affairs if you'd like, but I understand if you'd rather go with someone local."

"I don't want someone local. I want someone I can trust."
He stood, towering over me.

I remained perched on the armrest of the sofa adjacent to his
chair. A few more minutes and he'd give up. A few more
minutes and this would be over. Then I'd be free to go. I rubbed
the stubble on my cheek.

Free.

"Fine." His piercing gaze met mine. "Maybe one day you'll
tell me why the sudden change of heart. If you gotta go, you
gotta go. Gonna miss you, brother."

I let out a breath and rose to welcome his quick embrace. I
swallowed the lump in my throat and knocked back the rest of
my whiskey. "Believe it or not, I'm gonna miss you too."

For a moment, I considered telling him the truth. About the last
friend I had, and the last woman I loved. I sauntered toward the door.
He took my cue and followed me, his lips pressed together. He was
pissed at me. It wouldn't be the first time. In time, he'd get over it too.

A light knock saved me from having to say more. The door
clicked open and Valentina, Cole's soon-to-be bride, stepped in.
Cole's face went from gloomy to bright and cheery. Jeez, the guy
had it bad. He deserved this kind of happiness. Cole was one of
the good guys. Valentina strolled over to me and gave me a quick
hug. Three seconds was all Cole allowed before he possessively
put his arm around her and effectively made her blush.

"So, is he really leaving?" she asked, exchanging a meaningful look with Cole. I never understood couples like that. The
ones who had their own silent language.

I glanced at my shoes. I supposed I couldn't say never.
Emilia and I had that. No doubt it was why she never called
after I didn't show up last week. She knew where I was headed

and why. She understood enough to let me be. I strolled over to the wet bar and poured myself another two fingers of whiskey before I answered her question. "Yeah, I'm really leaving."

She treated me to a bright smile and then faced Cole. "Two peas in a pod."

"What does that mean?" I asked.

"Cole thought he could talk you out of it." If I didn't know any better, I'd say she was happy to see me go.

"Please don't ruin your mascara on my account."

She chuckled, and Cole adjusted his belt. "We should go, honey. Dom has a lot of things to do before his flight, I'm sure. Call me when you're settled in." Cole slapped me on the shoulder.

"Wait. Did you ask him?" Valentina braced her arm through his and stopped him mid-stride.

Cole ran a finger down her cheek. "No, I was kind of waiting for him to change his mind."

With a one-shoulder shrug, Valentina turned to me. "Vic said you were headed to Paradise Creek for a quick visit. I was wondering if we could tag along. I wanted to talk to Nikki in person. I never got to thank her for helping us."

"Yeah, sure." My gaze darted between the two of them. They meant well, but a two-hour drive to Paradise Creek wouldn't be enough time to talk me into staying. To let her die. "I'll meet you two downstairs."

Valentina stepped toward me and hugged me. "You're a good guy, Dom."

"Yeah, yeah." Cole snaked his hand around Valentina's waist and ushered her out of the room.

The events of the past week came crashing down on me. My chest tightened and blocked the oxygen to my lungs. I swigged from my glass until I swallowed nothing but air and then threw it across the room.

Valentina was wrong.

The door clicked again, and Vic strode in. "Car's ready. Why are you letting them come along?"

I had asked Mickey for two weeks before I made a permanent move back to Jersey. As it turned out, I only needed ten days to undo my life here. Also, if Emilia wanted to come here and do her best effort to make me stay, she'd done it by now. No, she wouldn't've changed my mind. It would've been nice to see her one last time though. *Coulda, woulda...fuck it. It was time to leave.*

"I couldn't think of a reason why not." I had more bad news to deliver to Nikki, but it had to be done. Maybe having a friend with me would make me feel less of an asshole. "Did Mickey send his plane like he said?"

"He did better than that. Or worse, depending on who you ask."

"What did he do?" A myriad of scenarios flashed through my mind. Did he find her? "Where is she?"

"Calm the fuck down. She's fine. I told you that." He rubbed the nape of his neck. "The Dragon Lady's got her. She'll be safe. I'll head back over there when you take off. You're in town for a few more days, right?"

I nodded, and Vic let the bellhop in to collect Emilia's luggage. I used the time to pour myself another drink. For some reason, I hadn't wanted them to touch anything in her room, where she slept, where she ate, or the sofa where she finally dropped her Little Miss Proper act and showed me all her scars. That day, I'd finally understood this irrational connection I felt with her since the day I first laid eyes on her.

The room went quiet again after the bellhop left. Vic poured himself a drink and sat next to me at the dining table. "He's going to push you to the limit. You know that, right?"

"I don't give a shit. Only Emilia is off limits. He understands that."

"Dom. There's only one thing he wants from you, and you know that. Are you ready?"

"To kill for him? I guess we'll find out when the time comes." The rush of adrenaline dropped into my stomach like a bunch of bricks. "What is Mickey up to?"

"He flew in himself. He'll be waiting for you at the small airport in Peoria."

"Fine."

Two days later, the black sedan pulled into the airport where Mickey, Vic, and my old-and-new-again life waited for me. I strolled the length of the hanger toward the Goldstream perched at the end of it. Its engine had already eased into a quiet rumble. I climbed up the steps as the numbness spread up my legs to the rest of me. For all of Mickey's mind games, he was never one to make people wait for the punchline—the payoff. It was a good feeling to finally be here and get on with it, find out exactly what he wanted from me.

Two steps into the main cabin, the punchline fell to my feet in a heap, with a swollen eye and busted lip. Levi glanced up at me with his one good eye. I barked out a laugh and rubbed the stubble on my cheek. "You know, usually people try to go for the lesser of two evils. You were better off dealing with me."

Levi grunted a chuckle, holding his ribs. "I had no choice in the matter. You know that."

"That seems to be the recurring theme when it comes to..." I met Mickey's gaze, who beamed at me. "Dad."

"This is me keeping my promise." He pointed at Levi. "She's free."

I turned to Vic, raising my eyebrows with the usual question. *Is she all right?* He slow-blinked once to assure me. With a nod, I stepped over Levi and strapped myself into a seat near the bar. The flight attendant, a young woman with long, curly hair and deep brown eyes, poured me a glass of whiskey. I shook my head as she set the drink down next to a bottle of water in front of me. She took her time, arranging the items on a napkin, her cleavage swaying with every move.

I drank the water and stared at nothing outside the window. The aircraft door closed and seconds later, Vic walked across my line of sight, headed for the black sedan waiting for him, back to Emilia. Where was she? Were they still hiding in Sedona? My vision blurred as he drove away, and the plane jerked forward. In my head, I replaced the roar of the engine with the drumming of percussion instruments like the ones that played the night Emilia and I had our first date. When I convinced myself Emilia and I could have something together.

The plane leveled off when we reached an altitude above the clouds. Across the aisle, Mickey unbuckled his seatbelt and turned to me. "As long as Levi is alive, she won't have peace."

That didn't take long. "Is that why he's here? Should I shoot him now or later?"

"That's up to you." He pointed a forefinger at me. "I can see you want to because then you'll be done with this. Levi goes away, and her problems go away, your promise to her is done. You know this. You keep waiting for me to make you shoot him, hold your hand. I won't do that for you. He's here. I can bring you to the well, but I can't make you drink."

A guttural sound escaped me. I hated it when he made

sense. I hated that he could read me so well. "What exactly do you think I'll be doing for you?"

"I need you as my second." He leaned back in his seat and for a moment, he looked like someone who actually needed me. "It'll be good for business to have a respected lawyer in the family."

"All those millions, and you can't find decent legal counsel."

He chuckled and relaxed his features, looking more like the man who raised me than the monster I knew he was. Slapping my shoulder with the back of his hand like we were old friends, he said, "Remember that time when Vic and I had to bail you out? We're no fancy lawyers, but we got the job done."

His words sparked a memory I'd long forgotten. When I thought a quick way to make a buck was to set up a gambling shack at the stadium. At the age of sixteen, gambling was illegal, but only if you started making a shit ton of money at it. My shoulders shook before I broke into a laugh. Mickey laughed along with me. "Those assholes just wanted their cut."

"You were in their territory. You earned that beating." He wiped a hand across his eye. "I was proud of you that day."

"I got thrown in jail. No, wait. I got the crap beaten out of me, and then I got thrown in jail."

"Yeah, but I knew then, you'd be all right. I knew that even though I wasn't your biological father, you were my son. You were family. You *are* family."

That day, I hadn't needed fancy lawyers. Mickey and Vic got me out, their way, and introduced me to the family business. The one he had hoped we would run together one day. I supposed today was it. The drums echoing in my head quieted down and I regained focus. Work. I needed to work if I was going to make it through this.

"I've seen that look on your face before. You got a new gig planned?"

He darted his gaze toward Levi and then nodded. "Guns."

"And?"

"I need a lawyer who never loses a case." There it was again. That look in his eyes, that fatherly pride that had the ability to suck me right in. The vortex.

"Well, as it so happens, my calendar is wide open." I sat back in my seat as the flight attendant refreshed my drink. She bit her red-lipsticked bottom lip and swallowed. I took the shot of whiskey and set the glass down.

"You don't remember me, do you?" She poured more amber liquid all the way to the rim. I shook my head. She reminded me of someone, but no, I was sure I didn't know her.

"She's Big Joey's kid," Mickey said as a way of introduction before he made his way to the captain's cockpit. "She wants to be a flight attendant. So here she is."

"Mia." She offered me her hand, and I shook it. Still not placing her face. "And I'm not a kid."

"No, you're not." I took another swig of whiskey. The numbness trickled down my throat and spread through my chest. I let out a breath.

Mia leaned on the seat in front of me, holding the bottle of whiskey as if she held the keys to some secret hideout. "Last time you saw me, I still had pigtails." She flashed me a smile and pointed at her soft curls.

Another shot. This time the liquid eased down my throat with a gentle burn and unlocked a tiny memory of a little girl. "My friend Joe's little sister. You put a toad in my coffee."

She made a big display of it, placing the bottle on Mickey's seat before she did a curtsy, long arms out, a wide grin on her face. "You deserved it. Gosh, you were insufferable, thinking you were all that, drinking coffee with the adults."

"I couldn't have been all that bad. Everywhere I went, there you were." More memories rushed to the forefront. I had a family before I left Jersey, where I belonged. No matter how fast I ran, how far I went, I was always meant to come back here. Every step I took since the day I left the hospital with a gunshot wound in my shoulder led me to this moment, this plane. I'd come full circle. Did Vic know I'd end up here? Mickey certainly did.

"You've been gone a long time." She sat on her haunches next to me and placed a hand on my shoulder.

"I know." I swallowed the knot in my throat.

"Welcome home, Dom."

27

ANGEL FACE

Emilia

The windowsill pressed against my ribs and knocked the wind out of me. All I could think of was that Dom needed me, that I needed to see him. I'd waited long enough. I relaxed my legs and focused on breathing. This was ridiculous. Mom and Vic had reduced me to this.

Sneaking out of my own home was childish, but what choice did I have? A whole month had gone by since Dom left me without a goodbye or explanation. No matter what arguments I threw at Vic, he wouldn't give in. Mom was worse. Freedom and my life, those were two things she wasn't willing to let go at this point. Or ever. But Dom needed me. I knew it.

I pointed my foot until my toes touched the edge of the bathroom sink, and then I squeezed through the small window, back into the house. Going out the window head-first hadn't worked. With a quick exhalation, I stood on my tippy toes and hooked my left leg over the windowsill. Twisting my hips, I pushed my torso forward. My right knee pressed against my forehead as I held my breath and wiggled myself through the opening.

When my head cleared the top of the window, I brought my right foot in and let myself drop to the ground. My getaway bag broke my fall as I fell with a loud thud, cursing Mom and Vic for not trusting that I could take care of myself. I rubbed my hip where I'd overextended it. There were bruises on my shoulder, and my wrists were already turning dark red. I ignored the throbbing on my side, slung my bag across my body, and headed toward the trees behind our cabin.

The walk to the main road was about half a mile away but going the long way following the creek added another mile. I checked the time again. I had another thirty minutes before sunup and before Mom woke and came to my room to check on me. Hopefully, by then I'd be on my way back to Phoenix and Dom. Emphasis on hopefully because the person driving my getaway car was someone I'd never met before—a stranger.

My heart pumped fast, fueling my aching muscles as I picked my way through the trail. I stopped in my tracks when I spotted a red Corvette near the road. Squeezing the bag strap between my fingers, I approached the car. Several steps in, the driver door opened and a woman climbed out. Her gaze darted from the road behind us to the rising sun, and then back to me. She smiled at me, which made me assume she'd been waiting for me.

Gravel crunched under her boots as she strode around the hood of the speed racer toward me. I met her halfway. "Hi. I'm Emilia."

"Valentina." She hugged me as if we were old friends. I supposed planning an escape together fast-tracked us from acquaintance to besties. "Sorry about the car. I know it sticks out like a sore thumb. I just grabbed the one closest to the garage door." She combed a loose strand of hair away from her face. "Let's go."

"Yeah." I jerked into a step toward the Corvette. "Thank you for doing this. I had no one else to call." I shoved my bag in the back seat and climbed into the passenger side.

"Glad we could help." Valentina bolted to the other side of the car and dropped in front of the steering wheel like she'd done this sort of thing many times. "This is a fun car." Flashing me a wide grin, she keyed the ignition. The engine roared as she shifted to second gear and hit the accelerator.

With the Sedona scenery zooming past us, I sank deeper into my seat. After all this time, I was going to see Dom again. I hugged myself to stop the butterflies wreaking havoc in my stomach. Even if he hadn't said goodbye or tried to contact me after he left me, I needed to believe he still wanted me.

Dammit. I should've told him how I felt about him when I had the chance. Deep in my gut, I knew he'd gone home to protect me because he had feelings for me. Did he understand how much I loved him? Did he understand that not having him in my life would be worse than a life on the run? I bent over and blew out air. I should've told him.

Valentina rubbed my back. "It'll be okay. If anyone can get through Dom's thick head, it's you. I know it. You can save him."

I turned to her. Jeez, she had a soothing smile. The gentle look in her dark eyes told me she meant what she'd said. "Did you see him?"

"Yeah, a few days before he left." She shifted her attention back to the road. "He acted like everything was fine, but I could tell he was hurting."

"This is all my fault."

"Don't say that. Cole filled me in on what you told him about Dom. Sounds like he left a lot of unresolved issues when he left home. This was bound to come back to him sooner or later."

"I certainly didn't help."

If Derek and Valentina knew the whole truth about Dom, they'd understand why Dom was in danger. When I first called Derek Cole, I couldn't bring myself to tell him the entire story. I couldn't tell him about Dom's scars, what he'd done to his friend, why he'd left home to begin with. Dom's past wasn't for me to share. So, I stuck to the events that transpired since the night Dom met up with me at the Roadrunner a couple of months back.

"We're here." Valentina pulled into the Peoria airport and parked. She glanced at her phone and smiled. "Looks like you're all set to go. Are you sure you'll be okay going on your own?"

"Yeah, you guys have done enough."

I grabbed my bag from the back seat and practically sprung out of her car. The sooner we were in the air, the better. The tiny voice in my head telling me this was a mistake kept getting louder. And I couldn't afford any more doubts. When we reached the hanger, Valentina rushed ahead of me to hug a guy that could easily be Henry Cavill's doppelganger.

"Emilia, this is Cole." Valentina squeezed Cole's biceps and giggled.

"Nice to meet you." Cole shook my hand. "Sorry. My fiancée is a little too excited about this whole thing with Dom."

"I'm just happy he found someone. We should be going with you." She spun to face Cole, and he nodded.

"No. Please. I don't want to impose any more than I already

have." If Dom didn't want me anymore, I didn't want his friends to witness it.

"We'll do it your way." He exchanged a meaningful look with Valentina and ushered me toward his private jet. "I arranged for a car to pick you up when you get there. If you need anything, just call, okay?"

I nodded. "Thank you."

Valentina walked me all the way to the top of the aircraft stepladder and hugged me. "Say hi to Dom for us."

"I will. Thanks again." I stepped into the small plane and sat by the window. My pulse hit overdrive when the engine came to life. Before more doubts flooded my mind, we hit the airport runway, and then we were in the air.

A couple of hours into the four-and-half hour flight, a guy tried to get me to eat a bagel with cream cheese, but I couldn't stomach anything. In the end, he settled for getting me the coffee and glass of whiskey I asked for. I drank the strong brew and let the smell of the amber liquid fill the air around me. As the only passenger on board the plane, the flight attendant insisted on making small talk. I nodded and smiled but didn't ask him questions of my own. His words swirled in and out of focus in mind.

"Anyway, I think we should start there," he said.

I peeled my gaze away from the window. "What?"

"I knew you weren't paying attention."

"I'm so sorry. My mind is somewhere else."

"I can see that. I'm your driver for as long as you need me. I've been to Jersey a few times, and I've got a phone." He grabbed his phone from the side pocket of his jacket. "Where are we going?"

"What?" Great question. Where the hell was I going? I'd

been so worried about what I wanted to say to Dom, I didn't stop to think about where I could find him. New Jersey was a big place. "Can we go back to the part where you told me where we should start."

At my words, the flight attendant took the seat next to mine. And I felt like the biggest jerk. "I'm so sorry. Um. What's...?"

"Tyler. And don't worry about it. I can see you have it bad." Tyler pointed at my untouched whiskey. "Dom just got here so there won't be much on him online. How about Mickey? We should go to his place of work. What's his full name? What does he do?" He leaned forward ready to type this information into his phone search engine.

"Mickey." That I knew for sure. "I don't know what he does for a living. I don't even know his last name." Unless there was a mobster's web page, finding Dom wouldn't be easy. The pressure on my chest returned, and I dropped my head in my hands to catch my breath. When I woke up this morning, I'd hope I'd get to see Dom before the end of the day, touch him, kiss him.

"I can tell you there'll be lots of Mickeys in Jersey." He typed something on his phone.

"I know." I took out my own phone and pulled up the search engine.

"There's some stuff here." Tyler beamed at me.

I logged onto the plane's WiFi and tapped on the search button. Slowly, a list of links and images came up. None of them rang a bell until I came to an image I knew well, an image I could draw from memory—Dom's tattoo. The one in the shape of angel wings covering half of his front. I'd always assumed the wings were a tribute to the freedom he guarded so much. All along, the ink on his chest linked him to his family.

"Let's go there first." I gave Tyler my phone with the address of a warehouse that doubled as a CrossFit gym.

"Sounds like a plan." He glanced at his watch. "Buckle up. We've already started our descent."

I gripped the armrest as the reality of the situation washed over me. I hadn't a clue whom Dom Moretti was or what he really wanted. My feelings for him made me see something that wasn't there. I'd convinced myself that everything he did was to save me.

What if he was back here because Mickey showed him this was where he belonged? Was my assessment of him back in law school the right one? Back then, he didn't try to hide what he was. Danger oozed out of his pores. Wasn't that what all the women in school were after? Wasn't his mobster connection the main reason that kept me away from him? Did I make a mistake letting Dom get to me? No, I couldn't let my fears get the best of me. I trusted Dom. He loved me. I knew it.

As soon as we deplaned, Tyler found the car Cole had called in for us. I had a feeling Cole wanted me with someone he could trust. No doubt Mickey knew I'd come looking for Dom sooner or later. I'd waited this long because I wanted to give everyone time to cool off and settle into a routine. Routines made people blind to their surroundings.

The drive to one of the warehouses we found on the web was only a short ten minutes from the Morristown airport. Unfortunately, the people working there had never heard of a Dom Moretti. Or so they said. I climbed in the black sedan and took my phone out of my purse again. Staring at Dom's tattoo brought me comfort.

"Should we try the next place?" Tyler asked buckling his

seatbelt. "I mean, we're already here." When I didn't answer, he tried again. "Let's keep going down the list."

Adrenaline surged through me. It filled me with want and dread at the same time as Tyler pulled into the parking lot of our next stop. For the most part, gyms tended to be crowded toward the end of the day. However, this place only had a few cars parked near the entrance. I climbed out and rubbed my throbbing hip. Other than the minor pains, the window incident from this morning felt like it'd happened days ago, not hours.

"Could you wait in the car, please?" I met Tyler's kind gaze in the rearview mirror.

I had no way of knowing what we were walking into. Truth was, I didn't want Tyler to see me make a fool of myself. Not that I had plans to beg Dom to come with me. Did I?

"I'll be here if you need anything. Take your time." He offered a warm smile.

I went up the cement steps that led to the steel doors on the side of the gym. The doors were rolled halfway up and cast a shadow inside the warehouse, where clanking noises and grunts echoed against the walls.

A woman in black leggings, a tight sports bra and killer abs met me two steps in. "Can I help you, doll?"

"Hi. I hope so. I'm trying to find a friend." Crap. I still couldn't figure out how to explain to a complete stranger that I was here because the company logo hanging outside their gym was tattooed on a guy I used to sleep with. "I'm sorry. Never mind." I spun around to leave.

"What's his name? I know a lot of people."

"Dom Moretti," I said with a confidence I didn't feel.

She chuckled and hollered over her shoulder. "Hey, Angel Face, there's someone here to see you."

In the corner of my eye, a guy punching a heavy bag stopped dead in his tracks. Dom moved away from the bag and the flutters I'd had in my belly since this morning exploded into a thousand pieces. In the month we were apart, his hair had grown longer, at least an inch, and the stubble on his cheeks was now a full beard. I'd never seen him in workout clothes. Of course, he looked crazy hot in jogger slim pants that showed every muscle on his legs. He appeared different, or rather, he seemed indifferent when his gaze met mine.

Sweat trickled down his bulging biceps as he prowled toward me, a half smirk on his face. The wraps around his hands showed red blotches around his knuckles. I fought the urge to run to him, wrap my arms around his neck and kiss that impossibly beautiful face.

His girlfriend, on the other hand, did exactly what I'd been dreaming of doing for the past few weeks. She snaked her arms around his waist and whispered something in his ear. And all I could do was stand there and watch them as tears burned my eyes.

Dom glanced at her. "Mia, I got this."

I froze. I never really thought Dom would move on. When Dom switched his attention back to me, I spun and darted out of the warehouse.

28

BUT I HAVE A BETTER IDEA

Dom

Mia squeezed my arm, but that wasn't enough to stop me from going after Emilia. Emilia had been here all of two minutes and I was already chasing after her like an idiot. This was why she couldn't be here, why she couldn't stay. When she was within reach, I wrapped my arm around her waist and held her against me. Fuck, she felt good. I buried my face in her vanilla-scented hair.

"Emilia, are you okay?" Cole's brother walked a wide circle around us until he was in front of her. Did I look so deranged that he felt he needed to use tactics on me?

"Hey, man, she came all the way out here to see me. Give us a minute?" I tried my best to sound casual, but the strain in my voice couldn't be hidden.

Emilia relaxed her stance, and I released her. She braced both hands on her hips. "Yeah, I'm fine."

"Okay. I'll be in the car if you need me." His gaze flitted

toward me, a tinge of warning in his eyes that said *Friends or not, I won't stand for it if you do something stupid.*

If I wanted to take Emilia away from here, he wouldn't be able to stop me.

Emilia watched him saunter back to his black sedan. When he was out of sight, she made no effort to turn around and face me. And all I wanted to do was hold her again. A month was a long-ass time to be away from her. What could I say to her? Sorry for leaving you? I wasn't sorry. Would she believe me if I told her I missed her every goddamn day we'd been apart? That I'd fantasized about this moment constantly?

I shot a glance over my shoulder toward the warehouse entrance. Mia glared at us, lips pursed, cheeks red. Of course, she was right. Emilia shouldn't be here. How long did we have before Mickey realized she was in town?

No, he already knew. This was the kind of thing Mickey kept tabs on. Why the hell did Vic not give me a heads-up? I would've had a better reaction to Emilia's presence than the one I had—ogling her like an asshole.

When I first saw Emilia standing next to Mia, I thought she was a hallucination. She visited my dreams so often, it was hard to tell the difference now. She had to go. Without giving it a second thought, I wrapped my arms around her waist, pinning her arms to her sides.

"Are you insane?" She struggled against my chest, but I gripped her tighter. Her smell was intoxicating.

"You're here to talk. Let's talk." I lifted her and carried her across the parking lot, back to the gym. Mia blocked the path at the top of the stairs, but I sidestepped her and kept going past the boxing ring to the office in the corner. My office.

"I can walk on my own, you know." She pushed down on my forearm and her back pressed harder against my chest.

"I know."

I opened the door and released her, using my body to barricade the entrance, in case she decided to run off again. She strode to the center of the room and ran her hand over my desk. The only piece of furniture I bothered to bring in. I opened my mouth to apologize for the condition of the building and the musty smell of sweat, but the words didn't come out. I hated seeing her here. This place wasn't for her. It was beneath her. I shut the door and threw the deadbolt.

"Why the hell are you here?"

She spun to face me. Red rose into her cheeks when she met my gaze. And that was my undoing.

"I thought—"

I closed the space between us and kissed her, burying my hands in her hair. I didn't want gentle or slow, and neither did she. She tugged at the hem of my T-shirt with urgency. Every one of my muscles tensed under her hot touch. Her hands traveled up and down my torso as she traced the edges of my tattoo. Like I'd done with her, she'd memorized every plane on my body. I deepened our kiss and groaned when she pressed against my hard-on.

"*Christ*, Emilia, I missed you." I moaned against her cheek, sucked on the cord of her neck, and kneaded her perfect ass.

"What?" she whispered against my temple while I nibbled on the hard peaks poking through the fabric of her top. "Stop." She sighed and pushed against me.

I took a single step back and placed both palms on the desktop behind her, caging her in. "I'm sorry. I shouldn't have done that, but a month is too long to be away from you."

She covered her mouth with one hand and shoved me with the other. I shuffled back to give her the space she wanted and to catch my own breath. "Seems to me you've made a home for yourself here."

"This is my home."

"Yes, I'm sure your girlfriend was glad to see you back."

I chuckled. "Who? Mia?"

"Is that her name?" The fire in her eyes filled me with an intense need to be inside her. How was I going to send her away? This was why I hadn't said goodbye when I left Phoenix. If I'd seen her that night, I never would've agreed to leave with Mickey. I needed her. I stepped toward her, and she backed away. "I'm such an idiot for thinking that you left me because you loved me."

"I do love you."

Using her hands for support, she leaned against the edge of the desk and met my gaze. "Then why are you with her?"

"What? I'm not. What makes you say that?"

"She kissed your cheek." She balled her fist and tapped her forehead.

I rubbed the spot where Mia's lips brushed my cheek. Yeah, when I got back, Mia had tried to be more than a friend. At first, I was willing to give it a shot and truly move on for Emilia's sake. I figured having someone in my bed would make all this bearable. But every time Mia touched me, Emilia and all her little details flooded my brain, my entire body, and I just couldn't go through with it. Emilia ruined me for everyone else. A smart girl like Mia, she caught on quick and let me be. She knew where we stood. "She's only a friend."

"A friend with benefits?"

"No benefits. Not even once." I searched Emilia's features.

Every inch of her was tattooed on my mind. The cluster of freckles on her nose, the pout of her lips, and the intense brown of her eyes. A grin spread across my face, and it filled every empty space in my chest. "Are you jealous? Why?"

Emilia opened her mouth to speak but the words didn't come out. The scent of vanilla infused the small office that had been my prison for almost a month. "Because."

"Say it." I stepped closer to her.

"Because I'm in love with you. I should've told you when I had the chance." She ambled toward me, her gaze on mine. "You shouldn't've left."

"Nothing has changed, Emilia."

She laced her fingers around my neck, and I let out a sigh. "There are a million other ways to fix this. You returning to the place that hurt you so much isn't the right answer. And you know it."

I gripped her wrists and pulled her arms off me. My mind went fuzzy whenever she touched me. And I needed to focus. This conversation was long overdue. "Okay. Let's talk about what we know. You think you know me, but you don't."

"Then tell me."

"You remember this?" I lifted my T-shirt to show her my inked torso.

"Yes. That's how I found you, actually." She shuffled away from me, crossing her arms over her chest.

"How do you mean?"

"I had no idea where to start looking once I landed. I Googled Mickey's name and this logo came up. We went to another warehouse like this one before we found you.

"That was smart."

"So was the tattoo some kind of initiation?"

"Not really. Growing up, the crew called me Angel Face. I didn't mind it. When I came up with the idea of opening a string of 'gyms' I used that name for the franchise. The angel wings became the logo."

"It's a big warehouse for just a CrossFit box." She regarded me. I nodded and gave her a minute to connect the dots, to understand that I was knee-deep in this, to see why Mickey needed me back. "What do you use the warehouse for?"

"It's a distribution center. For whatever the hell we want."

She put up her hand and shook her head. The lawyer in her didn't want details. This life wasn't for her. "So what if this was your idea? You can still walk away from it."

"I'm very good at this. I'm a fucking criminal, Emilia. A hired gun. Do you understand?"

"You're also a good lawyer."

"I'm way better at this."

She let out a breath. "You're being stubborn. You don't think I have those thoughts too? My life would've been so much easier if I'd caved from the beginning and dealt with Levi the first chance I got but these are the choices we make. We are who we choose to be. You taught me that."

"This world, my family, they're part of who I am. And that's never going to change. I spent five years of my life lying to myself, pretending I could be normal. A decent man. I earned my place here. Good or bad, this is exactly where someone like me deserves to be. You need to go."

Emilia smiled at me. "Yeah, I'll go, but you're coming with me." Not what I had expected after what I told her.

I cocked an eyebrow. "Look around you. There are no chains here. I choose to stay here."

"You're coming with me," she said matter of fact.

"You think I'm kidding?"

"No. I think you're serious about this, but so am I. I can be stubborn too. I made a mistake before. I shouldn't've let you confront Mickey alone. I should've been there for you. I was scared of my feelings for you and the future. I'm not anymore. I want a future with you." She kissed my shoulder twice and wrapped her arms around my waist. Hot blood charged through me as she molded her body against mine. I wanted this future too, but this whole thing had never been about what I wanted.

I cupped her cheek, running the pad of my thumb over her full lips. "I can't think straight when you're near." I leaned over and covered her mouth with mine. Maybe if we wished hard enough, we could make this work. Her tongue swirled against mine and woke each one of my senses. The same ones I spent the past month lulling with whiskey.

She pulled away first. "We can leave now. Cole's private jet is waiting for us at the airport. We'll deal with Mickey later."

"Cole? You called Cole? Dammit, Emilia." I paced the office. I was an idiot for thinking I could keep this under control.

"He's your friend. I didn't tell him the whole story. I didn't have to. When I said you needed help, he showed up, no questions asked."

"So that's why he was so pissed when I left. He had expected me to come clean." I rubbed the creases on my forehead.

"He offered to help me escape Vic and Mom that day. It would've been impossible to get to you then when everyone was on high alert." She placed a hand on my chest, and I covered it with mine. "I love you. I'm not leaving this place without you."

"Levi is here too."

"Why?"

"As long as he's here, you're free." I cupped the nape of her neck. I wanted nothing more than to be on the plane with Emilia, kissing every inch of her. To hell with the rest of the world. "He's a loose end."

"He was never your problem."

"Mickey made him my problem. He's alive because..."

"Because you can't go around shooting people dead. You taught me that too." She took my hand. "Where is he? Maybe we can work out a deal with him. His life for mine."

"We tried that, remember? Without the cartel backing him, he can't stand up to Mickey. And you and I both know that if he goes back to his boss to ask for help, he'll have to tell them you and your mom are not dead. How is that going to help us?"

"He could lie about us. He's been doing it all this time."

I shook my head. "He's a coward. If push comes to shove, he'll choose himself and tell them whatever they need to hear to save himself. And you know that."

"I know." She lowered her gaze.

We were back to square one. "There may be a million ways to solve this but only one where you get to be home free. Leave."

"No." She jutted out her chin in that way that was so Emilia, determined and final.

"Yes." I towered over her. "If I have to carry you back to the airport myself, I will. I mean it."

"Don't push me away." Her eyes filled with tears, and my heart broke in two.

"Don't throw your life away because of me." I advanced on her, and she stood her ground. *I'm sorry, Emilia.* I made a grab for her knees and hoisted her over my shoulder.

"Are you kidding me?" She took fistfuls of my shirt.

"I warned you." I unlocked the door and threw it open. I

squinted out of habit, expecting the bright light from the front entrance to hit me in the face as it always did this time of day. Instead, only the halogen lights high overhead illuminated the building. My pulse quickened. Every beat exploded like loud sirens in my head. I let Emilia slide down my front, but when she tried to move away from me, I held her tight.

"Stay close."

Mia moved to my side. "I called you, but I guess you two were busy in there."

I took my phone out of my sweatpants pocket and hit home. She had called ten times in the last ten minutes. She had also texted: "He's here."

The side entrance door creaked open and Mickey strode in. The creases around his mouth deepened as he pursed his lips. He pinned me with a dark stare before his gaze darted to the back of the gym and then to Emilia.

"So this is the famous Emilia Prado. We finally meet in person."

"Yes, finally," Emilia said in her best Little Miss Proper tone of voice.

"You have a lot of guts showing up here. I can see why Dom has this obsession for you."

I bit the inside of my lip and gripped Emilia's waist tighter. Mickey knew Emilia was much more than an obsession. "She was leaving."

Mickey shook a finger at me and offered a chilling smile. The hair on the nape of my neck bristled when he turned his attention to Emilia. "Yes, I saw that. You were making every effort to take her back to your friend's private jet. I appreciate that, but I have a better idea."

29

YEAH, THE GUN WAS LOADED

Emilia

Mickey regarded me with cold, greedy eyes. To him, I wasn't Dom's girlfriend or his obsession. I was the thing standing in the way of what he wanted. By the way his mouth twitched into a smirk every few seconds, I could only assume his idea had something to do with getting rid of me for good. Mickey scared the crap out of me, but all we could do at this point was let his game play out.

My muscles tightened, and I squeezed Dom's fingers between mine. He kissed my temple and stepped forward. "Let her go. You know very well that if anything happens to her, I will burn this place to the ground."

Mickey put his hand up. "I know. You're my son. In spite of all you've done, I want you to be happy. I'm here to do both of you a favor. Stop assuming my intentions aren't honorable."

"We didn't ask for any favors." I stood next to Dom, who shot me a glance that said *stay behind me* as if that would stop Mickey from getting his men to riddle me with bullets. Had he not noticed we were surrounded? That our only way out was his office, which was, quite fittingly, a dead end.

Five men stood at attention by the steel doors, two by the side entrance, another two behind us. And that didn't include the posse guarding Mickey. All of them with jerky fingers hovering over their unholstered guns. We weren't even armed. What were they expecting?

"That's because you don't know what I can do for you." Mickey smiled.

"I have a good idea."

"Does she always talk this much?" He turned to Dom.

"Yes," I answered for Dom. "Get on with it."

Mickey chuckled. "Get her a gun."

Without a glance to his boss or a glint of fear in his eyes to be giving a mad woman a loaded gun, one of Mickey's black suit-clad guards ambled toward me and handed me his weapon. As if I had men offering me guns all the time, I took it and did my usual checks on it. Yeah, the gun was loaded.

I wrapped my fingers around the handle, pointing it at the concrete floor. Clicks echoed around the warehouse. *Run.* My entire body screamed at me to run, but I couldn't move. When I met Mickey's gaze, all guns were aimed at my head. "I got it. Don't shoot the boss."

"Smart and pretty." Mickey pointed his chin at Dom. This entire display was for Dom's benefit. Every move Mickey made was to get a rise out of him, but Dom was used to these mind games. His face remained impassive. If I didn't know how much he loved me, I'd think Dom was bored.

My hand trembled, and I squeezed the metal between my fingers tighter. Dom's words flooded my mind. 'And you've decided? Is that what you're telling me? Emilia, killing a person will, in time, kill you.'

There had been a time when I wanted to kill a person in the worst way possible. I convinced myself that it was survival, that he deserved it, and that I was entitled to it.

The night Dom showed me his scars, he told me about how Mickey had made him kill his friend. That night, he lobbied for Levi's life. Not to save him but to save me. And that was what Mickey was banking on tonight. That Dom would do as he asked to save me.

"Enough. The suspense is killing me as they say." Mickey chortled at his own bad joke. "Bring him."

Again, one of his guards sprang into action. He didn't ask who or how? I didn't ask either because I knew exactly whom I had to kill today. Some favor. The guard strode the length of the gym on the opposite end and returned with Levi.

My stomach churned, hard as stone. The man who shot my dad and left Mom and me for dead over ten years ago stood in front of me. Regardless of his reasons, he was still the man who killed Dad. He'd lost weight since the last time I saw him. The cuts on his wrists from the wide cable ties binding them together weren't bleeding, but they were still fresh.

"Hello, cousin," he said in a hoarse voice. "I was wondering when you were going to show up."

The adrenaline rushed through me as images of Dad's bloody body flashed before me. I swallowed and replaced them with a new scene. Levi paying for what he did to my family. Dom's warm hand settled on my lower back. His tall frame towered over me, shielding me from Mickey.

"Give me the gun, Emilia," he whispered in my ear.

I shook my head. This was my problem. My fight. I didn't need Dom to save me. I didn't want him to.

"My son needs a gun." Mickey stepped forward, his gaze fixed on Dom, hands up to his lips as if he were praying.

As it happened every time Mickey spoke, his orders were followed blindly. In the corner of my eye, a weapon materialized in front of Dom. Without hesitation, Dom gripped the handle and aimed the gun at Levi's head. Then I saw a new scene in my head. Izzy crying over her dad's empty grave. The way I'd done countless times in the past ten years. Levi wasn't perfect, and in his own messed up way he had tried to help Mom and me.

"It isn't up to us to decide." I stepped in and faced Dom as Levi's hot breath brushed the back of my neck.

Dom lowered his gun but didn't loosen his grip. "I know, but this won't end for you until Levi is gone."

"Are you sure? Killing Levi won't end this thing with him." I pointed a finger at Mickey. He raised both his eyebrows. What did he think? That I would let Dom do this for me? "If you do this, it will start something new for you. And he knows it. That's why Levi is here. That's why Vic let me go." I met Vic's gaze in the back. The minute he'd walked in behind Levi, I realized he'd let me escape the cabin back in Sedona. I was here because he wanted me here.

Dom glanced over his shoulder and cursed when he spotted Vic's furrowed face among the other guards. "You let her go knowing she'd come straight here?"

"I'm tired of running, Dom," Vic said deadpan.

"You son of a bitch, I trusted you."

"And I earned that trust. I warned you to leave her be." Vic pointed at me.

"How do you think I knew Emilia was the key," Mickey

asked. "It was never hard to keep tabs on you, know your every move. There were things only Vic could know. Like the feelings you've had for her since the day you met."

"Vic." The whites of Dom's eyes turned red with unshed tears.

"I'm here to make sure this thing with Mickey ends tonight. I promised your mom I'd look after you. This is me keeping that promise."

My knees weakened. I wanted to scream. I wanted to cry. I'd tried to help Dom and made it all worse. I couldn't lose him to this world he didn't want. I shuffled back and collided with Levi's body. In a blur of arms, faces swirling out of focus, and a rumble of triggers clicking around us, Levi put me in a headlock, yanked the gun out of my hand and aimed it at Dom.

"Don't shoot them." The menace in Dom's tone made a couple guards lower their guns. "Levi, there's another way out of this. Let her go." Dom stalked forward, his arms raised in front of him.

"Tell them to lower their guns." Levi's erratic breathing crept through my hair and sent a terrifying chill down my spine. His grip tightened around my throat and white spots exploded in front of me. My feet dragged across the floor as he backed away toward the side entrance.

"Mickey, call off your men."

I slow blinked at the faces in front of me to gain focus. Ashen-faced, Dom prowled after Levi, hands still raised as we inched closer to the exit. Vic had his gun aimed somewhere over my head. The rest of the men didn't care if I got shot in the process or not.

"Stand down." Mickey glared at Vic.

Levi taking over the situation hadn't been part of Mickey's

plan. Had it been part of Vic's plan? Regardless of how Levi managed to break free, Mickey was no longer in control. He pursed his lips and all the wrinkles on his face bulged. His gaze darted across the room while he calculated his next step.

He could shoot both Levi and me and be done with this stupid game, but Dom had been clear. If anything happened to me, he would make sure everything Mickey had worked for all his life would turn to ashes. Everything Mickey placed value on hinged on his crew.

What was left for us? Would Levi take off and spend the rest of his life hiding from Mickey's crew? Or would he run back to the cartel to ask for help? For that, he'd need to tell them the truth—that Mom and I were still alive. I'd known Levi long enough to know that he would choose himself over my family any day of the week.

After ten years, if he went back to the cartel to explain he never finished the task he was given, would they have any kind of leniency with him? Or would they send someone else to take care of the loose ends? Even if they didn't kill him or his family, Levi would have to know that the life of privilege he once enjoyed because of his high standing would come to an end.

"What are you doing, Levi? Think of Jess and the kids." I was reaching. What could I possibly offer him to make him release me?

"You want me to kill him for you? Would you forgive me then? Would that make us even?" Levi whispered in my ear.

"No, I don't." My voice quavered as the realization of what this was for Levi washed over me. He was still trying to come out on top. I searched for the right words to make him stand down. "That's a suicide mission. They'll kill us both...I already forgave you."

A gray sky met us outside the warehouse. Levi tugged at me to make me fall in step with him. Dom put out his hand when he crossed the threshold to keep pace with Levi and me, while Mickey's crew spilled out of the building and followed close behind him—ready to make a move.

My mouth went dry while I played different scenarios in my head. If I fought Levi, he would no doubt start shooting. Dom would have to step in and kill Levi, which was exactly what Mickey wanted. And what if Levi ended up killing Dom? Mickey would never let us out of here alive.

"I don't deserve your forgiveness." He glared at Mickey, who looked like he was ready to do some shooting of his own.

"No, you don't but I needed to let all that anger go." I didn't recognize the shrill tone in my own voice. Levi was out of his mind.

"There's a car you can take. Emilia's driver can take you back to the airport. You can fly anywhere you want. We won't follow you." Dom stood so still, I couldn't tell if he was breathing. Levi relaxed his hold on me and glanced at Dom. "Get in the damn car, Levi, and never come back."

Levi pressed his lips to my temple. "What do you think are the chances Jess will name our boy after me?"

"What?" I met Dom's gaze. If he heard Levi's question, he didn't show it. He shook his head once. A silent plea to get me not to play the hero. He wanted Levi to go on his own but did that ever work? Levi would go through great lengths to ensure his survival. Wasn't that why he came to our house that night and shot my entire family even when it hadn't been his initial plan? When everything went to hell for him, he chose himself and the life he wanted with Jess. His best shot was to leave here with me and use me as insurance.

"Answer me."

"Good. I'd say good." I hated that I was right. Jess and I hadn't talked about baby names. But she was the type to want to name her boy after the baby's father. Even if Levi didn't deserve the honor.

"Promise you'll take care of my family."

"Get in the car, Levi."

"Promise me." He tightened his arm around my neck.

"I promise. They're my family too. I would do anything to protect them." Tears spilled down my cheeks.

"I believe you." He chuckled. The laugh of a man gone mad. "I'm sorry. For everything. I really am." He exhaled slowly. "Tell my kids I love them."

"Levi—"

His arm moved from my neck to my stomach so fast he knocked the wind out of me. The second blow came when he shoved me across the hood of the black sedan with one hand while he fired shots directly in front of him. Mickey's crew responded in kind before I hit the asphalt. I tried to find my footing, but a pair of hands gripped my shoulders and dragged me to the other side away from the rain of bullets pelting down on Levi.

The smoke and the shouts got muffled as my mind tried to sort out what'd happened. Was this about Jess and the kids? He must've done the math when Mickey pitted Dom and me against each other to see who would kill Levi first. He must've known he wasn't leaving this place alive. I rubbed my throbbing temple and curled against the back tire, my cheek pressed against the sooty rim. Levi was no longer my problem or my monster under the bed.

After what felt like hours, the gunfire stopped. The stench

of burnt metal stuck to the back of my throat, and the smoke stung my eyes. *Dom.* I wanted to get up and find him, but my legs wouldn't move.

"Is he?"

Tyler sat on his haunches next to me with a gun in his hands. He didn't shoot back at Mickey's crew, just stood his ground next to me while he scouted the area in the way only someone with experience would do.

"I don't know many flight attendants or personal drivers who can handle a hostage situation."

"I think it's obvious I'm neither of those things." He raised both eyebrows. "I apologize for not being forthcoming. My brother asked me to keep a low profile. He was right to assume you and Dom would need backup."

I should've known Dom's friend wouldn't let me fly cross-country on my own. "No wonder he was so understanding when I told him I didn't want him or Valentina to come with me." My voice sounded so far away, muffled by the ringing in my ears. My mind held on to the few details that made sense.

"Hey. Stay with me." He gripped my shoulders and turned my face to get me to look at him. "Can you tell me your name?"

I nodded.

"Hey. Do you know where you are?"

"What does it matter where I am? Where's Dom?"

"I'll take that as a yes." Tyler craned his neck to see over the trunk of the car. He pressed his knuckles to his nose and shook his head. "Ms. Prado. Don't look."

He surveyed my face and then the rest of me. "I think you have a concussion. You hit the asphalt pretty hard. Come on. We have to go before someone remembers you're still here."

"No, we can't go. I feel fine. We need to find Dom. Please." Every inch of my body hurt.

"I didn't want to say it, but your head is bleeding. I promise after you get help, I'll come back and find Dom for you."

I blinked several times, but the white blotches covering everything around me made it hard to focus. Arms lifted me into the back seat of the rental car. The cool black leather felt wet and sticky against the side of my face. His lips moved, but the words were a jumble of echoes I couldn't make out. I closed my eyes to make the shrill ring in my head stop. All I wanted to do was sleep.

30

TRAITORS NEVER WIN

Dom

What the fuck? I aimed my gun at Levi when he shoved Emilia out of the way and fired at Mickey. Vic used his own pistol to ram me in the shoulder. The unexpected blow brought me to my knees, and I dropped my gun.

"What the hell, Vic?" Why in the world was he helping Levi? The son of a bitch had taken Emilia as hostage.

"Get down." He pulled me away from Levi's line of sight. "Let those two finish this once and for all."

"What about Emilia?" I glanced up, but she was gone.

A few more shots rang out and then silence fell around us like a dark blanket. My heart slammed against my chest as my head snapped up toward Levi. I rolled on my side and cradled my shoulder when it throbbed in protest.

Twenty feet away, Levi lay in a pool of his own blood. Death by fire squad. What a horrible way to go. Why did he do it? With Emilia as a hostage, he could've gone anywhere. Or was that just it? Did he realize he'd taken a wrong turn when he partnered with Mickey, and he had nowhere to go? I scrambled to my feet and darted toward Emilia's black sedan.

Please be okay. Please be okay.

In the back seat of the driver's side, I found Tyler trying to wake Emilia up. "She hit her head hard." He climbed out of the car when he saw me. "I would've taken her to the hospital, but the front tire got hit pretty bad.

"Thanks. I got her." I nodded.

Her warm breath brushed my forehead when I pressed my ear to her chest. She was alive. I couldn't begin to imagine what all of this did to her. Cupping her cheeks, I turned her head to one side and then the other. She had a nasty cut on her temple, but the rest of her was whole. I held her tight until she moaned against my neck.

"I can't breathe with you on top of me," she mumbled against my neck.

"Fuck, Emilia. I've never been this scared in my life." I let my legs spill out of the car and helped her to sit up. "Are you okay? Do you remember where you are?"

"Why do people keep asking me that? I'm fine." She touched her palm to her bleeding temple and winced.

"I'll drive you to the hospital." I ran my fingers over the bruises on her arm.

"I don't need a hospital. I'm fine." She wiped the tears off her cheeks. "This was like déjà vu. Like the night Dad was shot." Squeezing her eyes shut, she dropped her face in her hands. "Did I pass out?"

"I think so. I'm so sorry you had to go through this again."

"You can't put this one on you." She glanced up at me.

Vic's words swirled in my head. I turned to him. He stood

there, eyebrows furrowed into a deep V. "You son of a bitch. You set this up?"

"I saw an opportunity and I took it. Mickey screwed Levi over. If Levi didn't die here tonight, the cartel would've gotten to him as soon as he landed in Phoenix. He was a dead man walking. At least this way, his death counted for something."

"You put Emilia's life in danger. You used her." I'd always appreciated Vic's calm demeanor, but right now I wanted nothing more than to punch the calm out of him. My insides twisted at the thought that this could've ended so differently for Emilia.

"I'm sorry, Ms. Prado, there was no other way."

"You cut the cable ties binding Levi's wrists, didn't you?" she asked, squinting at him, trying to make all the events that happened fit into a perfect box in her head. I sure as hell wanted to understand what exactly had gone down.

Vic nodded. "Traitors never win. I made sure he understood that."

Tears stained Emilia's face as she laced her fingers through mine. "Izzy will be crushed. How am I going to tell her?"

"We'll figure it out." I kissed the top of her head. What else could I say? How did I justify any of this? Mickey had gone too far with his insane thirst for control and his wicked mind games. Not even Vic could make excuses for his actions.

"I told you he'd push you to the limit." Vic grimaced. "He wasn't right anymore. You know? He lost his way a while a back."

I glared at Vic. He wasn't wrong about Mickey. Emilia let her feet fall to the ground and pushed herself out of the car. What was she thinking? Did she finally understand the kind of world I lived in? That being with me could never be a good thing?

"Is Mickey...?

I shook my head because I didn't know if he was gone or just wounded. The walls of my stomach felt like stone. Levi only had one shot to kill Mickey. If he didn't get the job done, Mickey would come after Vic. Would he damn it all to hell and also come after Emilia? I made it clear to him that she was off limits, but it was as Vic had said, Mickey wasn't right anymore.

I trudged toward the crowd near the entrance to the warehouse. Mickey's guys stood around him with stunted, pale faces. When I reached their circle, they stepped aside to let me through. I kneeled next to him and blinked tears away. Even if he deserved it, seeing him like this hurt. Mickey lay on the asphalt, eyes closed, mouth slack, with a single shot to his chest.

The blood, dark and thick, covered a large area around us. A copper taste mixed with fuel coated the back of my throat. I swallowed to make the tang go away, and my stomach heaved. Breathing through my mouth, I focused on Mickey. Other than the hole in his chest, he looked peaceful. I pinched my nose and let the pain spread through my veins. Mickey was gone.

I wiped my eyes on my shoulder where Emilia's hand rested. She'd come all the way to Jersey for me. For a while, Mickey had convinced me this was the life I was meant to live. He truly believed I'd be happy here because this mobster life was all he knew. That might have been true for him, but I had a choice. Where Mickey only had his crew, I had Emilia. I had a reason to choose something different for myself. Mickey had to choose the only family he knew—his crew.

When I glanced up, all of Mickey's guys stood at attention

in front of me in a semicircle. They regarded me, waiting for me to say something and to fix this fucking mess.

Big Tommy spoke first. "What do we do with the body, boss?" He pointed to the other side of the parking lot at Levi's contorted form lying in a pothole half-filled with rainwater —alone.

Boss? Was that who I was now? The new boss? They had it all wrong. I never wanted this. Didn't they have someone else to take over?

"Go home." I caught Emilia's hand and strode back inside the warehouse.

Behind me, Vic spoke fast on his phone, the way he always did when giving instructions. His guys would have to come in tonight and clean up because this mess was bigger than all of us.

When we reached my office, Mia jerked to her feet and bolted toward me. She crashed into me and hugged me tightly. "Dammit. What were you thinking going after that lunatic?"

"I was thinking he had Emilia and I needed to save her." I peeled her arms from around my neck. "Are you okay?"

"Yeah. I'm sorry. I was so worried. I thought you..." She rubbed her hands on her arms and turned away from me.

"We're fine. Levi's beef was with Mickey."

"What?" She spun to face me. "Is Uncle Mickey okay?"

"No. I'm sorry."

Her eyes glazed with unshed tears. "I told him he was pushing it with this arms deal. You mess with the bull." Mia covered her mouth and swallowed. When she regained her composure, she asked, "Now what? You sticking around?"

Emilia let out a heavy sigh. "Yeah. Now what?"

Up until now, I hadn't allowed myself to think it, to make plans outside of Jersey. There was nothing stopping me from getting on Cole's plane back to Phoenix. As far as the cartel knew, Emilia's family was killed ten years ago, and the only person who knew she was alive was dead. She was free to go home.

"Everything's changed." I put my arm around Emilia.

"You can say that again." Vic pushed the office door opened and strolled in. "I mean now that Mickey is out, you can run this place as you see fit. The crew is on board."

"Let me be clear." I met Emilia's gaze then turned my attention back to Vic. "I'm not staying. If it were up to me, I'd be on Cole's plane tonight."

"It is up to you, Dom. Your family is here. You and Emilia can stay. She'll be safe. We're home now." Vic glanced at Mia with a look in his eyes that said *Tell him. Make him stay.*

All this time, I'd assumed Vic had come with me because he was done with all this mobster stuff. In reality, it'd been exactly as he'd always said. He didn't agree with how Mickey ran the crew, with all his power plays and need to be the biggest, the big bad wolf.

"Those guys out there need you."

"He's right, Dom." Mia leaned on the edge of the desk, her gaze on Emilia. "You could make a home here. The two of you."

"No." Emilia let go of my hand. "Up until Mickey hunted Dom down and forced him to come back here, Dom had made a home for himself. You can't dump this on him now. This isn't what he wants."

"No, it isn't what I want, but I can't leave them hanging, Emilia." An entire crew of people depended on me now. Their livelihoods were at stake. They needed me.

"Are you serious?" Emilia's mouth went slack as tears pooled in her eyes. "First it was your dad, now it's Vic, Mia, the crew. Admit it, Dom. You want this life."

"You know I don't."

"Mickey did a number on you, didn't he?" Emilia stepped toward the door. Her icy stare cut me deep. When I reached for her hand, she slapped it away. "No. I'm leaving. Cole's plane is scheduled to leave tonight, and I plan to be on it. Make up your mind." Before her words had sunk in, she slipped out the door and slammed it shut.

Mia blocked me when I made to chase after Emilia. "Give her some space. We all need some time to think. What happened today with Uncle Mickey is tough to process. We have a lot of work to do."

She was right. For one, we had to figure out how to cover up Levi's death. If the cartel got wind he was abducted by our crew, they'd come after us on principle alone. We had to make sure they understood this was an even loss. One of theirs, for our boss.

Did Emilia not see that? I needed a little time. Though I had to admit, the idea of making a life with her here appealed to me now that Mickey was gone. Before he turned on me, trying to make me one of the crew, I'd been happy here.

I walked around my desk and plopped myself on the chair. I rubbed my temples to make the room stop spinning. We had work to do. Both Mia and Vic regarded me from the other side of the tabletop and smiled. They recognized the look on my face.

"Cleanup, cartel, and the new boss. That's what needs to be done. And in that order."

Business first then pleasure. I had to take care of this mess Mickey left behind before I could offer Emilia a life worthy of her.

"I already got started on cleanup. My guys bagged the...um, the bodies and are on their way to the crematory. We know a guy there that can help."

"Emilia's family would want to keep Levi's ashes. For Izzy. It's the least we can do." I put Emilia's tear-stained cheeks out of my mind. How would she tell Izzy? One problem at a time. "What about the cartel? How do we spin this tale so they don't come after our crew?"

Vic rubbed the nape of his neck. "Well, Levi let Mickey in on a new business venture, bypassed his own people."

I nodded. "A traitor. We could play that angle. We could say he came after the big boss and we had to respond in kind."

"Would that fly?" Mia asked. "Technically, Uncle Mickey is the one that screwed them over by going straight to the source and cutting them out of the deal."

"You knew about this?" I glared at Mia. Just how much did she know about Mickey's business?

"I've been shadowing Uncle Mickey for years now." She met my gaze. "I've been keeping tabs on everything. One time, he even trusted me to run a job for him."

"I thought you wanted to be a flight attendant." I sat back in my chair, seeing Mia under a new light.

"Uncle Mickey was old school. If I'd told him I wanted to run the family business, he would've told me I needed to go find myself a good man and have a few kids. A flight attendant job was something he could wrap his head around. It gave me an excuse to go places with him." She gave me a one-shoulder shrug.

"What else do you know?"

"I know the cartel doesn't know Levi wasn't in on Mickey's plan to cut them out of the deal. If they see him as a traitor, then they won't care that the deal he brokered on his own blew up in his face."

"Sounds like that could work. Do we still have people in Phoenix?" I should've known Mickey wouldn't waste a trip to Arizona. That was Mickey, always looking for the next gig, the upper hand, the way to make another million, even if it meant screwing people over in the process. Tonight, that got him killed.

"I'll handle that myself." Vic typed something on his phone. "I made connections while I was there. I promise. This won't come back to Jersey or Emilia."

"Thank you. So that's how you got Levi to agree to this suicide mission? You made him see how that was his only option."

"Yeah, he did it for his family. I promised this whole thing wouldn't touch them and that his daughter would have a place to visit him."

I placed the palms of my hands on my eyes and pressed hard to stop the tears. Tonight could've gone so differently if Vic hadn't interfered. If Levi hadn't been forced into doing, if not the right thing, at least the decent thing for his family. Because of him, Emilia and her family were free of the cartel.

I was an asshole for even considering that she might want to stay here with me. She deserved so much more.

"What about the crew?" Vic asked. "They need you. This is all they know."

I regarded Mia. She'd wormed her way into Mickey's circle of trust because she wanted to take over the crew. That took a lot of smarts and a lot of guts. "Would they follow Mia?

Mia's head snapped up. "They will if you back me up."

"Is that really what you want? This life?"

"Yes." A blush rose to her cheeks. Her eyes shone, wide with excitement.

"Are you sure you wouldn't be better off with a nice husband and a handful of kids?" I teased.

"Don't be an asshole. Kids. That's not for me. Not ever." She outlined a shape on the desk with her index finger. "I can do the job."

"Done. We'll talk to the guys. Just promise me you'll stay within the gray area."

"I don't know what kind of businesswoman you think I am. I would never do anything illegal." She clasped her hands to her chest, hiding her smile behind pursed lips.

I chuckled and met Vic's gaze. "Would you stay?"

"Yeah. It's good to be home. And someone has to keep Big Joey's kid out of trouble." He flashed Mia a toothy grin before he turned a more serious stare toward me. "You sure you won't stay?"

I would always be grateful to Mickey for saving me. He'd been there for me when I needed him the most when my dad died, and I had no home to go to. He gave me a family and a place where I could belong. I would always owe him for that. Now it was time to move on and find my own way.

"You got a new boss. You don't need me. Emilia's right. This place hasn't been home for me for a long time."

"You can't blame me for trying."

Shaking my head, I pushed away from the desk and stood. "I can't think of anything else that needs handling tonight. I think we're done here."

"Where are you going?" Mia asked.

"First, I'm going to take a shower." I scratched the bristles on my cheek. "And then, I'm gonna get Emilia back."

TECHNICALLY, WE'RE CHASING THE SUNRISE

Emilia

The bellhop tapped my room keycard on the card reader and ushered me inside. "Sorry. Turn-down service has already gone through, but I got you these." He dropped my overnight bag on the luggage rack in the closet and scurried to the bed to place two pieces of chocolate on the pillows. "Your friend is down the hall. Again, I'm sorry we couldn't find you adjacent rooms."

"No worries. Thanks." I was done with men trying to protect me. I sauntered into the bathroom. As much as I hated that the plane takeoff had been removed from the clearance list for whatever maintenance they had to do, I was glad for the chance to peel these dirty clothes off me and get cleaned up.

"You'll be happy you went with the upgrade. There's a complimentary bottle of wine, an extra-large couch." He pointed at the beige sectional in the living area shaped in a semicircle, facing a fifty-two-inch flat screen. This late and without a reservation, a junior suite was all the hotel had left. "And of course, a king-size bed." The smile on his face told me he was done with his spiel. I grabbed a few bills from my purse and offered them to him. He took the money and let himself out.

I didn't care about the extra-large couch. All I wanted was a bath and that bottle of red wine with my name on it. Moving around the room on automatic, I drew a hot bath, brushed my teeth, and poured myself some wine. I discarded my clothes and stepped into the hot, sudsy water. The clock struck midnight as I let myself submerge to wash the last few hours off my body. *Jesus*, I was glad this day was over.

Tears rolled down my cheeks as I washed away the last evidence of everything that happened since I left the cabin this morning. *Levi was gone.* I sat up in the tub and took a swig from my wine glass. I'd come to Jersey hoping to change Dom's mind and instead, I got Levi killed. Almost got myself killed.

Izzy, I'm so sorry.

I pressed my forehead on the lip of the tub and cried. I cried for Izzy, for Dom, and for all the things we could've had together. Why did Dom choose to stay? This life wasn't for him. Mickey was gone, and that meant Dom was free. Or did he stay out of guilt? Did he feel responsible for Levi shooting Mickey? After all, Levi ended up at the warehouse because of Dom's relationship with me. No, I combed my fingers through my wet hair. Mickey did that. His obsession with Dom brought him to this point. Mickey did this to himself. How did Dom not see that?

A slow burn swirled in my stomach. Dom didn't deserve this. I pressed my lips to the wine glass, but it was already empty. I climbed out of the bathtub, grabbed the bathrobe from behind the door, and padded back to the room to find the bottle.

The next sip warmed me to the core. I placed the drink on the nightstand and sat on the edge of the bed. The last of my energy drained from me, as the realization that I was all alone settled in my stomach like a ton of bricks.

In the morning, I'd return to Sedona and make a new plan with Mom and Jess. I still had a job in Phoenix. I could focus on that. We could buy a new house and start over. My chest tightened. I hated making plans without Dom, but I had to. In time, I would get over him. I'd forget his angel face and all the things he made me feel. In time, I could meet someone. Tears stung my eyes again, and I curled up on the bed. How would I ever get over someone like Dom? No one could ever replace him.

A knock on the door woke me with a jolt. How long had I been asleep? Adrenaline pumped hard through me from waking up so suddenly. A fist pounded on the door again, and I forced myself to take deep breaths to calm down. I tiptoed over and peeked into the peephole.

Oh, crap.

My heartbeat picked up the pace again when I saw Dom on the other side.

I glanced down at my bathrobe and spun in place looking for my clothes. Digging through my bag, I threw a change of clothes on the bed. Then I remembered I didn't have any makeup on. I scurried to the mirror. Jeez, did I always have such pink cheeks when Dom was around?

"Emilia, I know you're in there. Open up. We need to talk." Dammit. Makeup or clothes? I picked up my tinted moisturizer. Another knock. "Emilia, I have a key. Don't make me use it."

I threw the tube in my bag. "Are you kidding me? How did you get a key?"

"How do you think?"

No doubt he charmed the pants off the girl working the front the desk. I walked back to the door and squinted into the small opening. Dom stood there glaring at the door. He knocked again, and I jumped back. Fine. I flipped the latch and swung the door open.

"That's creepy."

"I know the girl working the counter. I told her we were on our honeymoon and that I had locked myself out."

Honeymoon? A hot current rushed through me when he smiled.

He was clean-shaven and for some reason, had decided to wear one of his suits. The royal-blue one, the one that made him look like a *GQ* cover model. If he was here to explain to me why he had to stay, this gorgeous thing he had going on was not helping.

I would be able to handle this talk way better if I were wearing real clothes and some makeup. I swept my fingers through my hair to get it away from my face, hoping he wouldn't notice that my cheeks had turned from pink to hot red.

His mouth went slack as he regarded me. "You're good for my ego." He pushed the door shut.

"What?" I crossed my arms over my taut nipples. "Leave the door open."

"Why? Do you want your neighbors to eavesdrop?"

"You didn't seem to care when you were about to tear down the door. You said you wanted it open. Leave it open." I returned to the glass of wine I'd left on the nightstand. Liquid courage seemed like a good idea. "What did you want to talk about?"

"Us."

"You made it clear there wasn't an us. Things changed. Apparently, they just didn't change enough for you. Is that right?"

"I'm sorry, Emilia. My head was all a big mishmash of gunshots and puzzle pieces. I needed a minute to process it all."

I swallowed my tears. "You keep leaving me. I came all the way out here to see you and from the moment I walked into the warehouse, all you've tried to do is send me away. Just leave. I can't do this right now. I'm tired." And all I want to do is cry and sleep.

"I worked it out with Mia and Vic. I want us."

Mia's name was the wrong thing to say to me right now. All the anger I'd felt since he left me in Arizona came crashing down on me, and I lashed out. "I don't want this. I made a mistake coming here. I was an idiot for thinking you'd submitted to Mickey because you loved me. You did it for him. For you. Get out." I pointed at the opened door. "Now." I spun to face away from him.

I wanted to be alone tonight but watching him leave me again hurt too much. He exhaled and stepped away from me. My body jerked when the door slammed shut. The silence filled every corner and left me breathless. I covered my mouth as the numbness spread through me.

"The day I left you waiting for me in Sedona to go home with Mickey..." Dom's voice froze me in place. I stood caged between the bed and his towering frame behind me, heart blasting. He cleared his throat. "That day, a heavy weight burrowed itself in the center of my chest. In that hollow space where I buried all my feelings for you. Some nights the crushing pain was so bad, it'd block all oxygen from my lungs and I'd wake up in a panic."

He snaked a warm hand around my waist and turned me toward him. "I'm sorry about before. All this has been surreal. Mickey getting shot. I never saw that coming. Believe me when I say that I want to be with you and spend the rest of my life making plans with you. If you want to go now. I'm ready."

That much I understood. My head was still spinning from everything that'd happened since Mickey showed up at the warehouse. I had lived with the threat that was Levi lurking in the shadows for so long that now that he was gone, I couldn't shake the feeling it was all a lie. That I missed something, and he was still alive, waiting for me. I tried to recall what I saw when I drove off the parking lot, but I couldn't remember if I'd seen Levi lying there or not.

"Is he really gone?"

Dom nodded. "Both bodies are being cremated tonight."

I gasped, and my knees weakened. Dom hugged me to him. "It's over. I know how you feel, but it's really over."

"Izzy will be heartbroken."

"Believe me. She'll learn to cope with it, and she'll have you and your family to help her through it."

"I'm sorry you got caught in the middle of this mess." I pushed myself away from Dom.

"First of all, you had nothing to do with Mickey using Levi to get to you, to get to me. And second of all, I wanted to help. I wanted you to be happy. I would've killed for you. I would've killed Levi if I knew without a shadow of a doubt that getting rid of him would make the problem go away. I knew that in time, you would've regretted killing your own family. He deserved what he got, but at the end of the day, he was still your niece's dad."

"He asked me to watch over them."

"I'm sure he thought he did it all for his family."

"You don't believe that?" I buried my face in the nook of his neck and shoulder.

"I believe he thought he did it for them, but he only sacrificed himself because he had no way out. He betrayed the cartel the same way he betrayed you and your family. Except this time, he met the big bad wolf."

"What do you mean?"

"He was doing business with Mickey. Mickey screwed him over. There was no going home for Levi."

The last piece of the puzzle fell in place for me. After all these years, Levi never really understood what he'd done to our family. Why did he apologize? To get me to take care of Jess and the kids? Then he truly didn't understand the meaning of family.

"Emilia, I love you so goddamn much."

"I love you too." I caressed Dom's cheek, letting my fingers slide down his strong jaw. He cocked his head and kissed the inside of my wrist. And just like that, the past, my anger, and all the days I'd spent without him vanished from my mind. "I wish we could go now, but they canceled my flight."

"I know." He flashed me a smile.

I hit his chest. "You did that? How?"

"You keep asking that. I run this town, remember? Or...I used to." He tightened his grip and pulled me to him. Heat spread between my legs when his gaze dropped to my bathrobe. "We can be airborne in an hour." He ran his hot tongue along the soft spot behind my ear. "Or we can be airborne in three hours."

I melted into him. "Three hours." I sighed.

"You are so beautiful. Do you know how much I want you?"

He kissed my neck as he tugged on the bathrobe tie. He pushed the terrycloth off my shoulders and let it drop to the floor. His gaze, dark with desire, lingered on my face then moved down to my chest and the rest of my nude body. My skin burned hot. I needed his touch. He reached out with his hand and kneaded my breast. Slow at first as if he were afraid I'd disappear.

"I was an idiot for thinking I could give you up."

With a moan, he captured my aching peak between his lips and sucked hard.

"I missed us." I hooked a leg over his hips when he let me down on the mattress. "I miss the suite."

I took fistfuls of his damp hair. When he lowered his body on top of mine, the silky wool of his suit coat rubbed against my bare skin and sent a rush of heat to my core. I arched my body toward him and grazed the leather of his belt on my mound. Goosebumps spread from my core up to my chest.

He continued his sweet torture, wet mouth on my neck, warm fabric against my breasts, and the smooth and cool feel of his buckle on my belly as he kneaded my backside. I cupped his face and kissed him, plunging my tongue past his lips. He responded with the same intensity, keeping up with my pace. His body felt so good, so strong.

My pulse pounded hot in my ears with all the desire I'd suppressed in the past month. Dom was here, and he wanted me. He wanted a future with me. After all we had been through, life was offering us a new beginning, a new world with no monsters under the bed.

"I want to see you." I pushed at his chest and then tugged at his buttons. He flashed me one of his half smiles, and my knees went weak. "Take it all off."

He did as I asked, starting with his shoes and socks. His coat and shirt came off next. I reached for the angel wings inked on his torso and traced every plane of hard muscle covered by smooth, fevered skin.

"I missed your hands." He caught my fingers and kissed the pads.

"You got bigger." I laughed.

"Intense workouts are the only remedy for blue balls. *Christ,* Emilia. I thought of you every day." He buried his hands in my hair and bent to capture my mouth again.

I unbuckled his belt and he made quick work of his pants as he swiped a condom from the front pocket of his trousers. In two beats, he brought my hips up to meet his erection and entered me. Raw, unrealized need took over. I ran my hands over his muscled shoulders and stomach. He worked me in this position until I called for him.

He puffed out air and let go of my hips. A small flip in my belly made me reach out to him to keep him from leaving again. But he didn't leave. Instead, he covered my body with his, spreading my legs so his hips would fit perfectly.

With one hand, he gripped both of my wrists over my head and cupped my breast with the other. His intense blue gaze locked onto mine before he plunged inside me, harder and deeper. The furrow between his eyebrows spoke of the danger we'd faced a few hours ago, of the love he'd always felt unworthy of, and the life he wanted with me. My eyes stung with tears. I wanted him to make me forget today and all the days we spent apart.

His lips moved to my neck, where he nibbled a path down to my shoulder. I buckled under him to make him look at me. We were done hiding our feelings. We'd earned this life together. I freed one of my hands and cupped his cheek, pulling him to face me. His features relaxed under my touch, and he let out a moan. He rocked forward and backward, cradling me, holding me tight. The way he filled me inside rippled through my body in hot waves.

This was my Dom. He understood we'd come so close to losing our second chance. The one we were given when we met again at the bar. I wrapped my arms around his neck. I'd almost lost the only man I've ever loved.

Tears streamed down my temples as my hips met his, keeping up with the new rhythm he set for us. Not as raw as before, but just as intense. With a groan, he captured my mouth in a deep kiss. He kissed me hard until the heat mounting inside me gave way and spread up to my navel. I cried out and let my climax take over. He sunk deeper into me and we both fell together.

"Fuck, Emilia." He gasped for air in my ear.

"I can't breathe." I pushed on his chest. He laughed and rolled onto his back, taking me with him. I sat up on his belly, trying to catch my breath.

"I definitely want to do that again." He raked a hand through his sweaty hair.

"Me too." I squeezed my legs around his torso, and his cock twitched inside me. "But I think it's time to go home."

"I like the sound of that." He frowned and reached under his back to remove a piece of gold foil. "What the hell?"

I chuckled, bringing my legs in to get off him. "Your body heat melted my chocolate." Settling myself onto the plush pillows, I unfolded the wrapper, fingered the softened mixture off it and into my mouth.

"I thought you wanted to go home." Dom gripped my butt cheeks and sat up. He kissed me until the sweetness in my mouth was spent. Sliding a hand up to my hip, he stretched his nude body across the bed and rested his cheek on my thigh. Like magnets, my fingers found his soft hair while I played with the muscled valleys on his back. I could stay like this forever.

"Let's go before I wake up and realize this was all a dream," Dom muttered against my skin, sending a rush of warmth up my leg.

"Not yet."

Hours later, Dom called the aircraft management company and within forty-five minutes, we were buckling our seatbelts and rushing down the airport runway. When we reached coasting altitude, the flight attendant prepared a dinner table for two, complete with several bottles of Valpolicella wine.

"I had the chef prepare an Italian fare for us. You seemed to like it the last time." He brushed my lips with his.

"This plane is overkill. We don't need this much room."

"We do for what I have planned. There's a private bedroom in the back." With a wink, he unbuckled his seatbelt and caught my hand. I did the same when he ushered me to the couch across the aisle from our meal.

I glanced out the window and squinted at the bright clouds puffing out of our way, covering a pink and orange sky. The last twenty-four hours had been one of the most insane in my life. After everything that happened with Dad, that was saying something. This peace and serenity were something I'd given up on.

"And they rode into the sunset and lived happily ever after?" I asked.

"Technically, we're chasing the sunrise." Dom wrapped his arms around me and pulled me toward him so my back rested on his chest and his warm breath teased the nape of my neck.

"A new day? I like that." I snuggled closer to him. "That's all want. A new day, a new life with you."

THE SECOND TIME

Emilia

Months later...

"What's with all the ruckus?" I strode into the room, buttoning my jacket. Dom stood by the kitchen counter, looking particularly gorgeous in his slim fit, single-breasted suit. The man could wear a suit.

"Good morning, sleepy head." He met me halfway and kissed me. A peck at first, and then a long, deep kiss that turned my knees to jelly.

I sighed and pushed him off me. "Okay. Stop that. I need to focus. Big day."

"I know. First day as a hotshot partner. The hours suck, but you're gonna love it." He returned to his workstation where several slices of wheat bread were spread out next to an overturned jar of apple jelly. "To celebrate, I'm making you a home lunch."

"In a dinosaur lunch box?" I hid a smile behind my fingers.

"Cole left it here last week. I thought you could use it."

"Okay, so what's for lunch?" I glanced at my watch. I had a good ten minutes before I had to leave for court.

"I'm not much of a cook, so it's just three PBJ sandwiches and carrots."

"That's a lot of sandwiches. Thank you." I kissed him on the cheek and grabbed the lunch bag he offered.

"There's also coffee." He opened a cupboard and then closed it when he saw only plates. Two cabinets down near the espresso machine, he found the travel mugs.

We'd been in our new house for all of three weeks, and I still couldn't get used to the idea that this life with Dom was real. We finally had a home of our own, no panic rooms or secret emergency exits. We had friends who visited and left their kid's stuff behind.

Dom's phone lit up with a text message. "That's my ride." He shoved a mug of coffee in my hand and hung the strap of my briefcase over my shoulder. "Come on, I'll drop you off."

On the ride to the office, Dom settled in on his side of the back seat and switched to his lawyer mode, which to me was yet another level of hot for him. He shuffled through papers as he scribbled notes on his legal pad. He'd said he was good at being a criminal, but he was wrong in that. He was always meant to be this, a decent man. Just as we were always meant to be here —together.

When the car stopped in front of my office, Dom leaned over and kissed my temple. "Oh, hey, what are you doing four weeks from Saturday?"

"No plans. Why?"

"Cole and Valentina are getting married, and apparently, we're in the wedding."

I giggled. "I've never been in a wedding before. Sounds like fun."

He pulled a strand of hair away from my cheek. "Look at us making plans."

"Yeah." I melted into him the way I always did when he looked at me like I was the most beautiful woman he'd ever seen.

"I'm so in love with you," Dom whispered.

"I love you too."

The intensity of his gaze reminded me how close we'd come to letting our fears rob us of a future together. I never thought forgiveness was something I was capable of, or that it could bring us such content. I never considered any of it until I met Dom. The second time.

UNRAVEL YOU

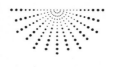

DIANA A. HICKS

THE THIGH-HIGH STOCKINGS

Valentina

"Mrs. Cole?" The maître d' slid into my line of sight.

My gaze jerked up at him. "We're not married."

"I'm sorry?" He stepped forward in that way super-fancy servers move in super-fancy restaurants.

I sat back on the blue-velvet couch and downed the rest of my champagne. "Mr. Cole and I are not married."

"My apologies. Mr. Cole...the ring...I assumed." He placed his hands behind him, standing perfectly straight.

"Not yet." I smiled, and his features relaxed some. Not all the way though. We were still in a very exclusive establishment. "Is my car ready?"

"Yes. Take your time." He poured more wine into my glass.

I glanced at my watch, placing a hand to my forehead. How did I end up waiting two hours for him again?

"Mr. Cole already took care of everything."

Of course, he did. "Thank you. I'd like to go home now." I scooted one spot over and rose to my feet. The silk of my dress skimmed down my legs, and images of Derek's hands inching up my thighs flickered through my mind. That had been the day he'd left on a business trip, roughly three weeks ago. God, I missed him.

"Of course." The maître d' ushered me to the entrance of the restaurant, where one of Derek's drivers waited for me, and swung the door open.

"Thank you." I climbed in and relaxed, running my hand along the supple leather of the seat. The car pulled out of the parking lot, and I kept my focus on the soft feel of the upholstery.

My phone rang in my purse, but I didn't answer it. Derek wasn't here. A call from him wasn't going to fix that.

"Mrs. Cole?" The driver was new. Derek had hired him to drive me and my son Max.

"It's Valentina," I said. "We're not married yet."

"Oh, I'm so sorry. I didn't realize." He cleared his throat. "Mr. Cole is trying to reach you. Can he try again?"

"Yes, that's fine." I fished my phone from the bottom of my clutch. Derek's incredibly handsome face and intense blue gaze lit up the screen. I stared at it for a few more rings before I swiped right to answer.

"Valentina, I've been trying to call you. Are you okay?"

"Yes." I glared at the tiny letters that said the connection was poor and video wasn't available. I wanted to see him. "Where are you?"

"I'm so sorry I missed our dinner. I'm still at the airport in Atlanta. My plane has an engine problem they thought they could fix right away. Turns out I'm stuck here 'til the morning. It's so late now. But I promise I'll be home as soon as I can."

His deep voice, the way he spoke every word with such

confidence, dulled all my senses. Suddenly, the disappointment of being stood up vanished. "Okay. I'll see you tomorrow." I started to say *I'm on my way home*, but he already knew that if he'd texted the driver to get me to answer his call.

"I gotta go. I love you."

My skin flushed, as it always did, when he said he loved me. I smiled at the phone. "I love you too."

The connection ended, leaving me with an odd sense of emptiness. I tapped on my messages and then on our housekeeper's name to let her know Derek wasn't coming home. After I typed a few letters, I gave up. Of course, she already knew he wasn't coming. Derek, the all-powerful billionaire, had a whole team of people monitoring and managing his entire life.

When the driver pulled into Derek's Andalusian-style mansion in the northern part of Tucson, I climbed out of the car and darted up the stone steps that led to the massive wooden door. "Good night." I waved to the driver.

"Good night, Mrs. Cole."

"We're... Good night, Tom." I let it be. We were as good as married. Derek and I were engaged, and I'd already lived in his home for all of four weeks. His idea, not mine. I would have stayed in the small cottage he leased to me after I graduated college two months ago.

Derek didn't like waiting. He wanted a life with me; he didn't see why we couldn't start immediately. For my part, I couldn't think of a single reason to stay apart from him, so I'd agreed to everything—the house, the ring, the fairy tale—though I kept waiting for the other glass slipper to drop. This was too perfect, too fast.

Except for the ones leading up to the stairs, the lights were off inside the house. I went straight to Max's room. He was already asleep in his perfectly made-up bed. Up until two months ago, I only got to see my son on weekends. I went to school while he stayed home in Casa Grande with my parents, about a forty-minute drive outside of Tucson. Yeah, small-town girl making the big move to the big city.

Some leap. Not four months after I'd arrived almost seven years ago, I got pregnant by a jerk who didn't want anything to do with me or my baby. For months, I told myself I never should have left home. I finished my freshman year, but after that I spent the rest of my pregnancy hiding in my room. A couple of random jobs and two semesters later, Mom talked some sense into me and made me go back to school.

Things made more sense after Max was born. He gave me the strength I needed to reapply at the university and finish my degree, though that meant being away from him for the next five years, at least during the week. Since the moment Mom had placed him in my arms in the birthing room, all I wanted was a home so Max could live with me, so we could be on our own together. Derek did that for us and then some. He didn't just offer a place for us to stay. He gave us a home, a family.

I kissed Max's cheek and pulled the sheets over his shoulder. After I turned off the nightlight, I strode to the master bedroom at the end of the long corridor and got ready for bed. It wasn't that late, but I didn't feel like spending the next hour or so looking for things to keep me entertained when all I wanted was to be doing something else with Derek. I missed him so much. I missed his hands in my hair, his lips on mine, and the way my skin felt alive every time he whispered something in my ear. His warm breath and deep voice never failed to send flutters down my back.

"Ah." I fell on my pillow facedown.

The next morning, I woke up to an empty room. I checked my phone and found a message from Derek.

Came in late last night, or was it early this morning? I found a flight from Atlanta to Phoenix. See you in the office? I miss you.

I didn't bother with a response. I tossed the phone on his side of the bed and got up to get ready for work. At least, we were on the same time zone now.

"Mom, we're going to be late." Max ran to the bottom of the stairs when I came down. He had his backpack ready by the door and a piece of bacon in his hand.

I glanced at my watch. "We have plenty of time."

In the kitchen, our housekeeper, Em, had coffee ready for me. This perk I could get used to. I sat on the barstool and sipped my latte. Em kept her gaze on me, her eyebrows slightly raised. She already knew Derek had stood me up last night.

"He gets caught in his own head sometimes. Give him time," she finally said when I kept my focus on my hot mug.

"It was an engine malfunction this time."

She smiled. "He's been alone for a long time."

I'd been alone too. "I know. I'm not mad. Just disappointed. Three weeks is a long time."

"Mooommm," Max called.

I rolled my eyes at Em and drank the rest of my coffee. "I only hope he keeps this enthusiasm for school when he gets to middle school."

She laughed and turned to grab his lunch bag. Another perk I could get used to. "Thank you. I overslept this morning."

"That's what I'm here for, dear. I like having company in the mornings now. He was up at five."

"I'm sorry."

"No, I was up before that." She patted my hand. "Go on. You don't want to be late. Car's already waiting for you."

I rushed out the door to find Max already in his booster seat. This kid was going places for sure. On the ride to school, he talked incessantly about all the work he had planned for the week. First grade was a crucial year, apparently.

"And Derek gave me his mason account, so I can buy all the books I want."

I chuckled. "You mean Amazon?"

"Yeah. He says they have everything there."

"Okay, I will talk to Derek about that. I need to approve all purchases." I grabbed a wipe off the middle console and cleaned his greasy face.

"Oh, I already put some stuff in the cart."

"Omigod. Okay, I'll look into that." I kissed his cheek. Derek and I needed to have a talk on parenting. Or maybe we needed to back up a bit and start with simpler things—for example, what were his mom and dad like? His brothers? He had four brothers who lived all over the country, but I'd never met them.

"Bye, Mom." Max waved when Tom pulled up to the drop-off area.

"Going to the office, Mrs. Cole?" he asked when we left the school. "Looks like Mr. Cole is running late this morning."

"Yes." My phone buzzed with another message from Derek.

Trip from hell. Running late.

The office was the usual morning chaos when I arrived, maybe a little more since everyone knew Derek was finally back. He injected the place with energy somehow. I didn't have meetings until midmorning, so I took my time getting to my office, which Derek insisted I move into, even though I was only a project manager in his department. He didn't care if people thought I was getting special treatment for sleeping with him, which I was.

As soon as he took over as CEO again, he sacked his ex-wife Bridget for embezzlement and for trying to sell his company out from under him. He'd also promoted me to manager. When Bridget ran the company, she'd hired me during a student job fair at the end of the fall semester. I started out writing code to update old reports for her. She was so intimidating; she scared the crap out of me. But she'd offered me the one thing I wanted most. A real job so I could afford a home for Max. Back then, I didn't know Derek, and I had no clue I'd fall for him so hard.

I fired up my computer and swiveled my chair around to see out the two-story window. The view of the city from up here was breathtaking, complete with a clear blue sky and a serene desert landscape. Since Derek moved to Tucson for one of his biggest clients, he'd acquired more office space. Cole Communications, Inc., owned all four buildings on the block. They all faced into a large courtyard lined with benches and water features throughout.

I felt the tremble on the windows and the floor before I spotted Derek's chopper. The one he used to commute to Phoenix on a daily basis. His client base was growing at a fast pace now that he was back in the CEO chair, so he spent a great deal of time there. We'd actually considered moving, but we loved it here so much that in the end we decided commuting every day wasn't a big deal.

The chopper landed on the helipad on the rooftop of the building across the way, and I held my breath for a moment, waiting for Derek to climb out. He was already dressed in a dark suit, hair perfectly styled, and wearing sunglasses. The scene in front of me could easily be a magazine photo shoot or an Omega watch commercial. That guy could wear a suit.

His admin met him by the door. By the way she talked with her arms flailing urgently, he was needed somewhere. I picked up my phone and typed a message for him.

Lunch?

He glanced down at his screen before he disappeared through the door. A minute later, his text came in with a loud ping.

Need a year-to-date report on recent acquisitions. Can you bring that by?

Right. I'd seen that request on my phone on the drive down. I giggled. Or maybe Derek only wanted an excuse to get me to his office. We'd been apart for so long, surely, I wasn't the only one thinking about sex. What did he have in mind? I glanced down at my skirt and blazer, glad I'd decided to wear a lacy bra, matching underwear, and thigh-high stockings. Yeah, three weeks was a very, very long time.

I headed for the door, then stopped myself. Not that Derek cared what people thought, but how would it look if I showed up at his office empty handed and stayed for an hour. Or two. I rushed back to my desk and grabbed my phone and the first file I found, a red one that stood out in my hand.

On the way to his office, I ran into my boss, who had a million and one questions about the acquisitions report. I was popular today. I answered his questions as quickly as I could. When he finally took a breath, I stopped him. "How about I email you the report when I get back to my office. That way you'll have it all in one place. I'm late for a meeting right now."

"Okay. I have what I need for now, but do send me that

report." He pretty much said that to the back of my head. Derek was all I could think of right now.

Derek's office was one floor above mine, on the opposite end of the building. I did my best to brisk walk through the maze of cube offices without looking too desperate. My blood rushed with anticipation. I could still feel Derek's hands sliding up my back from the last time we were together. The memory got me so wet it was all I could do not to take off running.

When I reached his reception area, his admin waved me through. I blushed, ears burning hot. As it always happened when he was around, a tiny flame flickered right smack in the middle of my chest. I blew out air and entered his office.

My face caught fire when ten different set of eyes, Derek's included, turned to look at me, holding a silly red folder. *Shit. He was serious about the report.*

The scowl on Derek's face stopped me in my tracks. Was his admin supposed to announce me since he had company? He glanced down at my hands. "Is that the report I asked for?" He used his this-is-a-business-meeting tone on me, and that sent a rush of embarrassment throughout my body. It still didn't do anything to fix the wetness between my legs. *Shit.*

"Yes." I peeked at the label on the front. I'd brought Max's summer-school projects. "But you know, I just remembered I have a more current file on my computer. I'll go get it."

His blue gaze moved slowly from me to the four men sitting across from him, then to his phone. He typed something on it, and tossed it on his desk. "No need. Just give us a quick update now." He gestured toward the only empty chair in his office.

I blew out air slowly through my teeth and slogged to my assigned seat. I'd put the update together over the weekend. I knew exactly what was on it, but for the life of me, I couldn't find the words. All I could see in my mind, flashing in neon pink, were the words *he didn't call you here for a quick office tumble.* I set my mobile down on the coffee table but kept the folder clutched to my chest.

His phone rang the second my butt touched the soft leather seat. He put up a finger. "One second. It's the urgent line." He put the handset to his ear and listened while I ogled him.

I'd missed his chiseled profile and full lips. The light made his blond hair look darker than I knew it was when the sun touched it. He leaned forward, and his suit jacket stretched around his shoulders and biceps. Gosh, the man was gorgeous.

I slanted a glance over to the men sitting next to me. They kept looking down at their watches, as if they had somewhere to be. After a few minutes, Derek finally dropped the phone onto the base.

"Gentlemen, looks like we'll have to reschedule for after lunch." He sat back on his executive chair, his long fingers gripping the armrest. "Something's come up. I need to tend to it immediately."

They all shot to their feet, assuring him it wasn't a problem at all. I stood as well, hiding the label on my red folder. I had a way out, and I had to take it.

"Valentina. Stay. I have a minute. If you can give me a quick update, I'd appreciate that."

"Sure." I nodded and stepped back to let the men through. If the floor opened now and swallowed me, I'd be okay with that.

Derek rose from his chair and sauntered toward the door to see his team out. When he returned, he leaned on the armrest of the long sofa in the lounge area of his office. I stalked over to him, and he extended his hand. "Let me see that."

"No."

"No?" He narrowed his eyes on me, a hint of a smile forming on his lips.

I looked up and then down before I finally conceded and shoved the folder into his hands.

He opened it and chuckled. "I thought I recognized this." He tossed it on the coffee table behind him, shaking his head. "Let's see it."

What was he thinking? "See what?"

"You had a plan when you walked into my office five minutes ago. What was it?" He gripped the edge of the armrest with both hands, crossing his legs at his ankles.

The tiny flame in my chest grew bigger and spread down to my core. "I had no plan." I admitted because the extent of my thoughts when he texted was to come in here and have sex. All I could think of was touching him and feeling his weight on me again. But now I was a little pissed. He could've been more explicit. Like, hey, I'm just here to work, bring me the report. No sex. Get your mind out of the gutter. He could also wipe that knowing smile off his face.

"What makes you think I had a plan?" I crossed my arms over my chest to cover my hardened nipples.

He rubbed the side of his face. "The thigh-high stockings. You know how they drive me wild. Even if I can't see them, I know that's the only kind you own."

If that was true, why was he still five feet away from me? Why had he not ripped my clothes off already and had his way with me on the couch? "I have a meeting to go to." I bolted to the door. Before I could open it, his large hand pressed against it, effectively blocking me from leaving.

"I don't think so." His voice was deep and so full of meaning. He walked me back to the living area until my butt hit the back of the sofa. "You had a plan. Show me." He gripped my waist and shifted so he was the one caged in.

I could go, or I could stay and get what I came here for.

I slipped my hands inside his suit jacket and pushed it off his shoulders. His dark gaze stayed on me as I removed his dress shirt. A low moan like a hiss escaped his lips when I ran my hands down his muscled chest. His pecs were harder than I remembered. It seemed Derek's hard body was directly proportional to the amount of stress he had at work. The more they pinned on him, the more time he spent in his boxing ring. These past three weeks must have been hell for him.

"Now you." His voice sounded strained.

Self-control was Derek's superpower. I gave up all pretenses and removed my blazer and silky top quickly. My skin felt hot from needing him so much. His lips parted when I finally let my skirt pool at my feet.

He cradled my face and kissed me hard. "Fuck. Valentina. You came to work wearing that underneath?"

His mouth was warm, and he tasted of cinnamon gum. I melted into him, fumbling with his belt. "The door." I panted in between kisses.

"I locked it." He gripped my ass and wrapped my legs around his waist as he strode around the sofa and sat with me straddling him. "Valentina. How do you do it? How do you make me forget about everything?" He freed me from my bra and sucked on my aching nipples, switching back and forth until I couldn't wait anymore.

"I need you now," I whispered in his ear. I didn't care that my voice was laced with desperate desire.

He cupped my butt cheeks and lifted me enough to give him room to lie flat on the cushions with his head on the decorative pillow. My thighs rubbed his sides as I rested on top of him, topless and without a clue what to do next. My confusion must have registered on my face because he placed both hands behind his head and grinned at me. His biceps bulged on either side of him.

"Your show."

"What?"

He bucked under me to get comfortable, as if he were getting ready to watch a movie or something. The grin that twitched his lip was both infuriating and such a turn-on.

"You want me inside you. Do it."

Made in the USA
Monee, IL
13 June 2020